Readers love
The Final Seduction
by ALLISON CASSATTA

"The author certainly knows how to make great characters and have them shine through with realistic situations. It is a powerful, seductive, intriguing read that will make the readers want to go after more of her books."

—MM Good Book Reviews

"If you haven't read any of this series, pick it up, don't wait, it is soooooo good. If you just need the latest release, I can't recommend enough that not reading this is doing an injustice to yourself. Allison Cassatta has graciously blessed us with an incredible series and I feel it would be a disservice not to pass it on to others."

—Mrs. Condit and Friends Read Books

"I highly recommend this series for everyone who likes their romance with a splash of danger and grit. A fantastic read."

—The Novel Approach

"This book had the right amount of everything guaranteed for an extremely engaging read. In a way, I'm kind of sad to see it all end, I'm going to miss these captivating characters. I could rightly say I was seduced."

—The Romance Studios

By ALLISON CASSATTA

With Tracey Michael: Beast
Dream 'til Monday
Kissing is Easy
Sins of the Heart
With Remmy Duchene: This is Love

DEAR DIARY
Dear Diary
Pride
Relationships 101

SIN & SEDUCTION
Sin & Seduction
Lies & Seduction
The Final Seduction

Published by DREAMSPINNER PRESS
http://www.dreamspinnerpress.com

DREAM 'TIL MONDAY

ALLISON CASSATTA

Dreamspinner Press

Published by
DREAMSPINNER PRESS

5032 Capital Circle SW, Suite 2, PMB# 279, Tallahassee, FL 32305-7886 USA
http://www.dreamspinnerpress.com/

Dream 'til Monday
© 2014 Allison Cassatta.

Cover Art
© 2014 Allison Cassatta.
http://www.allisoncassatta.com
Cover content is for illustrative purposes only and any person depicted on the cover is a model.

ISBN: 978-1-62798-980-0
Digital ISBN: 978-1-62798-981-7
Library of Congress Control Number: 2014943199
First Edition August 2014

Printed in the United States of America

This paper meets the requirements of
ANSI/NISO Z39.48-1992 (Permanence of Paper).

First and foremost, this book is dedicated to my readers. Without you, I would be a crazy person with a bunch of voices and pages of gibberish. You're the reason the gibberish becomes stories.

Second, I'd like to dedicate this book to two very special friends who rescued me from my hotel room and showed me how much fun San Francisco can be. Our outing to The Castro planted the seed for this story.

Thank you, Ron and Asher. I love you guys.

ACKNOWLEDGMENTS

As always, I would like to acknowledge the wonderful staff at Dreamspinner Press for all their work and dedication. I would also like to thank Kristi, Lynne, Tracey, and Raven for beta reading. It's painful, I know, but you guys do it oh so willingly, and I adore you for it.

CHAPTER ONE

THE PACIFIC Ocean crashed against the Malibu shoreline. Hot sun rained down on Miles's face as he watched his little girl run along the beach with her best friend. He couldn't believe how big Zoe had gotten and how much she looked like her mother. Her caramel curls bounced around her shoulders. A rose-colored hue filled her cheeks. Deep dimples framed her excited smile, and light freckles dotted her peach skin. No matter how fast she grew up, she would always be his little princess, the girl he'd held only moments after her birth and had instantly fallen in love with.

"Daddy! Daddy!" Zoe called out as she charged toward him.

Soon enough, she would become a young woman, and honestly, Miles wasn't sure how he would deal with that, with the things little girls needed to be taught. He couldn't talk to her about the changes her body would go through or boys or being a woman. Without her having a mother, those things would be hard.

The moment Miles had become aware of being a single parent, his sister had promised to help him in every way she could, but she wouldn't always be there. She couldn't always be there. So he'd vowed to baby Zoe to be everything she ever needed, to protect her and love her and never let her suffer. He vowed to make up for her not having a mother in her life. Everything he did, he did for her. She had the best of everything and wanted for nothing. She had all the love one child could possibly need.

"Daddy!"

She plopped down on the blanket beside him, pulling her bare legs to her chest. The bright pink of her bathing suit matched the bright pink of her face.

"Yeah, princess?"

"Gigi wants to spend the night. Can she?"

"Zoe, I'd hoped to spend an evening together before I have to take you to Aunt Karen's. You know I'll be gone for a long time."

Her smile faded. Her lips turned pouty. She tucked her chin against her chest. All those little moves turned her strong-willed father to mush, and nine times out of ten, she ended up getting exactly what she wanted.

"I know, but—"

He took a deep breath to steel his resolve, scrubbing at the nape of his neck with one hand. Like that would help. A little warmth at the collar was absolutely no defense mechanism when negotiating with a child.

"No buts, Zoe," he finally said to her. He had to keep his stare cast out to sea. Otherwise, those puppy dog eyes of hers would be his undoing. "You can hang out with Gigi tomorrow. Tonight, you're mine."

"Daddy," she whined.

"No. None of that. You promised me pizza and ice cream and silly movies."

She rolled her eyes. "You sound like such a girl."

Miles gave his daughter a sarcastic laugh, which she mocked perfectly. "And you're being a brat. Now, go tell Gigi good-bye so we can get going. I have to leave early in the morning."

"Yes, sir."

Zoe jumped to her feet and took off running, kicking up dusty clouds of beach behind her. She ran toward the ocean without stopping or slowing, and for so many reasons, that made Miles proud of her. At her age, he'd been terrified of the ocean, of the enormity and mystery of it, of the creatures living beneath the water's surface. Movies like *Jaws* and *Piranha* hadn't helped. No one had ever told him he was too young to watch those scary movies. No one had ever looked out for him. His mother and father had been typical Hollywood parents—the kind who forgot the fact they had a child because a nanny did the hard stuff for them.

Not his little girl. Zoe's life was absolutely the opposite of his. She had one parent who kept up with everything she did and gave her more attention than she could probably stand. And she was fearless. Most of the time, he loved that quality in her. Other times, it terrified him.

Miles pushed up from the blanket and brushed the sprinklings of sand from his jeans. He watched his daughter hug her best friend, then wave good-bye. It honestly broke Miles's heart that he had to be so firm on this, but for the next three months—possibly more—he would be on location in San Francisco filming his next big hit. Sure, a six-hour drive would get him home easily enough, but how often would he have the time to spend twelve hours on the road? Once filming started, he'd rarely have time to eat or sleep.

He gathered up their towels, her backpack, and the picnic basket he'd packed full of her favorite foods and waited as she ran back up the beach. In three short weeks, his little girl would turn seven.

Wow.

Where had the time gone?

Miles dragged his hand down his face, giving his tired eyes a thorough rubbing. Had it really been that long? Had it been almost seven years since his very best friend had died? That life-changing event was still so fresh in his memories, it felt like it had happened yesterday. He could still feel himself being shoved out of the delivery room by a handful of nurses—out into the hall so the doctors could save Anne's life. The heartbreak of being told she hadn't made it became fresh again. He'd never experienced pain and suffering quite like that, and the breakdown following would forever haunt him.

At times, the topic still came up in conversation with his sister. She worried about him and held nothing back when it came to letting him know exactly how much she did worry. He begged her not to, proclaiming he was fine. Years, promises, and lots of therapy hadn't convinced her he wouldn't break down again. He imagined she would never truly believe it, not until he gave up the past and started chasing her version of what his fairy tale should be. Zoe had survived. That was all the fairy tale he wanted or needed. And save for those first few months of him barely clinging to life and reality, every breath he'd taken had been for no one but her.

I hope I'm doing right by her, Anne.

"Ready, Daddy?" Zoe asked, popping up beside him.

She wrapped her small hand around his, and her gentle grip pulled his lips into a faint smile. Her mother had once elicited the same reaction from him. Every time she'd smiled in his direction or whispered his name, every time she'd told him she loved him, she'd tugged on his heart.

"Ready, princess," he softly said, still half-lost in the memories of his youth.

They climbed the sandy hill to the path leading up to Miles's Malibu beach house. Zoe had been a toddler when he'd bought the place. She'd been the main reason he'd picked a house so large. His daughter needed a room to sleep in and a room to play in, and they needed space to share together as well as space for his work, and of course, a room for Aunt Karen to sleep in when she came to visit. The Malibu beach house gave him all of that and then some. It was perfect, all the way down to the pink bedroom walls Zoe had made him paint over a few months ago because pink was *so* first grade.

"You know," Zoe said, "I can totally *be* a princess, but you don't have to call me princess anymore. I'm like… a lady or something."

Miles couldn't help laughing, though he tried to keep it restrained. Zoe put her hands on her hips and glared up at her father, and heaven help him, he had to fight even harder not to burst into hysterics.

"Daddy, you're trying my patience."

"Oh, I am, am I?" He crossed his arms and arched his brow. Where in the world had she learned that one? *Karen.* "Just how am I *trying* your patience, prin… little lady?"

"I'm just tryin' to keep it real, y'know?"

Keep it real? He blinked a few times. "Okay. I get it. No more 'princess' because you're a lady. Anything else I should be aware of?"

"Yeah." She started walking again, leaving her father standing stock still, a little curious and a little dumbfounded. Surely she planned on elaborating.

"Zoe?"

"Yeah, Daddy?"

"What else should I be aware of?"

Without missing a step or turning around to face him, she said, "I have a boyfriend. He's in third grade."

Miles could have fainted. His heart definitely stopped beating for a few breaths. That was a blast of news he wasn't prepared for, and while most children had their little elementary school romances, Zoe wasn't most children. She was his sweet little girl, his princess.

And he was now light years closer to those important talks he wasn't prepared for.

THERE WAS nothing more amazing than watching the sunrise through a warming filter. The blue of the sky had a hint of purple to it. The light on the horizon was as golden as the band Sawyer once wore on his very important finger, and it threw pink highlights against the clouds. This was his sanctuary—the only pure thing he had left in this world.

With a sigh, Sawyer slumped and let his camera gently fall to his chest. The strap around his neck kept it from tumbling into the sand. This heaven, his little piece of paradise, felt ruined now.

Exactly four months, one day, seven hours and thirty-three minutes had passed since Elijah had walked out of Sawyer's life and ripped his heart right out of his chest. Things had been going so great—like fairy-tale great—until the big M-word became a "Hey, here's the plane ticket" reality.

Sawyer's longtime lover had once claimed to dream of the day they could be legally wed like all the straight people who had been enjoying that right since the concept entered their minds. Sawyer had dreamed of it too—looked forward to it even—to the point of spending nights in bed holding his lover, talking about wedding plans and plans for the future. They'd loved each other so much, they'd had a commitment ceremony back in 2011, promising the day marriage became legal, they would take the next step. That historical day came when the Supreme Court decided DOMA was unconstitutional and new states were legalizing same-sex marriage.

Everyone they knew celebrated. Their committed friends were happy and ready to take the next step, just like Sawyer, but Elijah... well, something had happened. Elijah had changed. He didn't want to bind their union with legal documents anymore. "We're married in the eyes of God. Screw the state," he'd said, changing his tune so completely he'd sounded like a totally different man. Shortly after, all their plans went right down the drain. No more white picket fences. No more children playing in the yard. No more American dream. It was over.

Sawyer was alone for the first time since high school.

And all because Elijah wasn't ready to settle down, even though they'd been "settled down" together for over seven years already.

Come to find out, Elijah had been messing around on Sawyer for at least three years with a kid more than five years their junior. Normal people would've been pissed off enough to be over the heartbreak. Not Sawyer. He felt as lost as he ever had.

"Why the hell can't I get over you?" he whispered, raising the camera to his face.

Staring through the viewfinder, he could still see his beautiful Elijah posing in the morning sun as the waters of the Gulf of Mexico beat the white, sandy shore behind him. Every weekend they would waste hours upon hours exploring the beaches of Biloxi, Mississippi, while Sawyer snapped shots. He had some of the most amazing photos now, enough to build a portfolio to spur the interest of some big-time Hollywood movie company. They'd offered him a job... *him*—a nobody from south Mississippi, a nobody with a broken heart.

A nobody.

At first, Sawyer wouldn't even consider it. When he'd read the e-mail, a whole lot of "thanks, but no thanks" came in silent response. He thought up every great reason not to explore the option of leaving home for a better adventure, had even typed out the refusal e-mail. Never could hit Send, though. Something inside him told him not to do it, that he'd regret it later if he did.

One day—a few days or maybe even a week later—he sat on the front porch of his cottage in the middle of nowhere, sipping coffee and staring at a wall of trees while his best friend in the whole wide world gabbed on and on. He wasn't really paying much attention to what she was saying. More often than not, he didn't. Then for some silly reason, he decided to share his Hollywood story with her.

"Oh. My. God. Sawyer! You have to go. You have to do it," she carried on, more excited than he'd ever been about the news. An hour later, she still hadn't let it go. Two hours later, he was rewriting that e-mail and accepting the position. The closer the time came to pack up and go, the more excited Sawyer became. His emotions about leaving were a strange mix: concerned and eager, ready to move on, afraid to leave things behind. This would be good for him, though, he knew it. He needed a getaway, might even take Lucy's advice and get a little tail while he was on the west coast. Hell, he might even relocate his life, try for a new *everything*. Maybe that's just what he needed.

Sawyer lifted off his knees, stood, and brushed the sand from his jeans. He tucked his camera in the bag hanging from his shoulder, then turned to leave the beach. His bare feet sank into the sand; cool and gritty and everything *home* to him.

Biloxi was the only home he'd ever known. Not once had he ventured out of the South, not even for a vacation. He lived vicariously through *Lifestyles of the Rich and Famous*. Daydreams put him inside those mansions and limousines, and he'd been pretty certain, up until a few weeks ago, he'd never see any of that in reality.

Now's your chance to make a change, Sawyer Taylor. Make a name for yourself.

As soon as he stepped off the beach and onto pavement, the phone in his back pocket started to ring. The vibration against his ass gave him a start. He stumbled forward, toes fighting to anchor in the concrete. That didn't go so well. Grabbing a weathered wooden rail kept him from actually kissing the hard ground. He fished out the cell, and on the caller ID was a number he'd been waiting to see for almost a week.

"Mr. Rockwell?"

"I'm his assistant," a soft-spoken woman from somewhere out in the airwaves said. "He's ready for you to join his director in San Francisco. Your flight leaves in two days. I hope that's okay for you."

"It's fine."

"Because you really don't have a choice," she said as if Sawyer hadn't spoken. The woman babbled on and on and on about expectations, about the way things would happen and what he could expect when he got there. She spoke so fast Sawyer could barely keep up. He tried. Oh, how he tried. But he was certain a lot of detail would be lost by the time plans became action.

"Will you send this to me in an e-mail?" he asked.

At the exact same time, she said, "All of this will be sent in an e-mail."

"So, I guess everything's in order, then," he said.

"Just waiting on you."

"I'll be there."

"Good. Have a safe trip, Mr. Taylor. We'll see you in San Francisco."

"Right," Sawyer flatly said before hanging up and slipping the phone into his pocket.

He continued up the hill, onto the asphalt lot where he'd parked his beloved red Jeep Wagoneer before heading down to the beach that morning. Her hinges were rusted and her motor loud. She sputtered from time to time, but she was faithful and reliable and constant, which was a hell of a lot more than he could say for his love life. And yet, he still planned on leaving her behind just as he planned on leaving his old life behind.

Sawyer popped his hand on her thick, metal hood. He would miss her, but he had someone lined up to take care of her in case he ever decided to come back to Mississippi.

"It's time for a new life, baby," he said as he wrenched open the driver's side door. Everyone knew he wouldn't move on with his life and get over Elijah if he stayed in Biloxi, in the house they'd been sharing since they'd left their parents' places. Sawyer knew he would never forget Elijah if everything he saw reminded him of the love he'd had and lost.

Yeah, moving on was all he had left.

He had to do this.

CHAPTER TWO

CRACK OF dawn Thursday morning, Miles had to get his daughter ready to go to his sister's place for the next three months. Most of her things had already been taken there, or had been left there the last time Miles had gone on a directorial excursion. He would've taken her on every single one had his sister not convinced him a long time ago to let the little girl live a normal childhood. Well, nothing would ever *really* be normal for her. Sure, she had the continuity of being in a classroom and around her friends, and the closest thing she would have to a female role model was Miles's sister. She would have no siblings and her daddy… what was his deal?

His deal? Well, he worked his ass off and tended to his fatherly duties. That was his deal. Responsibilities didn't leave a whole lot of time for romance, and frankly, the one-night stands he often had would come nowhere near his child if he could help it. Single life worked much, much better for Daddy.

"May I have McDonald's for breakfast?" Zoe asked from the passenger's seat.

Miles shuddered at the thought of her polluting her little body with that crap. "McDonald's, sweetheart? Really?"

"I like the hotcakes."

"How about I take you for real belgian waffles from Daddy's favorite restaurant?"

She crinkled her tiny nose.

"Fine. McDonald's it is," he said with a sigh as he peeled down the first street on the right. The smile on his little girl's face was worth the fat and calories and cholesterol in one of those McMuffin things. At least now he could get it with egg whites and canadian bacon. Or better yet, he could just grab a not-so-healthy smoothie and call it a meal. Choices. Choices.

He pulled into the parking lot, where a statue of a nine-foot-tall clown greeted them with a smile and an immobile hand. Zoe popped up from the car and waved. She started in a mad dash for the door, and just as Miles was about to call her back, the phone in his pocket rang.

"Hello?" he said without checking the caller ID. Getting to his little girl's side was much more important than screening for unwanted phone calls.

"Miles?"

The voice stopped him dead in his tracks. He hadn't heard that sweet, velvety sound in six months, not since a wild weekend alone together left Miles wondering if many repeat performances and long, romantic getaways would blossom from the tryst or if he'd been used by yet another actor who wanted to get ahead.

"Gavin?"

"Hey."

"Hi."

"How are you?" the actor asked. As if he *really* wanted to know.

Miles caught up to his daughter and reached for her hand, cradling his phone between his ear and shoulder. That seemed like such a loaded question, all things considered. Gavin obviously had no clue what waking up in an empty bed after a magical sex-filled weekend did for a man like Miles's ego.

"I'm fine," he said flatly as they found their place in line. "Did you need something?"

"I just...." Gavin sighed. "I wanted to check on you. I know I haven't called, and that's very wrong of me. I've been super busy, but I've been thinking about you."

"I wouldn't know."

"Miles."

"Gavin, I can't talk right now. I'm with my daughter. I'll see you on the set in San Francisco."

"About that...."

"What about it?"

"I won't be there."

For a split second, Miles's heart stopped beating. A thread of panic wound through him. His stomach knotted and his temples pounded. God only knew what his blood pressure was doing right now. He was going to have to replace an actor not even four days before they were due to start filming. What the fuck?

"You're kidding, right?"

"No," Gavin said. "I got a better deal. I leave for Virginia tomorrow."

"Virginia." Miles nodded a bit convulsively. His blood pressure was definitely climbing toward stroke level, and fast. "That's nice. Just perfect. Don't expect any favors from me, and don't expect to be on any more of my movies."

"Miles."

"Go to hell, Gavin."

All the rage in him begged him to slam that phone down onto the tile and cheer as it shattered into a million little pieces. That phone, however, was his lifeline, like a vital organ, and he couldn't live without it. It connected him to everything important in the world of director Miles Eisenberg. Daddy, on the other hand….

Miles looked down at his little girl and found her wide, hazel eyes staring up at him like he'd turned into a monster. His heart sank. He never wanted to see an expression like that on her sweet face, and he certainly never wanted to be the one who put it there.

Sighing, he rubbed his free hand over the back of his neck, closed his eyes, and practiced steady breathing. He wasn't going to let an asshole like Gavin ruin the last few hours he had with his precious little girl.

"Daddy." Zoe tugged on his hand. Miles opened his eyes and looked back down. Her tiny pink lips curled into a soft smile. "I ordered hotcakes for me. Tell her what you want."

He smiled at the young lady behind the counter, a silent thank-you for being so patient. "I'll have a large strawberry-banana smoothie, please."

"Will that be all, sir?" she asked.

"Yes, please."

"Daddy, that's not food. You have to eat something," Zoe insisted.

"She has a point," the woman at the register said. With a wink, her once-subtle smile widened. She had the most perfect white teeth. A twinkle filled her blue eyes. She was quite beautiful and not what one would expect to find working in a fast food dive. Ah. Wait. Barely out of high school, came to California to become a star. Miles knew the type well, could spot them from across a crowded room. They always had that doe-eyed, hopeful look when they first arrived, and slowly, Hollywood sucked all the dreams and innocence right out of them.

Poor thing.

"Very well. Give me the yogurt parfait. It has fruit in it, right?"

"Yes, sir."

"That's perfect."

Miles fished out his credit card and handed it over.

After the woman swiped it and handed it back, Miles stepped aside with his little girl and guided her over to a table. The surface was sticky and crumby, but it was probably the cleanest table in the entire restaurant.

"Sit right here and don't move," he said before heading over to the condiment station. He grabbed a handful of napkins and returned to do the job of the people who'd failed the establishment.

A manly voice called his ticket number, and Zoe bounced excitedly in her seat. Miles gave her a look, and she said, "I know. Don't move." Miles grinned with pride, then returned to the counter to collect their food.

When he set the tray down and sat across from his daughter, he noticed her staring at him with a strange mix of curiosity and confusion, like she wanted to have one of those talks that often made him uncomfortable. He took a long sip of his smoothie to wet his palate.

"Daddy, why did you get mad at your phone?" she asked

He exhaled in relief at such an easy to answer question, not that he planned on giving her the whole truth. "The man on the other end upset me."

"Why?"

"Because he wasn't being a nice man."

"Why?"

"Because he…." *He screwed your father over.* "He did something that wasn't very nice, Zoe. He upset Daddy."

"Why?"

"Why do you keep asking me why?"

She shrugged and stuffed a small heap of pancakes into her mouth. "I dunno," she mumbled around her fork.

"Zoe, don't talk with food in your mouth, princess."

"I'm a lady," she declared.

"Well, ladies don't talk with their mouths full."

He lifted his cup and sucked down more smoothie. She shoved more pancake into her mouth. They quietly ate until all the food was gone, then Zoe looked up at him with more seriousness than a six-year-old child should ever display and said, "You shouldn't let mean people make you mad. Auntie Karen taught me that."

"Your Auntie Karen is a very, *very* wise woman."

"I know. She's totally making me into a wise woman too."

Miles choked on his drink. *Dear God, help me….*

After clearing their trash from the table and waiting outside the bathroom while Zoe washed the syrup from her hands, they returned to Miles's car to continue on their little journey. Miles would've prolonged the ride for hours, if not days, to spend more time with the most beautiful girl in the world, but he had somewhere to be. He had things to do. Filming wasn't due to start for four more days, but setup started the moment he pulled up to the inn. He had actors to check on, crew to scare into shape, and details to finalize… a lead role to fill, now.

"We're here!" Zoe squealed.

He barely had the car in park before she was trying to tear out the door and up to Karen's waiting arms. The only good thing about leaving her for so long was knowing she would be with someone who loved her almost as much as he did, someone who would take care of her and teach her things exactly like he would. And Zoe loved her Aunt Karen almost as much as she loved her daddy. She touted the fact quite often, and her feelings showed in her excitement when Karen's name was brought up.

"Hey, big brother," Karen said. She knelt down and wrapped both arms around Zoe's shoulders and hugged her tight. "And how's my little princess doing?"

"She's not a princess anymore," Miles warned. "She's a lady."

Karen arched her brow and Miles gave her a "yeah, you heard that right" nod.

"Daddy let me have hotcakes!" Zoe exclaimed.

"He did?" Karen stood elbow to almost elbow with her big brother. She gave him a look that alluded to his coming death if that child showed the first sign of being hopped up on sugar. "They better have been good," she said, more to Miles than to Zoe.

Zoe giggled while Miles hoisted her bags out of the trunk. He carried them over to his sister's front door and set each pink duffel bag by her feet; then he knelt down and spread his arms wide.

"Tell Daddy good-bye, sweetheart. I won't see you for a while."

Zoe threw her arms around her father, and he held her in a hug. Miles closed his eyes and kissed his little girl's temple, cradling the back of her head in his massive hand. Nothing in the world made him feel as wonderful as being a father; nothing made him feel so complete.

"I love you, sweetheart," he said softly.

"I love you too, Daddy."

Reluctantly, he let her go and turned her over to his sister, and then he rose to his feet to kiss Karen's cheek. He didn't have to tell her to take care of his pride and joy. He didn't have to worry about Zoe at all as long as she had Karen.

"Thank you," he whispered, leaning in to kiss his sister's cheek.

"You don't have to thank me, Miles. I love her too."

"I know you do."

With two fingers, she brushed a few pieces of his wind-blown hair back into place behind his ear. "Have a safe trip," she said. "We'll see you soon."

CHAPTER THREE

SAWYER STOOD outside the San Francisco airport, bright sun burning his eyes. He held his hand to his brow to shade his sight. Truth be told, the sun was welcome, as welcome as standing again for the first time in way too many hours. His stomach rumbled, reminding him once again the food on the plane should've never been considered safe for human consumption. One whiff of the mess they called braised fish and Sawyer couldn't make himself take the first bite. Now his empty stomach paid the price, loudly reminding him sustenance needed to be his first priority.

"C'mon, where are you?" he muttered, scouring the ramps and roadways weaving in and out of each other in front of the airport's massive wall of windows. He searched for something resembling a sedan sent by the movie company, something with markings or… *something*.

Nothing. Shuttle busses and taxis hurried by, cars and trucks and SUVs, crossovers and hybrids, and all the kinds of cars great amounts of money could buy. Nothing resembled a chauffeured sedan, and not a single one slowed down to pick him up. For a moment, he wondered if maybe he should've had the forethought to hang a sign around his neck like a lost puppy. That's certainly what he felt like right now—a lost puppy in a big, scary new world.

I am Sawyer Taylor, photographer. Please help me find my home.

Hiking up his bag full of equipment, he grabbed the handle of his wheeled suitcase and started toward the walkway leading to the line of shuttles and taxis, thinking he could get to the hotel faster if he just did it on his own.

As soon as his foot hit the pavement, a wailing horn sounded and a sleek red sports car whooshed by, kicking out a wind twice a strong as the pleasant California breeze. He quickly jerked back and pulled himself out of harm's way, only to discover the person behind the wheel wasn't a crazed lunatic, but rather a young blonde woman with high-priced taste. Her heels were the latest Jimmy Choos, and her dress absolutely had to be haute couture. Sawyer knew this because his very best friend in the entire world was the biggest label whore he'd ever met, and Lucy assumed just because Sawyer was gay, he loved designers as much as she did. Nothing could've been further from the truth. Now, put a top-of-the-line Nikon DSLR in his hand, and that was almost better than porn. Almost.

"I'm Penelope," the woman said, extending her arm. He recognized her voice right away. "I'm from Mr. Rockwell's office."

"Yes, I know."

"Good," she smirked. "Then we can handle the business of getting you settled quickly."

"That would be nice. I'm exhausted." His stomach rumbled again, reminding him of his other woes. "And I *really* need to eat somethin'."

She opened the trunk and reached for the bag he had hoisted on his shoulder. Sawyer immediately jerked away. No one—*no one*—ever touched his equipment. Some people got twitchy over things left out of place or having to touch the handle of a shopping cart without cleaning it. Sawyer got twitchy over people touching his gear, and he did his best to make that very clear up front.

"This doesn't leave my side," he said, white-knuckling the strap.

Penelope arched her little blonde brow at him.

"No one handles my gear but me."

"Understood, but when you get on set, you'll probably have an assistant. Your assistant is there to help you *handle your gear* and do whatever other menial tasks you see fit. Now, I suggest warming up to the idea of letting someone else touch your things, Sawyer. It'll help you acclimate to the fast-paced world of making movies."

She didn't wait for a response, but rudely swung her petite ass into her shiny sports car and slammed the door behind her. He glared from outside the passenger side of the car. The taxis were looking more and more enticing.

With a sigh, Sawyer resigned himself to having no other choice but to ride alongside Penelope, the ice queen from Mr. Rockwell's office, until she safely deposited him at his hotel. As long as they both kept to themselves, Sawyer felt pretty certain the ride would go rather swimmingly.

He planned to hide in his hotel room until Monday morning came along and he had no choice but to join the rest of the crew on the set. It sounded like a fabulous idea, and what better way to get prepared for the "fast-paced world" of working for Hollywood? Only problem was he'd promised Lucy he wouldn't lie around dwelling on the past and things he couldn't change. Oh, and she was totally the type to call and check in on him. A simple lie wouldn't cut it either. She would say something like, "I don't hear any background noise. You're in your room, aren't you?" That, of course, would be followed by her chewing him out about falling apart and letting himself go. It seemed easier to do what she expected of him and make the best of it if he could.

Penelope's car jerked and jostled over imperfect asphalt as she rushed him away from the airport. Each quickly taken loop threatened to bounce his head off the window beside him or spill him into her seat, even though the seatbelt cutting off his airway held him tight to the passenger side. If this kept up the entire twenty-five miles to his room, whatever remained of his breakfast might very well end up on her spotless floor mats.

"You okay?" she asked.

"No. You think you could slow down a bit?"

"This is how people drive here. You'll just have to deal with it or ride the BART."

"The what?"

"Bay Area Rapid Transport."

"What the hell is that?"

"It's a train. Sort of like the subways in New York. Sort of not."

"Oh," Sawyer said, turning his gaze back to the window so he could take in the scenery.

San Francisco was nothing like any other place he'd seen in his life, not that his travels had been vast and varied or anything. Flying over, he'd noticed how dense the neighborhoods were, but he got a whole new perspective from the ground. There was no such thing as a backyard to play in. Neighborhoods were hilly. Urban. Decayed. Well, at least that's how it appeared from the road. He could've been completely wrong about that, but compared to home, those were the first words that came to mind.

Sawyer knew right away he wasn't going to like San Francisco. The spray-painted markings on the interstate's sound walls gave off more than a hint of danger. Some of it was clearly gang graffiti. He swore he'd seen something similar in one of those *Gangland* documentaries on the Discovery channel. That's the only way he would've ever recognized it. Sawyer's very sheltered, very safe life hadn't prepared him for anything like this. Gangs didn't rule the beaches of Biloxi, Mississippi. The idea was so ludicrous, Sawyer snorted out a little laugh.

Penelope cut her eyes his way but didn't say a word.

He settled his head back against the seat, eyes closed, breathing easy, his tendency for motion sickness rearing its ugly head. Maybe if he didn't think about it and focused on his breath, everything would be okay, and he wouldn't hurl all over the upholstery.

Maybe....

"We're almost there," Penelope said, jerking to the right, then the left, presumably zipping through traffic. No way in hell was Sawyer going to open his eyes to check it out. Something about the idea of seeing his life flash before his eyes made his stomach tighten even more.

"If something happens, and we don't start filming Monday, someone from the studio will notify you," she said.

"Does filmin' get delayed often?"

"More often than the studio would like. Directors and producers— well, all the Hollywood types—are finicky people. Actors don't show up sometimes. Directors get in their moods. Weather might not permit. Anything could happen. Look at it this way, though. If it gets delayed, you get a vacation on the studio's dime."

Aren't we optimistic?

The car bounced up another hilly street that looked like every other hilly street he'd seen since he'd arrived. Penelope whipped around a corner and into a driveway that led back beyond two rows of thick trees. They arrived at a huge house that could've easily been a mansion hidden in the middle of San Francisco. Sawyer frowned as he took it all in. Nothing about the surrounding neighborhood would've alluded to this little treasure. Nothing about the urban decay right outside the ring of trees would've led anyone to believe paradise hid within those natural walls.

"What is this place?" he finally asked, eyes wide, mouth gaping.

A slow smile crept across Penelope's face, a smile of satisfaction for God only knew what reason. She didn't immediately answer, only pulled farther into the drive, then parked her sporty little car among all the other high-class hotrods lining the edge of the parking lot.

"This is the *only* place people working for the studio stay when they're in San Francisco. The paparazzi doesn't come around, and it's secluded enough no one will ever find you here. Be thankful. You could be in the Crown Plaza or Four Seasons or something like that."

"Four Seasons sounds nice…," he mumbled.

"This place is Pearl of the Bay, and it's sooooo much better than Four Seasons. Trust me."

Penelope slipped out of the car. The sound of her door slamming made him jump. He supposed she wanted him to follow her.

As soon as he opened the door, a soft cool breeze brushed along his face. Summer in Mississippi would've been hotter than hell, humid and difficult to deal with. Not in San Francisco. It was bright and beautiful outside, but the wind gave it the feel of a cool fall day. Each gentle gust lightened Sawyer's heart, and his smile grew wider. If the weather stayed like this, he could seriously see himself finding a beach to hide at and take pictures of.

Maybe San Fran isn't as bad as I thought.

"C'mon," Penelope said. "Get your things and follow me."

The trunk of her car popped open. She reached in and grabbed a Coach bag that wasn't his, then a second to match, and a third smaller bag. There were more matching suitcases in there, but she obviously wasn't hauling them in right now.

She eyed him for a long moment, clearly expecting him to do as she'd told him.

He eventually did, and she closed the trunk.

Sawyer waited to follow her up to the front of the inn. The double doors flew open, and a man in a penguin suit stepped out onto the porch. He was an older man, debonair from afar, with thin wire-rimmed glasses on the tip of his nose. Short salt and pepper hair hugged his scalp. A thin moustache hooded his tight lips. Rosy round cheeks framed a beady nose. He had a jolly look about him, welcoming and affable. Sawyer got the distinct feeling he'd be making friends with the gentleman before his trip ended.

"Welcome to San Francisco," the older man said, extending his hand. His voice was refined and eloquent, soft and warm. "I'm Martin, and I'll be here to help if ever you need anything."

"Thank you, Martin." Sawyer took his hand and gave it a firm shake. "I'm Sawyer Taylor, the photographer." *Like anyone has ever heard of me. Pfft.*

Martin smiled, and just like in his voice, there was warmth in his expression.

For the first time since Sawyer arrived in San Francisco, he felt like this little adventure of his wouldn't end up being some kind of horrible mistake. The West Coast might actually have more to give him than his lifelong home simply because one old man offered a little kindness.

Martin grabbed one of Sawyer's bags—the one hanging from his shoulder, the one he'd been so intent on keeping by his side at all times. Sawyer tightened his grip on the strap, and Martin retreated. Penelope had already disappeared into the house. Thank God, otherwise she might've accosted him for not letting Martin take the damn bag.

"Come," Martin said. "I'll walk you to your room."

"Thank you," Sawyer responded, relieved Martin didn't argue over the bag like Penelope had.

They headed into the house. The foyer was spectacular, large and beautifully decorated with an antique table right in the center. What looked like a crystal vase held an array of colorful flowers, reaching up toward a massive chandelier. Sawyer had only seen one like it in those historical Gulf Coast homes that managed to survive hurricane season every August and September. He'd always loved those old homes.

"So, I detect a hint of an accent," Martin said, tossing a quick smile and glance over his shoulder.

"Yes, sir. I'm from Mississippi—the coast, actually."

"I would've guessed west Tennessee or maybe Atlanta. Your accent isn't thick enough for Mississippi."

Sawyer couldn't help laughing. "Well, my father was a Yankee who married a southern belle. So, I s'pose I got a little bit of both."

"Yes, I suppose you did."

Martin climbed the stairs and Sawyer quickly followed. The soles of their shoes clicked and clapped against the hardwood flooring. He turned to Sawyer and said, "This is your room. As I said before, if there is anything at all you need, please don't hesitate to call on me. This is my home, and I like to take care of my guests."

"Thank you, Martin."

"Enjoy your stay, Mr. Taylor."

"Sawyer."

"Excuse me?"

"Call me Sawyer. It's only fair considerin' I'm callin' you Martin."

Martin gave Sawyer one last endearing smile as he placed a single gold-colored key in Sawyer's hand. "Sawyer it is," he said in a pleasant voice before turning on his heel. The kind old man disappeared down the stairs again.

The walls were bare, light blue. An oak chair rail separated plaster from nicely kept bead board. It was only a hint lighter than the hardwood floor below. From the look of it, Martin took great care of his home, took pride in his belongings. But what of Martin? Did he have family? Did someone take care of him the way he took care of his home?

Why do you care, Sawyer?

It wasn't that he cared, really. Mostly, it was curiosity. That was Sawyer's thing. People were his interest. Life was his interest. That's why he took pictures. They were a still study of life.

So, what about you, Martin? What's your story? Where are the family portraits? What about the kids? The grandkids?

Sawyer looked up and down the empty hall one last time, then pushed back his curiosity and slipped the key into the door. He gave the knob a turn and the door sprang open to a room that could've easily been a suite at a five-star hotel back home. The bed sat alone in the corner across from a settee and small antique table. Its posts rose high, and fluffy white blankets invited Sawyer to come on in and stay a long while. The colors were cool, just like they had been in the hallway—shades of pastel blues and greens. White trim and chair railing matched the white doors and windows. Sheer, white curtains barely kept out the daylight.

With a Cheshire grin, Sawyer dropped his suitcase at the door and hurried toward the bed, carefully lowering his gear bag onto the settee in passing. He raised his arms and dove forward, flying like an eagle with wings spread wide onto the fluffy mound of linens, pillows, and mattress. His landing was smooth and the surface as soft as it looked. His long limbs didn't even dangle over the edges.

Heaven.

As he reached for a pillow to settle in for a catnap, the phone in his pocket started to ring. *Jesus, not again.* Did Hollywood really require this much attention? Seriously, in the three years he'd had that phone, it hadn't been used as much as it had in the last two weeks.

It was Lucy. Oops.

"Yes, dear," he said rather sarcastically.

"Did you make it? Are you alive?"

"If I wasn't alive, I wouldn't have answered the phone, now would I?"

"Ha. Ha. Smartass."

Sawyer laughed.

"You were supposed to call me when you landed."

"Yeah, I know. This entire trip has been a whirlwind adventure already. Did you know forty minutes isn't enough time to find your gate, get on the Skylink, and get to said gate at the Dallas airport? I didn't even get a chance to piss before hoppin' on a three hour flight to San Francisco."

It was now Lucy's turn to laugh.

"Whatever you do," she said, "promise me you'll have some sort of fun, 'kay?"

Sawyer thought a moment. He rubbed his face against the fluffy comforter covering his very soft bed. Staying here all weekend sounded perfect... the perfect idea of "fun."

"I promise."

"I mean it."

"I know." He grinned wickedly to himself. It wasn't a lie. He planned on having a whole lot of fun... sleeping.

"You're gonna get up. Get dressed. And go out, right?"

Shit.

CHAPTER FOUR

"MARTIN, IT'S great to see you again," Miles said, clapping his hand against the older gentleman's shoulder. "What has it been? A year? Two?"

"Six months, Mr. Eisenberg," Martin responded flatly as he reached for Miles's luggage.

Miles frowned. "My last movie wrapped sixteen months ago."

"You weren't here for a movie, Mr. Eisenberg."

Brow arched, Miles thought back on what he might've been doing six months ago. Or rather, *who* he'd been doing. He used Martin's inn as a getaway when he wanted to do something lewd with a not-so-savory cohort. It allowed him to keep his misdeeds far from the impressionable eyes of his daughter while maintaining appearances for Hollywood.

A slow, devious grin tugged at the edges of his lips as a fond memory eased out from the recesses of his mind. The man in question had been exceptional, not the best Miles had ever had but certainly not the worst. He'd been an out-of-work actor looking for a part. The man in question had been none other than Gavin, the pretentious prick who'd bailed on him last minute. But he'd been one hell of a lay.

Yes. Yes, indeed, he had been.

In the aftermath of that porn-worthy weekend of carnal debauchery with Mr. Mystery Date, however, Miles did leave a hefty sum of money for Martin to take care of certain repairs needed in the suite.

Well, that certainly explains Martin's attitude.

Now, tell him you're sorry.

"Let me take that," Miles said in a sorrowful tone, avoiding two words he reserved for his daughter and his sister. Carrying his own luggage was the least he could do. "Am I in the same room?"

"As always, sir."

"Thank you, Martin. I can find my way."

"As you wish."

Martin disappeared through the double doors leading into the parlor, where the older man often sat behind an antique desk, reading a newspaper or a book. Miles casually stepped forward through the foyer toward the staircase leading to the second floor rooms.

As soon as his foot hit the hardwood upstairs, he heard the low hum of music coming from the first room on the left. It sounded acoustic, like that indie crap a lot of the new-agey Hollywood types listened to just so they could call themselves eclectic and artsy, or some shit like that. They were the types who sat in coffee shops, sipping lattes and reading the newspaper solely to find another cause to support. Those people were plastic. Fake. Just like Hollywood.

The room in question had been specifically reserved for Mr. Sawyer Taylor, an up-and-coming photographer whose eye for raw beauty fascinated Miles. Miles had accidentally gotten his hands on the kid's portfolio from one of those Tumblr things that always happened to come up when Miles googled for images. Over three hundred black and white photos taken around Mississippi and the Gulf Coast had caught Miles's attention and held it for over an hour. He'd known right then the studio needed to hire Sawyer as the set photographer. By the time the studio had gotten around to hiring him, Sawyer's photos had begun to appear in magazines. People around the art galleries were all abuzz with talk of the man who loved the camera so much but never appeared in front of it.

Was Sawyer a fake too? Was he one of those hip, yuppie douchebags Miles had come to despise in his years as a movie director?

God, I hope not.

To be honest, though, Miles was curious about the hot young photographer. No one ever showed the elusive Sawyer Taylor's face. No interviews were to be found. The man had been impossible to get on the phone. No matter. Once Miles had seen his work, he absolutely had to have *that* photographer for this movie. No one else would've done.

Miles turned toward the closed door and raised his fist. He planned on knocking, had even introduced himself three or four times in his head. But when it came time to put knuckles to wood, Miles couldn't do it. What if reality didn't live up to fantasy? What if Sawyer Taylor—the man— totally disappointed and made Miles not want to work with Sawyer Taylor—the photographer?

He abruptly lowered his hand and continued to the far end of the hall to the room where he always stayed. It was a large suite with huge windows looking out toward the bay. The room could've been split in two and old Martin could've doubled his money *if* he'd been a smarter businessman, but Miles certainly wouldn't complain. He had enough room to spend six or ten or twenty months in that suite, if he had to. He had luxury and comfort close to that of being in his own home, and that was perfect, but he would miss one very important person.

Miles fished his phone out of the pocket of his too-tight jeans. There were three text messages from his daughter. *Are you there yet? Bring something awesome back. I miss you, Daddy.* Each one made the smile on his face a little wider. Each one made him miss her a little more. He pictured her parked next to him at his desk with her Mac, pounding away at the keys. He would ask what she was working on so intently, to which she would say something like, "The book I'm writing, Daddy." He would sit in awe of her genius, and at such a young age. She was his best friend and the only girl he would ever love.

Grinning ear-to-ear, he opened her message and pressed the Call button. Some silly pop song played instead of a normal ringtone. It was one of her favorites, one he'd heard on their many trips to the mall with her friends. He didn't know the name or the artist but could hum along with it as if it was one of his favorites too.

"Daddy!" Zoe squealed from the other end of the line. She sounded so close, even though she was more than four hundred miles away. "It took you forever to get there."

"I know, sweetheart. Are you having fun with Aunt Karen?"

"She painted my toenails purple, and we're eating popcorn and watching movies."

"Sounds like the best evening ever."

"Would be more awesomer if you was here too."

"I know, sweetheart. Daddy will rush back as soon as he can, I promise."

Zoe continued to talk about all the things she wanted to do when her daddy finally made it home, things that included Justin Bieber albums and trips to the couturier. Apparently, her Aunt Karen had been busy teaching his child the latest fashions, and his wallet would pay the price. Anything for Zoe, though. Some called it spoiling. He called it trying like hell to make up for what she didn't have.

She went on to talk about something her best friend had done, and Miles listened closely until he spotted the entertainment section of the San Francisco Chronicle on the nightstand beside his bed. More specifically, a headline with his name, screaming for attention. His daughter's dainty, excited voice immediately faded away.

Miles Eisenberg to film latest A.L. Blake hit in San Francisco.

As far as he could remember, he hadn't done anything to warrant a headline, and no one was supposed to know anything about the studio filming anything anywhere. After the last book-to-movie gig bombed, Miles had wanted to keep this one quiet. Speculation was known to be a killer, and movie critics had a way of digging graves before the bodies even cooled. The last thing Miles needed was for this movie to flop just because his crew got a little nervous.

"Daddy, you're not listening," Zoe whined.

"I'm sorry, sweetheart. I'm here. Daddy's just a little preoccupied."

"What's preoccupied?"

"You know when you're watching TV and I try talking to you?"

"Yes, sir."

"That's preoccupied."

"Oh," she giggled. "But you didn't answer my question."

"What was the question?"

"When can I come see you?"

They had a tradition, Miles and his daughter. A month or so into filming, she would come to wherever he was staying and spend a week with him, hanging out on the set, sightseeing, staying up late, and watching movies. He would take her anywhere she wanted and buy her one of everything. She chose the restaurants. She chose the activities. Seeing her so happy rewarded him in ways his career never could.

"For your birthday. If Aunt Karen doesn't mind, she can bring you."

"Yay!" she squealed.

The sound elicited a laugh from him, despite the unexpected headline staring up in black and white. He tightened his hand around the newspaper, rough paper crinkling in his grip.

"Sweetheart, I have to go now. I love you."

"I love you too, Daddy."

"Tell Aunt Karen I'll call her later."

"Yes, sir."

With that, he ended the call and slid the phone back into his pocket. He unfolded the paper and read the article beneath the headline. It spoke of the last movie he'd made, another A.L. Blake book that been a bestseller and all the buzz in booklandia. It'd flown off the shelves faster than they could print it, and like all bestsellers, Hollywood had come aknockin'. Blake had been more than happy to see the masterpiece go to film. Of course, the second book in that series came out, and the studio already had its greedy hands on the film rights. The first movie had made all its money back, so the second would absolutely go to production despite the studio's soured name. Critics said Hollywood had ruined yet another book, and Eisenberg's bad direction was to blame.

Well, it hadn't *all* been Miles's fault. Blake had had a vision and the producer had had a vision. The studio had had their idea, and the actors.... God, let's not get started on the actors. Miles had been set up to fail, and when they'd called him back to do number two, he'd considered telling Hollywood to fuck off even if he had signed a contract.

Now, according to the entertainment rags, no one expected this one to be any better. They expected Miles to flop again, but he would show them. He wasn't going to take any shit from anyone this time around. This was *his* movie. Not some pretentious writer's. Not some high-strung producer's. Not some washed-up actor's. And damn sure not the studio's.

"I need a drink," he said, pushing up from the edge of the bed. He tossed the newspaper in the wastebasket by the door on his way to the bathroom, silently swearing he wouldn't pay any more attention to critics and reporters. They would see, just like the rest of the world. Miles Eisenberg wasn't a flop. His movies weren't flops.

CHAPTER FIVE

THAT HAD to have been the worst night of sleep Sawyer had ever gotten. The clock on the nightstand blared in stark red the predawn hour of way too damn early in the morning. Back home it would've been around 6:00 a.m. Not here. In California, the sun hadn't come up yet, and normal people still had half a night's sleep to get. The two-hour time difference didn't matter to Sawyer's internal clock, and sleeping in wasn't an option.

He flung one leg over the edge of the bed, then the other, and sat there for a long moment, rubbing both hands over his face. That didn't help the burn of sleep in his eyes. It didn't help sunny up his mood either. Already, it was looking like he needed to call the day a bust.

Once he'd convinced himself there was absolutely no chance of sleep in his immediate future, he pushed to his feet and resolved to do the showering, dressing, eating thing, then maybe go in search of something epic and uplifting, something as inspirational as the beaches back home.

He didn't spend a whole lot of time in the shower, despite the heat and the pressure against his muscles. Oh, it felt amazing, and he could've happily spent the next three or so months hiding there with no problem, but he'd made a promise to his best friend. He always did his best to keep his word once he gave it.

Sawyer pulled on a plaid button-down, pushed the sleeves up to his elbows, then dragged a brown leather belt through the loops of his faded jeans. He shoved his feet into a pair of tattered brown boots, then grabbed his camera bag and headed downstairs.

His boots hit the hardwood foyer floor with a thud, and almost immediately, Martin appeared from around the stairs. The shadow of him moving caught the corner of Sawyer's eye and Sawyer softly gasped, gripping his chest.

"You scared me," he said with a gasp.

"I'm sorry, sir," Martin responded with a slight bow.

"That's okay. Everything's fine now."

Sawyer tightened both hands around the strap of his gear bag, glance shifting around the dark foyer. He smelled food cooking in the back of the house. The scent of bacon frying and coffee brewing wafted down the hallway. His stomach started to rumble. Sawyer grimaced.

"Breakfast will be served soon, Mr."—one edge of Martin's lip twitched—"Sawyer. Will you be joining us?"

"Perhaps. I wanted to go into the city today. Maybe take some photos."

"You shouldn't leave on an empty stomach. Come, let me feed you. Then I can enlighten you on the ways of the beautiful Bay Area."

Martin spun on his heel and started down the hall. From the back, Sawyer noticed the slight bald spot in his salt and pepper hair. He also noticed a faint limp in the older man's gait. Surely to God he didn't run this place by himself. It was too big, had too many rooms, too many duties. Surely he had help.

"Have a seat at the table. Pearl will bring a plate to you."

So he did have help. Good.

"So, you and Pearl run this place alone?"

"No." A twinkle filled Martin's dark eyes. "Our son helps us. He's in college during the day, but he does all the hard stuff at night."

"Ah, Pearl's your wife."

"Not exactly, but that story is for another time, my friend. Let me get the coffee; then I'll tell you about San Francisco."

"Sure." Sawyer folded his hands in his lap, sitting back in his chair. Martin left the dining room, old-fashioned double doors swinging behind him. The aroma of freshly brewed coffee rushed toward him, riding on the gust of air left in Martin's wake.

Funny, Sawyer thought, when he realized how at home and at ease he felt in Martin's lovely house. The place was warm and inviting, even more so than the place he'd once shared with a man he'd loved with every ounce of his being.

Footsteps thudded in the background. Sawyer raised his head in time to catch two women in workout suits jogging toward him, platinum blonde ponytails swinging at the crowns of their heads. They could've been twins. They looked like actresses. He wasn't sure why he assumed such, but it seemed safe, all things considered.

"Hi," the one on the left said in a high-pitched voice.

"Hi," the one on the right promptly repeated.

"Hi," Sawyer said with a nervous smile.

"Breakfast, ladies?" Martin asked.

Sawyer's head jerked back around, surprised his new friend had come into the room without making a single sound. Before, the swinging doors had creaked on their hinges. Maybe this time Sawyer had been too wrapped up in his thoughts and the female joggers to notice.

"No time, Martin," the first woman said.

"Plus, we have to watch our figures," the second said.

"Hollywood doesn't like fat actresses," the first added.

It was like watching a Ping-Pong match.

They both waved, then disappeared out the side door. Martin took the spot across from Sawyer, sliding over a piping hot cup of coffee as he settled into the chair.

"So, San Francisco," Martin said, circling both hands around his coffee cup. "You *must* visit Golden Gate Park and have a meal in Chinatown. Maybe shop downtown and take some photos in Yosemite. But at the end of the night"—he leaned closer, voice lowering a decibel or two—"finish up in The Castro."

Brow arched, Sawyer took a sip of his coffee. The Castro was considered the mecca of the gay community, the place prominent gay rights leader Harvey Milk had called home before he was assassinated. Sawyer and Elijah had once planned to make the journey to the West Coast, to see all the sights California had to offer and pay tribute to a man who'd impacted so many lives. Sawyer hadn't known he would end up making the trek alone.

The thing was, how had Martin known Sawyer would be interested in The Castro? He didn't think he'd let on about his sexuality. It wasn't like he put it on display. He didn't fall into any of the stereotypes, not that he could tell. He was a quiet guy who kept to himself. So how had Martin figured it out?

"Have you ever been to The Castro?" he quietly asked.

"Many times, my friend. I listened to Mr. Milk speak on more than one occasion."

"Really?" Sawyer perked up. "That must've been inspiring."

"It was." Martin laid his hand over the one Sawyer had flattened against the dining room table. He looked Sawyer in the eyes. "Go there. You'll enjoy it. Lots of beautiful things to see."

"I will." And that little conversation had Sawyer twice as confused about Martin as he had been before.

Right then, Pearl appeared at the swinging doors, as if she knew Sawyer had been wondering about her and the kind old man who ran the inn, not to mention the son they'd had together. She was a lovely woman, slender with high cheekbones and snow-white hair. The same brand of kindness Sawyer had seen in Martin's eyes filled her soft gaze. She smiled as she carried two heaping plates of food to the table. She set one in front of Sawyer, the other in front of Martin, and she added a kiss to the older man's forehead.

Without a word, she left the men alone to mull over their thoughts as they tossed back eggs and caffeine. The silence was only broken by the sound of bacon being chewed or coffee being swallowed. After the food had been put in front of their faces, conversation no longer seemed so important. It wasn't until the first plate was empty and the fork hit the porcelain that Martin began speaking again.

"If you want to explore the city, I can have a car take you downtown. You can take the BART all over San Francisco and just call me when you're ready to come home."

"BART. Right. Penelope told me about that."

"It's a lot like the subway systems in bigger cities. There's a map on the wall of each car. It's fairly straightforward. However, if you'd rather, I'm sure we can arrange for a car to stay with you all day."

"No, I like the idea of ridin' on a train. I can get more photography done that way."

"I assumed. Regardless, you have my number just in case, yes?"

"Yes, sir, I do."

"No 'sir.'" Martin patted Sawyer's hand as he stood from the table. "Just Martin."

"Thank you, Martin."

"You're most welcome, my friend."

CHAPTER SIX

THE HOT water rolling down Miles's back felt absolutely amazing. After the uninterrupted night of sleep he'd had, he felt like a million dollars. Petty actors and whiny ex-flings wouldn't ruin the intense happiness he enjoyed. Not today. Today was going to be awesome!

He ran a soapy hand down his chest, across his navel, and over his upper thighs. The suds tickled the fine hairs dancing along his legs. He reached farther, down between his legs, to grip a large helping of morning wood and achy sac. A hard groan rumbled his throat as he tightened his fingers. His eyes rolled back in his head. He laid his forehead against the steamy tile and got down to business, jerking and tugging until his shaft thickened against his palm.

God, this feels so good.

The great thing about not being at home was he could do all the jerking and moaning he wanted without the threat of his little girl bursting in on him. As a rule, he didn't have *any* sort of sex at the house if she was going to be around. He just couldn't do it. Fucking with her in the next room felt wrong on so many levels, not much different than trying to have sex in his parents' house with them watching *Andy Griffith* or some shit in the living room. So when he had an opportunity like this to get his rocks off, he would take it every damn time, and take it nice and slow so he could enjoy every second of it.

He ran his moist hand slowly down the sensitive skin of his cock, gripping a little tighter as he slid it back up. Eager nerve endings reached out for a taste of the pleasure. Low moans rumbled in his chest. He pictured the last man he'd screwed: the art of their bodies twisting, the roll of their muscles beneath flesh, sweat beading on their skin, and the sounds of pleasure filling the air as they both came. Gavin might've been an asshole, but he was beautiful. Remembering their weekend-long tryst was like watching high-dollar porn. No one with any sort of libido would've gotten through that memory without getting turned on.

And it made Miles even harder.

He turned on one foot and pressed his ass to the tile—legs spread, knees slightly bent. Every breath he took burned a little hotter, became a little shallower. The longer he gripped his cock and the faster his fingers played over the length of his erection, the quicker his heart beat. He licked his lips, letting his shoulders relax and his head hang as his fist pumped its way toward feeding his body one hell of an orgasm.

It didn't take long. Within minutes, thick, pearly happiness burst from the tip of his cock, and the kind of relief only to be had from getting off spread through all his limbs. The remnants of his personal wake-up call swirled down the drain. His eyes hooded. His lips spread. Yeah, happiness was a good word for it.

He finished cleaning and showering, going through the motions: lather, rinse, repeat if needed. Nice and clean. Dried. Teeth brushed. Body lotioned. Hair combed into a meticulous coiffure. He considered himself too old and too refined for that messy look boys on the sunnier side of thirty wore. He considered himself too professional and too much in the limelight to not look his best before going into public, especially on location. The thin, white cashmere sweater he'd chosen to wear enhanced his tan. The dark jeans hugged his ass and thighs in all the right places. Even if he wasn't considered Hollywood beautiful, he still looked handsome, debonair. It worked for him.

Now, to go hire another actor.

Coming from the kitchen he smelled the lingering scents of a breakfast he'd clearly missed, not that it mattered much. He wasn't a huge fan of eggs and refused to put a strip of bacon in his mouth no matter how wonderful people claimed it to be. No, not in his body. He had too much to live for not to take care of himself. The one guilty pleasure he indulged in was coffee. No one on God's green earth would *ever* take that away from him.

"Good morning, Martin," he said in his most sing-song voice. "Pearl."

The odd couple was in the kitchen washing dishes. Miles had to squeeze by them both to get to the industrial-sized coffeemaker and the carafe filled half-full of the good stuff—leaded, not that decaf crap the more health-conscious members of society consumed.

"Travel mug?" Martin asked, handing the thermos to Miles.

Miles gave him a wide, thankful grin. "You're an amazing man, Martin. Thank you."

"You're welcome."

Martin returned to the dishes. Miles returned to concocting the perfect mix of java, cream, and sugar while mentally arranging his day. It would probably start with a conference call to the studio and the casting director. He had about twenty-two hours to find someone twice as hot and twice as talented to replace Gavin, twice as well known but not a fading star, and someone he could count on not to flake for a better gig.

"That son of yours isn't around, is he?" Miles asked.

Martin gave him a suspicious look. "And what might you want with my son?"

"Well, he did some acting, didn't he?"

"No offense, Miles, but I'd rather you not engage him. He's finally got acting out of his head and moved on. He's in college and working on his life. One call from you about a movie, and he'll ignore his classes and come rushing to play movie star with you."

"That's a shame," Miles muttered. "He's beautiful enough."

"While I appreciate your admiration of mine and Pearl's genes, I'd rather you leave my son alone. He's a good kid and has a huge heart, and it breaks very easily. You're not the type of man I want for Henry."

Sipping his coffee, Miles blinked at Martin from over the rim of the mug he held to his lips. He hadn't thought about Henry in a romantic way at all. Now that Martin mentioned it, though, Henry was certainly worth taking to bed. He had a model-perfect body and silky brown hair with light brown eyes to match. Beneath a sun-drenched tan, he had gorgeous olive skin.

"Stop that," Martin barked.

Miles choked on his coffee. "What? What was I doing?"

"You're thinking about Henry."

Miles laughed. "No, I wasn't."

"Lies."

Shaking his head, Miles topped off his coffee and pushed his dirty thoughts of the innkeeper's son aside. His brain returned to work mode. On his way out of the room, he reached into his pocket and pulled out his vibrating phone. A reminder in red and white screamed from the screen. He turned back to Martin. "Has Sawyer Taylor shown up yet?"

The wistful smile on Martin's face might've caused alarm had it not been so damn strange to see. Smiles like that only graced the old man's lips when his son came home. "Yes, he arrived last night." Even Martin's voice changed, taking on a distinct lilt.

"Well, where is he?"

"He went to do some sightseeing."

"What?" Miles frowned. "I wanted to meet with him today. Jesus Christ." He sighed and bit back a stream of curses. "How long will he be gone?"

Martin shrugged. "I told him I would send a car when he wanted to come back to the inn."

"How is he travelling without a car?"

"BART."

"What?" Miles couldn't contain the astonishment in his voice. How dare Martin send Sawyer—a naïve country boy—out into the big city without a car? "Where did he go?"

"Just to the touristy places. The car took him. He wanted to travel on the BART." Martin's grin returned. "I told him to finish the day visiting The Castro."

"The Castro? Why?"

"Really?"

"I'm asking."

"He's a gay boy visiting San Francisco for the first time. Why wouldn't he go to The Castro?"

Gay? What? Wait. How had Miles not known this? How had Martin known this? "He's gay?" Miles frowned.

One thin salt and pepper brow over Martin's dark eyes arched, causing a ripple effect of wrinkles on his forehead. He crossed his arms and stared at Miles as if he were the most preposterous bastard under the stars. Even his head tilted to the side.

"What?" Miles asked.

"You didn't know about him?"

"No."

"I thought you'd hired him simply because he was gay."

"No, Martin. I hired him for his talent. Have you seen his work?"

"No. Have you had a conversation with him?"

"No."

"You should." Martin dropped the condescending tone, and the wide smile returned. "He's very nice, unspoiled by the likes of Hollywood."

"Well, that's great." Miles meant it. "But I need him here for a planning meeting. I *planned* on meeting him and getting to know him today."

"Well, I suggest you get a move on it."

One of many foul, four-letter words found its way to Miles's mind, despite his respect for the older man and the woman who always seemed to be with him, and he let one of the less offensive curses slip by his pinched lips. He tightened his fingers around his coffee mug as his brain rearranged his checklist. *Studio first. Find an actor. Then, somehow retrieve Sawyer Taylor before the big bad city eats him.* One problem.... Miles had no clue what Sawyer looked like, and as of two days ago, not one single person at the studio had been able to find a picture.

But hell, this would be easy. All he had to do was look for a doe-eyed country boy with a thick Mississippi accent. How many of those could possibly be roaming around San Francisco?

CHAPTER SEVEN

"ALABAMA, HUH? We're neighbors." Sawyer laughed before sucking down the remainder of his coffee. "And it took comin' all the way to the West Coast to bump into each other."

Funny thing about having an accent in a place with no accent: people noticed. Even the subtlest hint of an accent had a way of making friends. As soon as Sawyer had opened his mouth, ears perked up. He'd ordered a plain black coffee to go, and yet, thirty minutes later, he hadn't been able to leave the little coffee shop on the busiest street Sawyer had ever seen in his life.

They sat outside, watching trollies and busses go by. The occasional bum would stop and ask for change. Natives zoomed right by those restless vagabonds without noticing them. Sawyer had wanted to pull out all his change and hand it over, but his new friend had stopped him. "You don't wanna do that," the man had told him, placing his hand over Sawyer's. "Most of 'em'll just go buy booze or drugs. Soup kitchens feed 'em. Missions give 'em a place to sleep. Don't be givin' 'em your money."

"So, what made you come to San Francisco?" Sawyer asked the stranger.

"I hated Alabama. Mostly, I hated bein' so close to my parents. They wanted me to give up my dreams and settle down, have a family, and all that bull. I just wanna paint and write stories. That's what makes me happy." The stranger took another sip of his coffee. "What about you?"

"I didn't leave Mississippi." *Oh, but didn't you?* "Well, not for good, or that's not the plan. I'm just here workin' on a movie set."

"A movie set?" The guy sat straight up in his chair, eyes wide with interest. "You an actor?"

"No." Sawyer snorted. "I'm a photographer." He held up one hand, offering it to the stranger for a proper introduction. "I'm Sawyer Taylor, but you probably haven't heard of—"

"I've heard-a you! Your work was featured in one of my favorite art magazines. Great stuff. You've got some pretty amazin' pictures of the Gulf." The stranger took his hand and gave it a good, hard shake. "It's such an honor to meet you. I'm Wes. Wes Booker."

Finally, a name!

"It's a pleasure," Sawyer said. He checked his watch, a gift from his best friend, Lucy, after things had gone south in his life. She'd told him he needed a pick-me-up, and nothing was better than a brand new piece of jewelry. The morning was quickly dwindling away, and he'd only managed a few shots as he'd walked the streets of downtown. "I hate to do this, but I should get goin'. I wanted to get some pictures and do a little sight-seein'."

"Wanna tour guide? I ain't lived here long, but I can get 'round a'ight."

Normally, Sawyer would've politely told the guy he liked to work alone. Not exactly a lie, not a harmful one anyway. But considering he didn't know anything about San Francisco, and the idea of taking public transportation left a nagging worry in his gut, he'd take the offer and run with it.

"Sure. Sounds good."

Never in his twenty-six years had Sawyer seen such a glowing expression on one man's face. He had a kid-in-a-candy-store look, complete with sparkling eyes and a bright, white smile. Laughing to himself, Sawyer hoisted his camera bag up on his shoulder, and Wes grabbed the messenger bag he'd set down on the ground beside him, and the two headed out of the little iron gate surrounding the coffee shop's patio and headed to the nearest BART station.

Down below the city, people waited for the train to come jetting through. The digital sign above the railways said they had a whole ten minutes before the BART arrived. That ten minutes could very well end up being the longest of Sawyer's life. He hated standing around and waiting for things to happen.

"You're gonna hafta learn a lil' patience here," Wes said. His voice echoed against the concrete walls. It had more boom, more power than it had before.

"What? I'm bein' patient," Sawyer said.

"No you're not. You're shiftin' back and forth on your feet like the swayin's gonna bring the train any faster."

Sawyer hadn't noticed it until Wes mentioned it, but he was doing exactly what Wes accused him of. He forced himself to still, looked back up at the clock, and frowned. Eight minutes to go.

With a sigh, Sawyer turned around, and right in the middle of his sight appeared the coolest urban art he could've ever imagined. It was the angle and the lights, and the looks on people's faces as they rode down the escalator. Every single person wore an emotionless expression, like the daily grind had ground them into bodies without souls or hearts, like the world had finally become such a burden they simply moved through it without enjoying it. He'd never seen such a thing. He *had* to capture it.

He fought to get his camera out of the bag, while struggling not to move from that spot. The damn bag didn't seem to want to let go of his gear. The lens caught on the edge. The camera strap knotted with who knew what. A growl rumbled in Sawyer's throat. The train would arrive in four minutes.

When the fabric finally set his equipment free, it took less than sixty seconds to position the camera and set the right angle. He snapped a few shots in quick succession, then changed the f-stop and the shutter speed to play with the scene a little. Later, when he went back to look at the photos, he'd note the changes and how they'd affected the pictures. That's how he learned what worked and what didn't. In all, that one scene probably resulted in close to twenty pictures, and he finished just as the light for the BART train appeared in the dark.

"It's here," Wes said.

"I know." Sawyer said. Satisfaction filled his voice.

The train squealed to a stop in front of them. Two mechanical doors opened up to a grimy, decayed interior. No one with any sense would feel comfortable sitting on the half-fabric, half-plastic seats, not in Sawyer's mind anyway. Staying on his feet sounded like the best idea… until the train lurched forward and nearly sent Sawyer toppling right into Wes's lap. They both laughed. Sawyer braced himself against the rail, but he didn't stay there long. There were too many fascinating things to see on the BART, too much life happening around him.

He eased away from the safety of the bar and carefully walked the narrow aisle, using the hard edge of each plastic seat to help keep him on his feet. Hip keeping him steady, he held the camera with both hands and aimed it at a man in glasses who had an old, hardback book in front of his face. He wore an intense expression, lips moving along with the words. What made the shot so cool was his reflection, and the reflection of the words on the page, in the dark window beside him. Sawyer snapped off the picture just before the train left the tunnel and the reflection disappeared. The man in the seat looked up as soon as the shutter clicked. He gave Sawyer a "what the hell?" look.

"Sorry," Sawyer whispered.

The man went back to his book.

Sawyer returned to his safe handrail. Wes had been watching him the whole time. His new friend said, "You can't just go 'round takin' pictures of people. They don't take kindly to that type-a thing here."

"I didn't know," Sawyer said.

"Now you do. Just… be careful, 'kay?"

"Sure."

The train pulled to a stop at the Civic Center station, and Wes promptly stood. He told Sawyer it was the best way to get to Golden Gate Park from the BART. They'd have to take a bus or the MUNI, or a taxi if Sawyer felt like spending the money, but the Civic Center was the closest station to where Sawyer wanted to go.

Outside, while Wes and Sawyer waited for a cab to drive by, Sawyer snapped off a few more pictures. Nothing in the world looked anything like San Francisco. Not that he'd seen much of the world. In fact, Sawyer had never really left the South. The farthest west he'd been was Louisiana, and *nothing* about that state even remotely resembled California. This place felt like a whole new world.

"So where all you plan on goin' today?" Wes asked, dragging Sawyer's attention back from the cityscape.

"I don't know." Sawyer exhaled. "I know my final stop is The Castro."

"Castro." Wes curled his nose. "Why would you wanna go to *that* place?"

"Why wouldn't I?"

"Because." The other guy looked around, then leaned in close and whispered, "That's where all the gays go. You don't wanna go there."

"But I do."

When Wes pulled back, the expression on his face screamed disapproval and disgust, like many of those backwoods assholes back home who'd called Sawyer an abomination. Sawyer hadn't seen a look like that in a while.

"You one of 'em?" Wes finally asked.

Two thoughts flittered through Sawyer's mind. He could tell Wes the truth and risk being beaten and left for dead in an underground train station. Or, he could lie and hope for the best. Obviously, Wes hadn't figured it out, so Sawyer must have done a decent job hiding the fact. But he'd already come out of the closet once. No way in hell was some stranger going to shove him back in.

"Maybe we should go our separate ways," Sawyer finally said. It seemed better than admitting a truth Wes clearly didn't want to hear.

"I think you might be right." Wes turned toward the track.

Sawyer stepped onto the escalator, keeping one eye on the stranger who'd managed to hide his bigotry for a good portion of the morning. At least he'd helped Sawyer find his way this far. He could find The Castro later, and when it came time to go back to the inn, he'd call Martin for a car. Sounded like the perfect plan.

CHAPTER EIGHT

"HE'D BETTER be good," Miles said before hanging up the phone. The meeting with the studio hadn't gone the way he'd wanted. At least with Facetime on his iPhone, he'd been able to kick back in the bed and relax while actors mutilated the main character. They'd pulled together and scraped the bottom of the barrel for someone who could handle the role. Only one guy came remotely close to holding a candle to Gavin's talent, and he was a far cry from a good replacement, but the best they could get on short notice.

This movie will not flop.

He stood from the bed and grabbed the button-down shirt he'd ironed for going out that night from the back of the chair beside him. It was soft and white and looked great against his olive complexion.

"You're a handsome devil," he said to himself, fastening the third button from the top.

That bit of pep talk wasn't meant to sound vain, not by a long shot. His therapist called them daily affirmations. Something about telling himself how wonderful he was gave him the self-esteem he needed to compete in the cutthroat business of Hollywood moviemaking. The fact of the matter was Miles didn't have a vain bone in his body. He put on an act for this world, an act he could've lived without if fate had afforded something different for him. It hadn't.

Downstairs, a black sedan with pitch-black tinted windows and a guy in a tuxedo waited to take him wherever his little heart desired. Since Sawyer hadn't come back yet, Miles assumed he was still touring the city. He knew the last stop for Sawyer was supposed to be The Castro and thought a surprise encounter would be the kind of first impression that would make Sawyer want to be his photographer on a more permanent basis. And if that chance encounter didn't happen, oh well. The Castro had the kind of scenery that made Miles proud of who he was. He could let loose and have some fun, bury himself among a crowd of gay men so the paparazzi would have a harder time catching him doing something he maybe shouldn't be doing.

Yes, this plan sounded phenomenal.

With traffic, it took close to forty-five minutes to get from the outskirts of San Francisco to the more colorful end of Market, where commercial America died down and gay history picked up. The buildings didn't change much, nor did the atmosphere in general. Everything still looked much the same, but the feeling of being in The Castro hit Miles hard as soon as he stepped out of the car at the corner of Market and Castro. He absolutely loved everything about this place, loved seeing men holding hands so openly, even loved the lesbians. There was an air of pride on Castro, pride Harvey Milk would've been proud of.

The first bar he ducked into wasn't much more than a hole in the wall. The room was dark and disappeared somewhere in the back. Clothes lines zigzagged the ceiling, displaying underwear of all makes and models, from boxers to speedos and everything in between. Men lined the bar. Mostly bears. Mostly bearded, bellied men in jeans. They were young and old. Some already engaged in conversation with other men. Some not. The reason Miles liked this place was because he could talk to someone if the mood struck and not have to scream over the thumping of club music.

He sat down at the one free seat at the bar, and almost immediately, the man beside him turned toward him to engage in conversation. Miles hadn't had enough alcohol to go there yet. "Social butterfly" didn't exactly describe Miles. The pomposity of Hollywood tended to rear its ugly head when he opened his mouth unless he silently coached himself away from being that brand of jackass.

"I'm Trevor," the guy said, offering Miles his hand.

"I need a drink," Miles responded. Trevor didn't seem to be impressed.

The bartender appeared from out of the dark abyss at the back of the cramped room. He had nothing on but a pair of bright green speedos. A single black bear claw had been tattooed over his navel, ruining the view of what looked to be the beginning of a six-pack. A black trail of fuzz dipped down into his underwear, leading the way to an absolutely impressive bulge and thick hairy thighs. Not exactly Miles's type, but he was handsome in his own right.

"What can I getcha?" he asked, plump pink lips moving behind a dark mustache and thick beard.

"Scotch and water?" Miles eyed the backbar, looking for his favorite brand. "On second thought, give me a rum and Diet Coke."

"Coming right up."

The man beside him, the one who'd introduced himself as Trevor said, "Yeah, they don't keep good scotch here. Doesn't move very well."

"You a regular?"

"Pretty much. Have been since my partner died."

"Sorry to hear that."

"Eh, it was four years ago. No one seems to be as good as him, you know?"

"Boy, do I," Miles said before sucking down half his drink. He held up a finger to go ahead and line up his second round.

Now, he'd never been in love with anyone enough to consider them a "partner" and certainly not enough to introduce them to his little girl. The only person who'd come close was Anne, the woman who'd given birth to Zoe and died before he could vow to give that woman everything she wanted in life. He didn't love her in a heterosexual, "let's get married and have a million babies" kind of way, but he loved her as a best friend and the mother of his child. As far as men went, no one had ever equaled what Anne had given him, and he felt pretty certain no one ever would, so empty, meaningless sex did a fine job of filling the void in between.

"Let me buy you a drink," Trevor said, turning his entire body toward Miles. He let his knees drift apart, spreading his legs like an open invitation to take a look at what he was offering—which was a hell of a lot more than just a drink.

"It would be rude of me to accept," Miles said. "You see, I'm meeting someone here"— *maybe*—"and I would feel like I'm taking advantage of your kindness if I accepted then ran off with someone else."

"That's very… honest of you."

"I do my best."

"I could keep you company until he arrives."

Miles opened his mouth to let Trevor down as nicely as he could when the front door opened and evening sunlight spilled in from the street. Haloed in that bright blue light was a beautiful man with a kind smile and strong physique. He looked lost or scared, or maybe surprised to see a room full of the kind of men who hung out at this particular bar. Maybe he was looking for the nightclub around the corner and had gotten lost on his way to the dive. Whichever the case, he caught Miles's eye.

Silently, Miles prayed for the seat on the other side of him to open up so the boy in blue could squeeze in beside him. Big and hairy didn't budge, though, and from the looks of it, he had no plan to move anytime soon. He had his large nose buried in an e-book reader and flipped through the pages so slowly, Miles wondered if the man struggled with even the one-syllable words.

The new guy squeezed up at the end of the bar, and a plan quickly formed in Miles's head. He jumped from his seat and said loud enough for Trevor to hear, "I'm so glad you made it." He had a hand out and aimed for the guy to take, and as soon as their palms touched, Miles leaned in and said, "Just go with it. I sort of lied." He frowned. "Or maybe I didn't. What are you drinking?"

"A, um, a beer, I guess."

"Any kind?"

"Um, sure."

"Bartender," Miles called, holding up his hand. When the fuzzy little bartender returned, Miles ordered the new guy's beer, another rum and Diet Coke, and a round of shooters he would most certainly regret later.

Drinks in hand, Miles guided the new guy to a table in a dark corner at the very back of the room. The only light came from a naked red lightbulb. It cast eerie shadows on his new companion's features but somehow didn't take away from his more than pleasant appearance. He had an adorable boy-next-door quality about him, a quality not found in the plastic Hollywood types Miles spent most of his time interfacing with. Miles approved… very much approved.

"Sorry about that scene at the bar," Miles said. "I won't keep you if you had something else to do."

"Nope. I'm good. Surprised, but good."

"Perfect. As I said, I told the man I'd been sitting beside I was meeting someone, which wasn't exactly the truth. It just seemed easier to lie than hurt his feelings."

"That was very kind of you."

"He told me the story of his dead lover."

New guy made an O-face, like he understood without needing any more details. Miles appreciated his understanding and wished he had such astute people surrounding him on any given day. Already, he liked this man.

The shots and beers and booze kept coming. Miles picked up the tab. He didn't mind. The conversation was well worth it, and the longer he watched those lips move, the more he realized a sudden and overwhelming urge to kiss them. They were close enough he could feel warm breath against his cheek when the beautiful stranger spoke or laughed at Miles's antics. Their words slurred, and Miles suspected making a move had a wonderful chance of ending well.

He made the first move, laying his hand over that of his unexpected date's. Their fingers slowly wove together, locking them in the moment. Everything inside Miles screamed for him to go for it. He needed this, whatever *this* ended up being. A tryst before filming always made him much easier to deal with on set, made his disposition a bit sunnier. Getting laid would definitely start things off on the right foot.

He lifted the stranger's hand and brought it to his lips, stopping whatever he was saying midsentence. Their stares were fully engaged, heat and lust filling their eyes. Miles kissed the tip of his new friend's thumb, then the knuckles. He said, "I can have a car come get us. We're about forty minutes away from my hotel."

"Please" was whispered in a breathy rush.

CHAPTER NINE

"PLEASE," SAWYER said. He couldn't believe the very first bar he'd passed on Castro landed him in a compromising situation with a stranger. For a man still on the fence about getting laid, he seemed to have Lady Luck on his side tonight. Lucy would've been proud.

Speaking of…

Though he could hear Lucy cheering him on and telling him to get his man parts played with, his sex education teacher from high school contradicted his best friend. In Small Town, Mississippi, abstinence was the lesson, and never once would any of the esteemed educators touch on gay sex. But the rules were generally the same: if you're going to do it, be safe about it.

Safe. Right. Sawyer could do safe.

God, he hoped this guy had condoms. Sawyer didn't carry them. Had never had to. He'd lost his virginity to Elijah, and he'd only been with Elijah. They'd never strayed from each other. Until four months ago, their lives together had been set in stone, and he'd never even thought about being with another man. Sure, he'd gone window-shopping many times, but he'd never made a purchase. Never wanted to.

"You okay?" the man at his side asked.

Sawyer didn't remember how, but they'd managed to get out to the curb and were both standing on their own feet. "S'great," he slurred. When he turned to check out the sights of this beautifully historic district, the lights and people and buildings moved in a blur. A silly little chuckle spilled from his lips.

"Here, let me take your bag for you."

"No," Sawyer insisted. Even drunk he wanted to handle his gear and felt more than capable of taking care of it. "Mines."

"Yes, I know it's yours, I just thought…."

"Gots it."

"Okay. Very well."

A sleek, black car pulled to the curb in front of them, and out of instinct, Sawyer reached for the handle. A man who very much resembled an oversized penguin stopped him. He held open the door and waited for Sawyer to climb in. The man behind him gave him a nod, signaling for him to go ahead. Sawyer realized the danger of climbing into a vehicle with a man he didn't know, but right now, he didn't really care. Right now, he was going to get laid!

He plopped down in the seat. "Too tight," he muttered, tugging on the crotch of his jeans.

"Let me fix that for you."

"Okay." Maybe, if he got lucky, he would remember doing this tomorrow.

With the whining of his zipper, the pressure began to ease. Sawyer's head rolled back against the seat. A hand dipped down inside his pants about the same time he felt cool air roll across his chest. Then a warm mouth grazed along his abs. He looked down to find a dark head of hair easing up his chest. He raised his ass to pump against the hand wrapped around his cock.

"Kiss me?" he asked, voice so hoarse it surprised him.

"Babe, I'll kiss all over your gorgeous body, but I don't kiss lips. It's too intimate, something people in love do."

"Love." Sawyer snorted. "S'a myth."

"Truer words were never spoken, babe."

That magical mouth returned to Sawyer's chest. His head rolled back again, eyes closed as the gentle pressure returned to his groin. He subdued a moan as fingers fondled his sac, bit down on his bottom lip when those same fingers wrapped around his shaft and started to stroke. His legs spread of their own volition, eager to give this man, this stranger, all the space he needed to do whatever he wanted.

"Oh, God," Sawyer said, voice trailing off into a moan he could no longer hold back when a tongue flicked over his nipple. The hand gripping his cock tightened, pumping harder, faster. "Oh, my God," he rasped. His sac tightened.

"Stop resisting. You want to come for me. Just do it."

Not yet. No, not yet. "Don't stop."

Teeth grazed his nipple, gently bit and tugged. It was a new experience for Sawyer, an experience that broke down all his resolve to hang on to the orgasm brewing in his balls. He locked his hand over the back of the leather seat and squeezed so hard it hurt his fingers, and the material creaked as their tips bit into it. He jacked his hips and would've sworn he heard the man who was palming his package snort out a laugh.

Holding back wasn't an option anymore.

The hand jerked faster and faster, but it was the thumb stroking the hard ridge of his cock that finally did it. Sawyer's release pushed through his thickened shaft. He bucked his hips again. "I'm coming. I'm coming," he chanted in rhythm with his thrusting. Before he knew it, pearly ropes of eager sperm were painting the back of the sedan's leather seats, and Sawyer was left boneless and barely able to breathe.

"Feel better?" the man asked.

"Hell, yes," Sawyer panted.

They both laughed.

"You're not going to fall asleep on me now, are you?"

"Honestly?" Sawyer sat up in the seat as much as he could. "I think I'm almost sober, actually. But no, I don't plan on fallin' asleep on you."

"Good. I have some fun planned for us."

The car pulled into a neighborhood Sawyer remotely recognized, even if it was dark outside. He would bet money he'd been through it once or twice already, but he could've been wrong. After all, most of those neighborhoods looked exactly the same to him. He couldn't distinguish one from the other. He kept his mouth shut, watching out the window as they meandered along hilly roads.

"Where did you say you were stayin'?" he asked.

"It's a quaint little inn nestled back behind the neighborhood. No one really knows about it. I'm friends with the innkeeper and request it anytime I'm filming in San Francisco."

"Really?" Sawyer sat up farther, closing the fly of his jeans after tucking away his spent cock. This was bad. The man who'd just given him a hand job obviously worked on the same set Sawyer did. "What did you say you did for a living?"

"I didn't. I'm a movie director."

"Miles Eisenberg?"

The man frowned and cocked his head, clearly surprised Sawyer knew his name.

"I'm Sawyer Taylor."

Miles's face deadpanned. Literally. All expression faded like a ruined painting. He stared at Sawyer like words were failing him. He may have even blanched. It was hard to tell in the dark of the sedan. They pulled up to the hotel, and sure enough, it was the exact same one where Sawyer had been deposited the day before.

"Shit," Sawyer muttered.

"Shit's right."

Miles dragged his hand down his face. When the car stopped and the door opened, all the interior lights came on, showing the remains of what they'd done in the backseat. Spots coated the leather. Spots stained Sawyer's jeans. But the biggest evidence of how far they'd gone was the very thick bulge tenting Miles's slacks.

Miles didn't allow much time to stare. He abruptly reached down and locked a hand over his crotch. Their eyes met, and Miles's held a weird mix of anger and disappointment. Sawyer didn't get it. If he wanted to keep going, Sawyer was game. Why not finish what they'd started?

"I'll see you on set Monday morning," Miles gritted out before hauling himself out of the car.

Sawyer sat speechless, waiting for a door to be slammed in his face, watching as Miles climbed the front steps to the house. Miles didn't remove his hand, and he didn't look back. Even with so many feet between them and the only light being a small lantern at either side of the door, Sawyer could see the hard set of his shoulders.

"Sir?" The driver looked inside the car.

Sawyer forgot he'd been waiting there. "Sorry."

"No need for apologies. Would you like some assistance?"

"No, I think I can handle it."

Sawyer collected his camera bag and slid across the leather seat until his feet reached the concrete. He stood, tested his legs, and when the world didn't start spinning and he didn't sway, he knew it was safe to keep going, though he wasn't as sober as he'd thought. The experience with Miles hadn't completely overridden the solid buzz he'd found himself with before leaving The Castro.

"Thank you," he said to the driver before marching up the steps and walking through the front door.

He made it to the table in the center of the foyer before a voice calling his name stopped him. He'd have liked it to have been Miles so he could apologize for what happened in the car, but the gravelly voice belonged to someone much older than the man who'd jerked him off. Sawyer lifted his head. Martin's salt-and-pepper brow furrowed deep in his wrinkled forehead.

"Dear God, son, what's wrong?" he asked, closing the space between them.

"I got drunk in The Castro," Sawyer admitted.

Martin laughed softly. "That's certainly easy to accomplish, but why do you look so down about it?"

"I let a strange man give me a hand job."

"Again, things like that often happen, especially in some of those bars. You didn't have unprotected intercourse, right?"

Sawyer shook his head.

"So what's the problem?"

"The man was my new boss."

"Ohhhh," Martin drawled. "I see."

"Yeah." Sawyer lowered his gaze.

Without uttering another word, Martin hooked his arm around Sawyer's and walked up the stairs with him. He guided Sawyer all the way to his door, even waited as Sawyer fished out the key. Martin reached in and flipped on the lights.

"Miles Eisenberg is a very finicky man. I've known him for many years now. He's been coming to my inn since the first time he filmed in San Francisco. It had to have been close to a decade ago. He had the same wide-eyed, eager innocence you do. Hollywood has sullied that. In my heart, I believe he's still a good man, but he's not the same man I met. He does his level best not to mix business with pleasure, and the man has the best intentions, but things... well, they don't always work out the way we plan." Martin patted Sawyer's shoulder. "The best thing you can do for yourself is go about business as usual and pretend none of this ever happened."

"Thank you, Martin."

"It's no problem, young man. As I said before, if there's anything you need, anything at all, you can call on me. I meant that."

"I see."

"Rest well, Sawyer. I'll see you in the morning."

The door closed, and Sawyer was alone again. If he had any idea what room Miles was in, he might've marched right down there and told Miles there was no need for what happened in the car to interfere with their work. Business came first, and Sawyer didn't have any intention of letting anything come between him and his big break. But the other part of him had had so much fun tonight, fun he'd needed to forget about Biloxi and Elijah, fun he'd promised his best friend he would be sure to have.

Instead of making a bigger fool of himself, he sat down on the edge of the bed and stripped away his soiled jeans and the T-shirt that smelled of booze and some cologne Sawyer had never worn in his life. He tossed it all to the floor, thinking he'd deal with it tomorrow. Tomorrow was Sunday—a whole day before they had to meet on set to begin shooting Miles's movie. Maybe a day would do some good and come Monday, neither one of them would even think about what they'd done. It would be the past, and their future ended after making a movie.

CHAPTER TEN

AS SOON as Miles closed the door to his room, he froze. Where the hell had his brain been when he'd reached inside Sawyer Taylor's pants and gotten up close and personal with his cock? Why the hell hadn't he bothered to introduce himself before he'd started drinking with that very handsome, very unavailable man? Because he'd become tangled up in a harmless little lie.

Because I didn't use my stupid fucking brain.

His head dipped forward, cracking against the solid surface of the wooden door. He pulled back then let it hit the door again, over and over and over. The dull ache blossoming in the center of his forehead deadened the pain knocking on the back of his skull. He'd started to sober up, and the prehangover headache had already begun to set in.

Miles stopped with the banging, considering it would only make matters worse, but it echoed and for a moment, he swore he was losing his mind. The tap, tap, tap on the door didn't come from him pounding his forehead, not this time. The knocking came from outside, and despite having no desire to speak with anyone right now, he opened the door anyway. He found Martin standing on the other side with a look of disapproval on his face.

"What?" Miles asked, moving out of the doorway with his back to Martin.

"Sawyer seems like a good kid," Martin said, closing the door behind him. "Wouldn't you agree?"

Miles shot a curious look over his shoulder, targeting Martin and his not-so-subtle suggestion. "Why are you telling me this?"

"Whatever happened between you two, don't treat him like all the whores you bring here to bed. He's different. He's special, okay?"

This time, Miles did turn around. A thread of aggravation wound through him, tugging at the guilt he'd felt not five minutes ago. "What did he say to you?" Miles asked. "Did he tell you something happened?"

"Does it really matter?"

"Yes."

"Why?"

"Because, I don't want rumors spread about me before we even start filming. I don't want word to get to the rest of the cast that something is going on between Sawyer and me. I don't need or want that kind of publicity. I just want to make my movie and go home to my daughter, Martin. Is that too much to ask?"

Martin didn't say anything, but it wasn't really a question that required an answer—more like a plea for a little sympathy, not that Miles could honestly say he deserved it. He'd started this whole mess in the first place, a fact he wouldn't bother trying to deny.

A hand gripped his shoulder, and he looked up to find Martin staring at him with a fair amount of sorrow and maybe even a little understanding. "You've changed so much," the old man said. "I met you right before Zoe was born, and I'd never seen anyone so full of life. Then you changed."

"I lost my best friend," Miles reminded him.

"And you gained a beautiful little girl."

Miles hung his head again. "I know," he said in a quiet voice. "And I wouldn't trade her for the world."

"No one is asking you to, but you're lonely and you're trying to make up for that with empty sex. *That's* what has changed you."

"What does this have to do with Sawyer?" Miles asked.

"Nothing at all. He was the catalyst, I suppose. Seeing the way he looked tonight, it made me angry enough to say something to you about the way you act."

"The way I act. Right." Miles raised his head and squared his shoulders. He started unbuttoning his shirt, keeping his stare cold, daring, and aimed at Martin with contempt. "Is there anything else you need to say to me?"

"No, I suppose there isn't."

"Then have a good night, Martin."

Martin took that wish for a good evening as a polite dismissal— exactly what Miles intended it to be. He didn't need a man who hadn't been in a relationship in the seven years they'd known each other telling him about love. What the hell did Martin know about being with someone and feelings and empty sex? The way Martin had told his story over the years, he'd chosen to do the same thing Miles had. He'd chosen to take care of his child rather than sating the needs of his libido. Only Martin had the benefit of having the child's mother in his life, and Miles didn't.

He sank down on the edge of the bed, shirt hanging open, shoulders slumped. All the anger slowly turned to self-disappointment. Shame. He could've handled the situation with Sawyer a little better. He could've been kinder to Martin. Martin deserved an apology. Maybe tomorrow he would even find Sawyer and apologize for the way he'd acted. Have a polite and intellectual conversation with the kid. He would explain that this was for the best, that Miles couldn't give him anything deep and meaningful because all his love and energy went to the most important person in his life. With his work and his daughter, he didn't have time or desire for anything more than one-night stands. Nothing against Sawyer, of course. None of this could be blamed on him.

Closing his eyes, Miles lay back on the bed and settled into his soft pillow. It didn't take long for sleep to consume him, for images of his little girl to dance through his head. She wore a sparkly pink tutu, but it paled in comparison to the glow of her innocent smile. The tiara on her head had been bought for her fifth birthday. In fact, so had the tutu. She'd wanted to be a ballerina princess, so Miles had done everything in his power to give her a *Swan Lake*-like birthday. Real ballet dancers showed up in full costume. The cake was as grand as a wedding cake. A swan ice sculpture sat on a table in the middle of the room. But the look in his daughter's eyes when she'd seen it all had been the memory that stuck with him. Even now, that's what he remembered most from that day.

Before he was truly ready to let go of the memory, the alarm on his phone sounded. The noise was so shrill it could've raised the dead, and *dead* certainly did a fine job of describing Miles's state of being.

The sun pushing through the curtains made the pounding in his head much worse than it probably would've been otherwise. A hangover the size of Texas beat him about the skull. And the thick taste of ick on his tongue made him gag. He silently swore to himself he'd never do that again, at least not anytime soon. Because of his lovely hangover and the death in his mouth, he swore he'd take advantage of the quiet patio behind the inn and replenish his alcohol-laden bloodstream with caffeine and sunlight.

Miles pulled a plain green T-shirt over his head and thin, gray lounge pants over his legs. He slipped his feet into a pair of canvas deck shoes, grabbed his shades and his laptop, then headed down to the kitchen.

Thankfully, when he arrived at the table, no one save for Pearl was there. Not even Martin had shown his face. Judging by the smell in the air, the coffee had already been brewed and waited to wash Miles's misery away.

He poured a huge cup as he hugged his laptop to his chest, gave Pearl a grateful smile, then continued out to the back deck to lounge by the gardens.

Martin and his son really had done an amazing job with the scenery. It transformed a suburban San Francisco home into a semitropical paradise. A privacy fence kept the outside world from soiling its beauty. Tall palm trees transported the mind from a bustling metropolis to an exotic island getaway. Large, colorful flowers painted an amazing backdrop. A towering waterfall structure beneath the trees made the retreat a reality more than the product of an overactive imagination.

This was one of the many, many reasons why he loved Martin's place.

He sat down on one of the multiple wooden chaise lounges at the back edge of a garden and settled his laptop on his thighs. He lowered the sunglasses perched on his head and placed his coffee cup on a side table to await its chance to wet his palate and massage his mood.

He'd just opened the lid and settled in with the script for another read-through when he heard the familiar sound of a camera shutter clicking in the distance. His heart stopped midbeat. *Sawyer.*

One of two things could happen here: Miles could hide behind his laptop and sink down in the chaise, keep the sunglasses on his face, and pretend like nothing had ever happened, or he could man up and apologize for ditching Sawyer the way he had. Maybe he could explain that fucking the employees wasn't on his agenda.

What about Gavin?

Gavin didn't count. He hadn't hired Gavin until after they'd spent the weekend together, and frankly, the sex hadn't landed Gavin the lead role. The actor's talent had.

The shutter clicked again, and when Miles turned his head, he saw Sawyer standing right behind him, back facing Miles. He had the camera held up to his eye, and looked to be taking close-ups of the flowers. Miles had a decision to make, and fast.

But Sawyer made the decision for him. When Sawyer spun around to focus his sights on something else, his eyes locked on Miles. The photographer had a deer-in-headlights look, like he wanted to run and hide but couldn't because his body took control and decided to freeze where he stood. Miles certainly sympathized.

"Hey," he said.

"Hi," Sawyer responded.

Awkward. Now what?

Apparently, neither one of them had the balls to speak first. Sawyer shifted his gaze around the gardens, clearly fighting not to look Miles in the eye. Mile closed his laptop and set it aside; then he stood so he could face Sawyer like a man.

"Look," he said, "I'm sorry about last night. That was inappropriate of me, and I apologize. Had I not been—"

"Don't apologize, and please God, don't blame the booze for it."

"Okay…." Confusion set in. Usually, when men did dumb things, it was so much easier to admit to being a screw-up thanks to booze. Yet, this beguiling creature wanted the opposite. "I'm sorry, but… well, why did you say it *that* way? Wouldn't it be easier to blame the alcohol and never broach the subject again?"

"Maybe for you, but I don't get drunk and fuck around with strange men. It's not my style. Plus, I'd like to think there was some sorta attraction there, otherwise you wouldn't have ripped me away from the bar."

"I ripped you away from the bar because I saw an opportunity."

As soon as Miles spat those words back at Sawyer, he wished he hadn't. A touch of what Miles would've sworn was devastation filled the photographer's big brown doe eyes. All the years of pretending to be cold and uncaring didn't lessen the blow of seeing someone have their feelings hurt the way Sawyer so obviously had. Maybe because the Hollywood types Miles usually fucked didn't seem to care one way or another about feelings.

"Sawyer, I'm sorry. That's not what I meant."

"It's okay." Sawyer shrugged. "You don't owe me anything. We're not friends. You don't know me. I don't know you. You're my boss. End of story."

Before Miles had a chance to explain he wasn't the kind of guy to intentionally hurt people's feelings, Sawyer made an abrupt about-face and stalked out of the gardens and into the house. He slammed the door so hard, the sound vibrated Miles's bones. He'd never had someone walk out on him like that before, and frankly, it didn't sit well with him.

CHAPTER ELEVEN

"YOU'RE JUST gonna avoid him as much as you can," Sawyer mumbled to himself as he stormed back into the house. "You're not gonna let him get to you because you're here to do a job, not make friends and impress people, and sure as hell not to find somebody to sleep with." But hadn't that been part of the plan? He distinctly remembered the thought of getting some tail while he was in San Francisco.

Well, plans could always change. So far, San Francisco had been one major heartburn after another. Public transportation was the only way to get around, and yet it was scary as hell. People weren't kind and considerate. They didn't lounge on beaches and take their time to smell the flowers. Hell, there weren't many flowers to speak of anyway. The only upside had been his trip to The Castro, and even that had been ruined because one megalomaniacal prick hadn't been able to keep his hands to himself.

Yeah, but be honest with yourself, Sawyer Taylor. Part of that was your fault too.

He spent the entire trip through the dining room, the foyer, up the stairs, and into his bedroom mentally kicking himself in the ass over what had happened with Miles Eisenberg last night, then again out in the garden. Sawyer knew good and damn well he couldn't handle hard booze, and yet he'd had more than his fair share of shots. Now he wanted to turn his anger on Miles? How did that work? Miles hadn't poured those shots down his throat. Miles hadn't made him say yes to the hand job. Miles hadn't taken away his freewill.

"So stupid," he grumbled, gently dropping his camera bag on the bed.

Now he had to spend the next three months not only walking on eggshells on the set, but at the hotel too. Nearly every single waking hour would be spent either taking orders from the director or hiding from his ill-considered hookup. Boy, this was going to be an adventure to write home about.

Not!

The quiet in his room had already begun to push the boundaries of his sanity. The few and faint little noises weren't enough to take his mind off things.

A bad recording of a great indie song sang from his back pocket and punched a startling hole through the silence. The phone vibrated his right ass cheek. There was exactly one person on the face of the earth he wanted to talk to right now. Anyone else could suck it up. The caller just so happened to be that one person he absolutely *needed* to hear from.

"God, I miss you," he said. He held the phone tight to his ear.

"That bad?" Lucy asked. Her voice came through crystal clear, as if she were standing right in front of him.

If he closed his eyes, he could actually picture her sitting beside him on the bed, holding his hand while she gave him the kind of look that often led to him spilling his guts to her. "It just got better."

"Yeah? How's that?"

"I think I'm gettin' homesick."

Even her laughter came through without the interruption of static and the feeling of being so far away. "You've been gone exactly two days. How are you homesick already?"

Sighing, he sat down on the edge of his bed, careful to make sure his camera didn't fall off. He lay back against the pillows and tried to force his body to relax. The tension just didn't want to let go.

"San Francisco is beautiful and inspirin'. I can't lie about that. But the people here are…. I don't know. They're different, Lucy. The innkeeper, Martin, is the nicest person I've ever met, but everyone else…." Sawyer shook his head, not that Lucy could see him. "I met a homophobe from Alabama. Then there's Miles. He's—"

"You finally met the director!" She sounded so excited for him. When he'd told her Miles Eisenberg wanted to hire him for a film, she'd fangirled for a solid hour, going on and on about his movies and what the tabloids had said about him. She made a hobby of keeping up with famous people, mainly who they dated and what designer they wore.

"Yeah, and trust me, he's not everythin' he's cracked up to be. I've never met such a pompous—"

"Oh my God, Sawyer, don't ruin the fantasy for me. Jeez."

"Sorry to burst your bubble, love. He's an ass."

Silence spread out over the airways. He heard every single breath she took and could almost picture her giving him that droll expression she liked to use when he was being a special brand of difficult asshole.

"I know how you're lookin' at me," he said.

"You need to relax. Let go of life in Biloxi. Let go of Elijah… and have some fun for chrissake, Sawyer."

"I tried havin' fun and it didn't work out. No, I think I'm gonna stick to the plan and focus on work. In three months, or whenever this hell is finally over, then I'll decide what I wanna do."

"Sawyer—"

"Don't, Lucy. Don't 'Sawyer' me. Just stop. I'll figure this all out in my own time, in my own way. Just le'go and stop worryin' 'bout my life."

Silence screamed louder than the bitter words Sawyer had hurled at her. He'd hurt her feelings. Hurt had been the only thing to ever quiet Lucy's rambunctious mouth. Now he felt like shit.

"I'm sorry, Lucy. I'm—"

"It's okay, Sawyer. I understand, and you're right. I don't have any business buttin' in your life." She paused as if waiting for him to agree or disagree. He didn't say a word. The thing about Lucy, she seemed to be her happiest when she had a certain amount of control over everything. Everything including Sawyer. Though Sawyer had never had a problem with it in the past.

"You probably need to go," she finally said, a modicum of restraint returning to her. "I'll call you later."

"Please do. I love you, Lucy."

"I love you too, Sawyer."

The line died and Sawyer set his phone on the nightstand. He spent the next fifteen minutes staring up at the ceiling. When that gave him too much room to think, he stood and reached for the bags he had yet to unpack. Traditionally, he wasn't the kind of man who hung his clothes in the hotel closet, nor did he use the drawers to stow away his lesser belongings. When he traveled, he tended to live out of a suitcase, but he'd also never stayed away for more than a few days.

When he finished putting away his clothes, he grabbed his laptop bag and sat in a chair at the table in the center of the room. He set his computer up, then placed his camera right beside it. If nothing else, the pictures he'd taken around San Francisco might entertain him.

A knock at the door pulled his attention away from the rough cityscape he'd spent yesterday taking pictures of. He debated not answering, pretending to be asleep or something so he didn't have to face people he wasn't ready to face. Then again, it could've been Martin, and Sawyer hadn't thoroughly enjoyed anyone's company like he enjoyed Martin's in quite a while.

"Come in," he said, waiting to see whose head popped into the opening.

It wasn't Martin's or Pearl's snow-white hair, wasn't either of the blondes he'd seen yesterday morning. No, the head of hair was thick and dark, almost black, neat and well styled. Sawyer's heart slipped down inside of his chest and hit his stomach hard enough to make him feel like he needed to hurl.

"What do you want?" Sawyer said, turning back to his laptop and pictures, hoping his lack of interest would put Miles off.

"We got off on the wrong foot," Miles said.

Something in his voice sounded so different from when they'd been making out in the car, even different than it had this morning. He almost sounded humble, but Sawyer knew damn well the director hadn't seen the error of his ways or learned any lessons, not that fast. Miles didn't seem like the type.

"I accepted your apology. What else do you want?"

"You accepted my apology because you wanted me to shut up. You wanted me to leave you alone."

"Maybe I did." Sawyer didn't bother to raise his stare from the laptop's screen.

"Do you want me to go now?"

While Sawyer had the urge to blurt out a solid and unarguable yes, the moment he looked up and saw Miles's concerned expression, Sawyer couldn't make himself do it. He saw something much deeper, warmer than Miles had shown before, something *almost* worthy of compassion.

"No. Stay," Sawyer said and regretted it as soon as the last word rolled off his tongue.

Miles slipped down into the other seat at the tiny table. Sawyer closed his laptop and forced himself to meet Miles's stare. For the first time since they'd met, Sawyer noticed the incredible magnetism of Miles's eyes. The hazel irises had a crystalline glow Sawyer had never seen in another's eyes before. But Miles's beauty didn't end there. His highly kissable lips were framed with facial hair. Not a crude amount, but a short, tight dusting of dark hair. It made Miles's brand of handsomeness more rugged, the kind of *manly* look Sawyer appreciated.

"If I'm completely honest with you," Miles said, "will you promise not to use it against me? I normally do my best not to get close to people, and I'm not trying to get close to you. I just…. I feel like I need to explain myself."

"You don't need to explain anything to me."

"Yes, I do. I don't know why, but I do."

"'Kay." Sawyer crossed his arms and gave Miles a tight nod, a silent go ahead.

"Nothing can jeopardize this movie," Miles carefully began, but Sawyer believed his words were far different from what he wanted to say, a mask to cover some other truth. "The last one didn't go so well, and the critics brutalized it. This one has to be perfect. I can't afford another flop."

"I thought you were gonna be honest with me."

"That was honest."

"Right."

Pinching his lips tight, Sawyer stood, gathered his camera into his arms and started toward the hotel room door. A silent prayer went out into the air, a prayer for whatever barrier kept Miles so guarded to come tumbling down, a prayer for things to change before Sawyer walked out of that room. He didn't want to spend the next three months wishing he'd never come to California and avoiding his boss like the plague.

His hand locked over the doorknob. Sawyer hesitated before giving it a twist. In the few seconds after Sawyer walked through the door and away from his employer, Miles would have lost his chance to change the horrible first impression he'd left Sawyer with.

Three. Two. One….

Miles didn't open his mouth

Sawyer didn't give him another chance.

CHAPTER TWELVE

MONDAY MORNING the alarm on Miles's cell phone went off way before anyone with any sense would even consider climbing out of bed. If he wanted to get his workout in and enjoy the Hollywood rag mags over a cup of piping hot java before his shower, he had to get his ass out of the bed and into high gear. Though he had to admit, hanging out with the pillow and soft linens sounded a hell of a lot better than beating his feet along a hidden gravel path behind the inn—or beating his head against a wall over the latest rumors of his demise. At least they still talked about him. When one was forgotten by the tabloids, they tended to be forgotten by Hollywood too.

Unfortunately, he hadn't gotten much sleep last night, and the idea of getting out of bed right now sounded downright criminal. He hadn't been able to get Sawyer's disgusted expression out of his mind. The photographer shouldn't get to Miles the way he did. People gave Miles a variety of looks on any day of the week, and he let their opinions of him roll right off his back. Now, why couldn't he do the same with Sawyer?

Because somewhere in the pit of your being, you know how much you respect him.

The fact that Miles respected Sawyer meant he was something special. Very few people garnered the level of deep respect that engendered genuine kindness and consideration on Miles's part. Sure, he respected many people for their business acumen or their talent, or any other variety of prowess both outside the bed and in, but not very many for the person they were inside. Sawyer was different. He had a devastating, heartwarming innocence Miles rarely found in Hollywood. It reminded him of being home in the valley, growing up with Anne. Anne had that same innocence, the same love and appreciation for life.

Well, he couldn't very well spend the day lying in bed and wishing he'd made a better impression on the young photographer. He had a smash-hit movie to make. He had a life and a child to support, a crew waiting for his direction… a shower calling his name.

He didn't waste too many valuable minutes beneath the spray of hot water, though he knew he could've been happy staying there for hours.

Enough time was given to hair and body that when he finished, he felt squeaky-clean. He lotioned up and spritzed on some cologne, then grabbed his lucky shirt. He had worn the thin, white pullover on the first day of filming the movie that had cemented his name in Hollywood stardom. Film students all over the world would hear his name in lectures because of it, and thus, his lucky shirt had become a staple.

Downstairs, he'd hoped to catch the first car over to the film site alone. He had a habit of reading out loud when he went over the script, and some people found it to be an annoying practice. Not that he cared much, but their stares tended to be distracting. What he hadn't expected was to find the photographer waiting on the porch.

As soon as he stepped down onto the wooden flooring, the old porch creaked, and Sawyer's head whipped around. Their eyes met for a split second before Sawyer turned away. From the side, Miles could make out Sawyer's pinched lips, clenched jaw, and the skin rippling over rigid bone. There was something incredibly sexy about a man with a jawline like that. It held the kind of power most envied. It gave an air of manliness and strength to an otherwise subdued personality. Miles could see himself plying that rigid jaw with a thousand kisses.

The thought widened his eyes. Where the hell had that come from?

"I don't have to take the first car," Sawyer said.

It took a few times swallowing, then clearing his throat, before Miles trusted his voice not to come out hoarse and lusty. "You don't have to do that," he finally said. "We can share a car, Sawyer. Hell, we'll be working close together on set. We might as well learn to get along."

"Who said I wasn't tryin' to get along?" Sawyer didn't turn to face Miles. He didn't have to. Given the harsh sound of his voice, his expression would've broken Miles's heart.

"Please. You take everything I say and do the wrong way. I'm not used to that."

This time, Sawyer did turn around. He stood so close Miles could feel Sawyer's breath brush along his cheek. Sawyer said, "I don't take you at all, actually."

Exactly what happened next was a total blur for Miles. If someone asked him ten minutes or ten years down the road, he knew he wouldn't be able to recall the train of thought that led to him reaching up, grabbing Sawyer by the cheeks, and crushing their mouths together. But it happened. His rule about not kissing people became a distant and fleeting aspect of his life. No, intimacy didn't apply here because he'd spent half the weekend fighting with Sawyer, and that took a certain level of passion. Passion he poured into the kiss.

He held Sawyer's face tight as their lips melded together. Sawyer opened his mouth, granting Miles the entrance he sought. His tongue delved deep inside, licking and lapping as much of Sawyer as he could get. Nothing had ever tasted so sweet, and he swore he would hold on to that taste until he could steal more of it.

Eyes closed, he moved his hand down, down, over Sawyer's arms and down to his waist. Their bodies pressed together. The firm edge of a budding hard-on pressed against an equally hard bulge between Sawyer's legs. He would've given anything to take the photographer inside and finish what they'd started the other night.

You have a movie to make.

The kiss broke with a gasp. Sawyer's lips were red and swollen and glistened in the sunlight. Even as Miles lifted his hand to brush his thumb along their erotic beauty, he knew he'd made another mistake.

"I shouldn't have done that," he whispered. His hand found rest in the curve of Sawyer's neck. He couldn't make himself pull away.

"No, you probably shouldn't have. And yet, you still have your hands on me."

"I know."

"Why is that?"

"I don't know."

"I deserve better."

"I won't argue that."

Sawyer laid his hand over Miles's. His fingers were gentle and caressing, his touch nearly as kind as the look in his eyes. Miles felt himself sinking into that handsome stare. Before he could drown, though, Sawyer removed Miles's hand from the side of his neck and abruptly, not so kindly, let it go.

"Take the car," Sawyer said flatly. "I'll catch the next one."

He walked away without speaking, back up the steps and into the house before Miles could ask him not to go. Miles supposed he deserved that. He'd just planted a kiss on a man he'd told himself he couldn't be intimate with. He'd broken every single rule he'd made for himself, and for what? To be pushed away exactly like he'd pushed Sawyer away Saturday night.

Touché, Sawyer. Touché.

THE DOOR slammed behind Sawyer and he couldn't move from the spot. He'd barely been able to walk away from Miles, and the silent cheering in his head didn't make him feel any better about it.

That kiss had been utterly amazing, swoon-worthy and heart-stopping. No one had kissed him like that since Elijah, before Elijah had decided they didn't love each other anymore.

So, what did this all mean? Why was Miles being so persistent and distant at the same time? And what about the kiss? Why would Miles do that? Was he crazy? Yeah, that had to be it. Miles Eisenberg was a lunatic. It made sense now.

Liar.

Eyes closed, Sawyer leaned back against the door and fought to steady his breath. If anyone came down the steps or through the foyer, they'd find him disheveled and wrecked, with his lips all red and swollen, and they would know exactly what he'd done, even if they didn't know who he'd done it with.

He licked his parched lips and listened to the sound of his heart slowly finding the right tempo again. He waited for his breaths to stop feeling like fire. He waited until he trusted his body not to embarrass him.

"Are you okay?" one of the blonde women from yesterday asked.

"Yeah, you look totally trashed," the other added.

"I'm fine," Sawyer said.

"So um… okay, can you move so we can get outside before the car gets here?"

"Sure."

Sawyer pushed up from the door and cleared the way. The women left him standing there as if they'd never spoken to him. He supposed that was the way it worked in Hollywood. People only seemed to care when you had something they wanted. He watched the girls bounce down the steps to join Miles. The expression on his face instantly changed. What once was a frown turned into a warm, welcoming, entirely plastic smile. The smile didn't fill his eyes with happiness. They didn't sparkle like they had Saturday night when Sawyer had been with him on Castro.

Fingers knotted around the strap of his camera bag, Sawyer hid in the window, keeping his sights on Miles through the cover of a sheer curtain. Occasionally, Miles would look up, and Sawyer feared Miles could see him standing there. It took a lot of effort, but Sawyer eventually convinced himself Miles couldn't. So what if he could, anyway? Miles had no control over him

Oh, be honest, he does have a little control over you. Otherwise, you'd be out there waiting for the car with them, not hiding behind a curtain.

"For fuck's sake," he growled as he wrenched open the door.

The car had just pulled up outside. He wasn't going to let the weirdness between him and Miles Eisenberg keep him from performing his duties to the best of his ability. He wasn't going to let the director soil his work ethic. A soft smile—not the fake one he'd been wearing—spread across Miles's lips as if he were happy Sawyer had changed his mind.

The chauffeur opened the door and the two blondes climbed in: one in front and the other in back, leaving only two more places to sit. Miles waited, expecting what, Sawyer couldn't say.

Instead of immediately climbing in, he stood nose-to-nose with Miles and said, "Save your smiles. I didn't come back because of you. I came back 'cause I have a job to do. The studio is payin' good money for me to be here, and I'd like to not waste it."

CHAPTER THIRTEEN

AS SOON as the car stopped at the location, everyone piled out as fast as they could. No one waited for the chauffeur to open the doors. No one had spoken the entire ride. The radio hadn't even been turned on. In fact, the only sound had come from one of the blondes' earbuds, and it'd been a garbled mess of noise. That had been the most uncomfortable hour of Sawyer's life, and he couldn't abandon ship fast enough.

Miles marched straight up to the building without saying two words. It seemed like he'd gotten into his zone long before their arrival, and now he had his director's face on. From the looks of it, the day would be all business and no screwing around. Sawyer certainly hoped it turned out that way. Work always made for the best distraction.

The building looked like an old abandoned warehouse from the outside. Rusted metal walls formed the exterior. Not a single window could be seen from the driveway. A set of dirty, off-white doors was the only opening on that side of the building. It wasn't exactly what Sawyer had expected when he'd signed up for this gig. He'd expected pristine working conditions and high-dollar lounges, a little city full of different studios and golf carts and trailers and famous movie stars meandering about—just like he'd seen on TV and in movies. This looked nothing at all like TV's version of Hollywood… unless they were on the set of a horror movie.

Inside, the large, open area was sectioned off into what appeared to be multiple sets. Each cube looked like a different room in a house or office. One even looked like an adult toy store. Sawyer wished he'd read those books before signing up. Lucy had sworn it wasn't anything he'd be too embarrassed to watch, and now he was starting to doubt how truthful his friend had been with him.

"This is a romantic comedy, right?" he asked one of the blondes.

She giggled and nodded. Her eyes were as wide as his, like this was her first time on a movie set too. He distantly wondered what her role was in the film.

"May I start taking pictures?" he asked, aiming the question at Miles, who was now many feet ahead of them.

"Please wait until we've had our opening meeting," Miles responded, voice flat and official, all business—as if nothing had happened between them.

A sharp sigh pushed through Sawyer's lips. This would *definitely* end up being the most miserable three months of Sawyer's life. And that statement had turned into a freaking mantra in the last three days.

The doors behind him whined and scraped the concrete floor as they opened. The sound inspired a shiver, much like a teacher raking her nails down a chalkboard or a knife slicing the wrong way across a porcelain plate. The hairs on Sawyer's arms stood at full attention.

Another group of people he hadn't yet met spilled into the warehouse, bringing with them the warmth and light of the sun. Sawyer would've given anything to be on a beach right now, taking pictures of blue tide rolling in around the feet of a beautiful man. The thought took him back to the last time he'd shot pictures of Elijah—nude pictures for their private collection. They'd spent hours on the quiet beach, making love on a ratty old comforter Sawyer kept in the back of his Wagoneer. As he recalled, the thing was still back there.

If that thought didn't dampen his already soggy mood....

The people who were obviously already familiar with making movies circled in around Miles, leaving the only open space to the right of the ill-tempered director. That was the last place Sawyer wanted to be, rubbing elbows with a man who ran so hot and cold it made Sawyer's head spin, a man who'd been making him utterly uncomfortable since they'd met.

As best he could, Sawyer kept his eyes front and center, not daring to look at the man beside him. Oh, but something about Miles tugged at the core of Sawyer's being. He was that man in the crowd of a million mundanes who shone like a diamond, the one no one in their right mind would turn down. He smelled so good, and his voice was velvety smooth and so damn commanding. Sawyer could almost hear him demanding, "Strip for me. Roll over. Open your legs. Let me fuck you." He had to catch himself before the silent purr floating around in his head became a real, and very embarrassing, sound. He had to stop thinking of his boss that way before his body made real, and very embarrassing, decisions for him.

"… that being said"—Miles's voice broke through the euphoria of Sawyer's fantasy—"we're going to have fun making this movie. It's going to be a chart topper, a star maker, and the best damn film of the year."

Everyone but Sawyer rallied in celebration. Truth be told, Miles Eisenberg made one hell of a motivational speaker. Even Sawyer secretly wanted to cheer along with them. The stubborn man he could be when his feelings were hurt wouldn't allow him to, though.

"Sawyer." Oh shit. Miles had singled him out.

"Yeah?"

"You can take pictures of anything you like. The more, the better. Just please, keep in mind that nothing is allowed to be released to the public. All photos must be sent to the studio at the end of filming."

"Understood."

"Good. Now"—Miles clapped both hands together —"let's make a movie."

Immediately, Sawyer headed toward a table against the wall, one not already loaded down with fruit and pastries and bottles of juices. He set his bag down and proceeded to dig around. Inside were his camera and various lenses, the different kinds of flash, and other little tools of the trade. He had his hand wrapped around his beautiful, top-of-the-line Nikon, had it halfway out of the bag, when someone called his name and startled him so badly he nearly dropped it. His heart seized the moment it left his hand. Thank God he still had it mostly in the bag.

And Penelope was going to get her ass chewed out for that one.

"What?" Sawyer gritted out, keeping his shaking hands off his equipment.

"This is Tabby. She's going to be your assistant while you're on the set."

Sawyer shot a glare over his shoulder. The girl in question had chestnut brown pigtails high on the sides of her head and close to the back, like she wasn't making any effort to look cute, just trying to efficiently keep her hair out of her face. She wore sandy-colored cargo pants and a tight-fitting shirt. The logo on it, he assumed, belonged to her alma mater... if she was old enough to even be in college. She was delightful, but homely. Everything about her looked adorably mousey. He appreciated her simple style. It was functional, rather than fashionable.

He offered her a hand. She was way too thrilled to touch it.

"It's such an honor to work with you, Mr. Taylor," she squeaked. Her high-pitched voice would end up driving him insane. He could tell already.

"I don't know 'bout all that," he said. "Just do me a favor and don't mess with my cameras. Remember that rule and we'll get along just fine."

"Sawyer," Penelope barked.

Tabby frowned.

"What?" Sawyer said. "I told you I didn't want no assistant. I handle my own gear."

Tabby lowered her head.

"Too bad," Penelope all but growled at him. "You're *going* to have one. End of discussion." Before he could argue again, Penelope was storming her way toward Miles.

Sawyer looked at Tabby, who had been staring at him while he wasn't paying attention. She immediately averted her eyes when he caught her.

"That wasn't about you," he said.

"I know."

"I don't like people touchin' my things."

"I know."

"I told Penelope—" He paused. "You know?"

"I don't like people touching my stuff either, but I really need this internship to go well, so please let me stay. I'll do whatever I'm told."

"Right." Sawyer sighed as he slid the bag her way. "I'll handle my cameras. You handle the extras. Just make sure everything goes back where it belongs, 'kay?"

She beamed, nodding convulsively. "Thank you, Mr. Taylor."

"It's Sawyer. Call me Sawyer."

"Sawyer. Right."

For the first few hours, Sawyer and Tabby stood back and listened as Miles directed the crew and the actors. Watching the man in action was one of the most impressive things Sawyer had ever seen. Miles looked completely at home in the director's chair, and he made everything look so easy. If an actor didn't do exactly what he wanted, Miles exercised a fair amount of patience, and they tried the scene again. One take. Two takes. Three takes. The smallest changes caused the scene to be run from the beginning. Sawyer watched in awe, and before he knew it, they were breaking for lunch and he hadn't snapped the first picture.

Shit. He'd have to explain to Miles what happened, and hope like hell Miles understood.

The crowd dissipated, and Sawyer dismissed Tabby for the day, leaving a whole lot of vacant air, one scared shitless photographer, and one very intimidating director. After everything they'd said to each other, the kiss and the… well, hand job in the back of the sedan, Sawyer felt like a dolt approaching Miles in such an adoring way. Maybe adoring was the wrong word. What he felt really didn't resemble adoration, but more professional respect.

Stop stalling.

"Hey." Sawyer spoke softly, unsure of himself in a high-school crush sort of way. Miles raised his head and closed the leather binder in his lap. He folded both hands over the top of it and gave Sawyer one hell of a knee-knocking look.

"I, um…." Sawyer stumbled through his words. "I…. I haven't taken any pictures yet."

"Why not?"

"Do you wanna honest answer, or one that makes me sound less pathetic?"

Miles thought on that a moment, or that's what he looked to be doing. "Honest."

"You're impressive to watch. I…. I found myself lost in everything goin' on around me."

"It wasn't me. You were lost in the magic. I had the same feeling when I worked on my first movie set. The magic fades, I promise."

"Okay." Sawyer nodded slowly, exhaled, and turned to walk away. But he didn't want to go. He couldn't deny the feeling he needed to say so much more. Yet he wasn't sure how he would even begin… until he turned around and caught Miles staring at him with what Sawyer imagined to be a healthy dose of regret.

"Can we start over?" Sawyer said, taking a step closer.

Miles arched his brow. "Start over?"

"Yeah." Sawyer held out his hand. "I'm Sawyer Taylor. I'll be your set photographer."

A soft smile tugged at the edge of Miles's lips, faint dimples hugging them tightly. To Sawyer's surprise, Miles took his hand. He didn't so much shake it, but held it tight like he wanted to feel a connection with Sawyer that meant more than backseat hand jobs and forced kisses.

"I'm Miles Eisenberg. I'll be your director." Miles didn't let go of his hand. His smile slowly faded. "And I'm sorry for being such a miserable ass with you."

"I don't know what you're talkin' 'bout. We just met." Sawyer winked.

Miles quietly laughed. "Very well. May I buy my photographer lunch?"

"That sounds perfect. Your photographer is starvin'."

Miles stood and set the leather binder he'd been perusing down on the seat. He joined Sawyer, close by his side, and almost acted as though he wanted to take Sawyer's hand but thought better of it. That was fine. They weren't together, and keeping up professional appearances would better serve them both. No need for anyone to get the wrong idea about what was going on between them.

What exactly *was* going on between them?

Chapter Fourteen

On a stretch of Folsom, far enough from the convention center that people rarely ventured down that way, was a tiny diner. The atmosphere was homey, the service good, and they had some of the best deli sandwiches Miles had ever had the pleasure of shoving into his mouth. It wasn't five-star dining, nothing elegant—maybe not even as good as what craft service was offering—but it was close and discreet. They could get away from the set and the busy-bodies, and no one would go looking for a Hollywood director and his new crush there.

New crush? Really?

Yes, in a way, he supposed he had a crush on Sawyer Taylor. He'd had a crush on the photographer even before Sawyer had arrived in San Francisco. He'd fallen in love through photographs, through images so beautiful and romantic anyone who had a taste for art could easily love them. And now, after meeting the man behind such beauty, Miles loved his work even more.

He pulled out a chair and nodded for Sawyer to have a seat. Being chivalrous came easy with Sawyer. Chivalry had never mattered with the other men. They were there to sate a carnal need. Sawyer was so much more than that.

"Can I have an ice water with lemon?" Miles asked the waitress as he took the seat across from his companion. "And a Caesar salad, please."

"And I'll have a sweet tea, no lemon, please. Oh, and the salad sounds good. I'll have that too."

Smiling, she gathered the menus, then disappeared. Before the men could engage in conversation, she returned with their drinks. Thankfully, she didn't hang around to chat. The only talking Miles wanted to do was with Sawyer.

"I have to tell you something," he said.

Sawyer raised his head. Their eyes met, and Sawyer's stare took his breath away.

"I meant that kiss," Miles admitted. Holding his breath, Miles waited for Sawyer to say something—a "get over it, it'll never happen, I don't look at you that way," maybe. Nothing. Not a single word was spoken.

Sawyer's expression didn't change. The fact remained, Miles had absolutely meant that kiss. Not one man to ever cross Miles's path or partake in a salacious rendezvous with him had ever been kissed the way he'd kissed Sawyer. His lips had been saved for his daughter's forehead when he laid her down to sleep at night or for his sister's cheek before they said their good-byes. Men got sex. They didn't get the tender kisses reserved for the special people in his life.

Sawyer absolutely seemed to be one of those special people.

"Please say something," Miles whispered. "Tell me to fuck off if you want to."

"I don't."

"Then tell me something. Tell me how I'm supposed to feel right now."

The waitress came back and deposited two generously sized salads in front of them. Each man thanked her. Then she disappeared again. Miles's request still hung in the air, waiting like an eager child on Christmas morning. Would Sawyer surprise him? Did he have a chance in hell of making up the last few days to Sawyer? His companion picked up his fork, eyes trained on his food. He began pushing lettuce around in the bowl.

"I don't know what to tell you," Sawyer muttered without looking up. "We've known each other for three days, and you've taken me through a range of emotions I've spent four months trying not to feel."

"I don't understand."

The fork clanked against the bowl when Sawyer dropped it. The sound startled Miles, kicking up the beat of his heart. Sawyer finally looked up, and for the first time since they'd crossed paths, Miles saw true heartbreak in the photographer's eyes.

"What happened four months ago, Sawyer?"

"I lost eight years of my life."

"How?"

Confusion and curiosity were a bitch, sometimes. Clearly, Sawyer didn't want to elaborate. Miles had a burning need to know, and yet, he didn't want to push or prod. He didn't want Sawyer to hate him for trying to dig into his past, but his curiosity wouldn't let go.

He reached across the table and laid his hand down, palm up, fingers curled. If Sawyer wanted to hold his hand, he could. It was there for him to take, to comfort him, to help him if he wanted it. A man with such a beautiful heart and mind, and an eye for the truly romantic, deserved so much, and Miles sincerely wanted to give him anything he needed.

"I've been with one man," Sawyer began. His voice wavered enough Miles knew tears were fighting to break free. "He was my first and only love."

Miles started to pull back his hand and casually tuck it away, feeling like an ass for the hand job, for the kiss, for the fighting, and for wanting to hold Sawyer's hand right now. But before he could hide his empty hand under the table, Sawyer hooked his fingers with Miles's. He held on with desperation, like he needed Miles to not let go. Miles wouldn't, not for anything in the world.

"I thought I was enough for him. We started dating in high school, even had a commitment ceremony and talked about adopting. We bought a house and everything. Looking back, I don't know if he ever really loved me. We were supposed to get officially married, but...."

"I have a daughter," Miles blurted. Something about Sawyer's candid honesty made him want to share too. "Not to belittle your pain, I swear, and I'm incredibly sorry for interrupting your story. I just.... I felt I needed to tell you about her. I don't talk about her with anyone other than my sister."

"Why did you share it with me?"

"I don't know." Miles moved his hand in such a way his fingers became intertwined with Sawyer's. Holding hands helped him, and seemed to help Sawyer as well, like each one needed a level of companionship only the other could give.

"It felt like the right thing to do," Miles continued. He swallowed. "Her mother was my best friend." He closed his eyes and lowered his head, squeezing Sawyer's hand tighter. "I was in the room, waiting for my daughter to be born. The heart monitors started going crazy. Doctors rushed in. I was shoved out of the way, and I didn't know if my daughter and Anne were going to be okay, or if I was going to lose them. Had my sister not been there, I probably would've fallen apart."

"I'm sorry, Miles. I...."

"It's okay. My daughter is the light of my life. She's exactly like her mother, and just as beautiful. She's the reason I work so hard. I want her to have everything she could ever want or need."

"But not a mother."

"No." Miles looked back up. "My sister is playing that role. It's the best I can give her."

"She has your love, Miles. Clearly. Every child should be so fortunate."

"Thank you. Sincerely. I never know if I'm doing right by her. It's hard sometimes."

"I always wanted to be a father. Elijah swore we would have kids. We had a surrogate ready and everything. My friend, Lucy, said she would have our child, but…." Sawyer laughed. "Actually, she still wants to have my baby."

"Consider it," Miles said. "The only thing in this world that truly makes me happy is my little girl. She makes breathing easier."

Silence fell between them. Miles couldn't help noticing the way Sawyer looked at him now. It appeared, in Sawyer's eyes, that Miles wasn't just some director who'd hired him to photograph a movie anymore. Maybe Sawyer even saw a man capable of loving someone other than himself, not a hustler giving out drunken hand jobs and unwanted kisses. He realized then just how much importance he put on Sawyer's opinion of him.

They finished their conversation over salads. Miles learned more about Sawyer in those two hours than he had in the three days they'd known—or rather, fought not to know—each other. For instance, he learned Sawyer never went to college, that he gave up on a higher education to help his parents in their store. His family had lived hand-to-mouth and never really gotten ahead. He hadn't had a relationship with his parents since he'd come out of the closet. That had happened six short months before Elijah had called it off with him. The most astonishing thing of all, Sawyer hadn't been ruined by his past. He'd grown from it, and he'd blossomed into a beautiful man.

Miles's heart broke for Sawyer, genuinely broke. And his heart broke for himself. His story was actually very similar. Not being impoverished and setting dreams aside, but the part about his parents turning their backs on him after he'd come out. The only people who'd stayed by his side after that had been Anne and Karen.

Anne…. Her name still twisted his stomach.

The perky little waitress returned with her sunny smile and her "I'll do what I can to make you tip me" demeanor. She looked at the table, and Miles followed the line of her sight. He found his hand still entangled with Sawyer's, holding on with an unwillingness to let go. It surprised him to find himself engaged in such a thing.

"Check please," he croaked.

CHAPTER FIFTEEN

THE FIRST day of filming wrapped. Sawyer had an impressive collection of shots, mostly of Miles, with a varying spread of behind-the-scenes action coming in a close second. He'd spent a few hours after dinner going through them on his computer, discarding the ones he would never, *ever* allow to see the light of day. In all, he had fifty—give or take—memory-worthy shots to save for the studio and more than a hundred and fifty throwaways. Not bad for the first day.

He sat back in his chair, arms tucked behind his head, watching as the slideshow of shots played across the computer screen. A wonderful sense of pride came from seeing his work so beautifully displayed, but the feeling of satisfaction would've been so much sweeter shared with someone special, someone who appreciated his art as much as he did.

Standing, Sawyer closed the lid to his laptop and disconnected his camera. He gathered the machine and its myriad cables in his arms with the intention of going right down to Miles's room. He didn't even make it to the bedroom door. What if Miles had something else going on? What if Miles was doing someone else?

Oh, God, I can't handle that.

He sat down, stood, then sat again. If his brain kept yo-yoing this way, he would lose his mind for sure.

Okay. Okay. You can do this.

He stood, hugging his laptop tightly. This time, when he reached for the doorknob, he planned on going all the way. Nothing was going to talk him out of it.

Out in the hallway, once he'd braved the barrier of the doorjamb, he was met with low lights and cool air. A few short steps, and he would be at the director's bedroom door, with a contrived reason to be there, a lie to cover the truth that Sawyer really only wanted to be close to him. Before he knew it, he'd walked the entire length of the hall and stood front and center at his intended destination. He raised his fist, swallowed his worry, and knocked on the door.

Not much sound came from the room, no rustling of sheets, no moaning or groaning. Sawyer didn't even hear a television. Miles didn't say "Hold on" or "I'll be right there." In fact, he didn't say anything, and Sawyer worried maybe Miles had already gone to bed. He had turned on his heel, ready to run like the wind, when the door behind him opened.

"Hey," Miles said, voice surprisingly soft. "Where are you going?"

"I thought…." Sawyer smiled nervously as he hugged his computer tighter. "I thought you might've gone to bed or something."

"No, I was just reading the script." Miles looked at the device barricaded in Sawyer's arms. "What do you have there?"

"Just a few pictures from the set. I thought I'd show you."

"Perfect. Come in."

Miles held the door wide open and stepped out of its frame.

Inside, the bedroom was dark, save for the blue light radiating from the TV screen. It cast a rich royal glow over the mussed sheets on the bed. The pillows were stacked high against the headboard. The script lay open, facedown beside them. Even though the TV was on, Sawyer heard no sound, not even the low hum of white noise.

"If I'm bothering you…."

"You're not," Miles said. "Stay. Please."

"Thanks."

Sawyer set his laptop on the table, but didn't bother lifting the lid. He hoped whatever spark he'd felt at the restaurant at lunch held true here at the inn, in the dark privacy of Miles's bedroom.

When Sawyer raised his head, he found Miles watching him with the kind of unwavering interest one lover watched another. But they weren't lovers, not yet. They'd shared a hand job, a kiss, and a magical lunch date, one argument and a make up. None of which deserved the look one lover gave to another. And Sawyer had no clue what to say.

Not true. *Kiss me. Kiss me. Kiss me.*

"Do you, um…. We, um…."

"The most comfortable place is on the bed." Miles's eyes widened. He held up both hands. "Not that I'm trying to get you in bed. I just—"

"It's okay. I didn't take it that way."

"Good," Miles said, though his expression resembled disappointment more than it resembled relief. "Didn't want you to think I was trying anything."

"I didn't." *No, but you wished.*

Swallowing hard, Sawyer looked at the bed, then back to Miles. He didn't want to make the first move. Something about doing so seemed so presumptuous, even if Miles had made the suggestion. It felt wrong and awkward to climb into his boss's bed. He reached for his laptop, but Miles intercepted his hand.

Silently, they stared at each other. Neither man seemed willing to make the first move. Sawyer wanted to feel another one of those hot, dominating kisses.

As if Miles knew exactly what Sawyer had on his mind, Miles wrapped one hand around the back of Sawyer's neck and guided him closer. Their lips connected. Their eyes closed. Sawyer's heart melted, pouring heat throughout his body. Every inch of him caught fire when their tongues twisted together.

For the first time in a long while, Sawyer felt butterflies when he kissed someone. It was the fluttering in his chest and the chills running down his arms, the tingles rippling along his back and the tightness in his most sensitive places. Butterflies. Like feeling something so genuine it didn't matter how much time they'd spent together or how much they knew about each other. Like their souls had made a decision logic couldn't change.

When Sawyer finally realized what he felt and what those feelings meant, he gasped and broke the kiss, wondering if Miles had felt the same thing.

"What just happened here?" he asked, voice airy and raspy.

"We kissed…." Miles didn't release his hold on Sawyer's neck. The tips of his fingers tickled the fine hair at Sawyer's nape.

They'd kissed. Sure, but had Miles felt anything? Or was it an empty, meaningless kiss like the hand job had been, like the first kiss had been? Maybe coming to Miles's room had been a mistake. Why had he ventured down that hallway anyway?

The pictures.

Right.

"I should go back to my own room," Sawyer said, grabbing his laptop from the table. His mind was made up. He needed to go back to his room and pretend the second kiss hadn't happened. Then Miles locked his hand around Sawyer's forearm.

"Don't leave," Miles said, hushed and needy in a nonsexual way— something he couldn't have imagined hearing from Miles prior to this.

Sawyer silently debated staying or going. The kiss had left him with a lot of questions and a lot of confusion. This would've been easier if he knew how to sleep around and not care, but he'd never been that guy and didn't think he could be.

"Stop overthinking it," Miles said. "I'm not asking for anything more than your company, I swear."

"I'm not overthinkin' it."

Miles smoothed his thumb over the crease in Sawyer's forehead. Apparently, he *had* been overthinking the situation, so hard in fact, his brow had furrowed.

"Okay, maybe I was overthinkin' it."

Laughing, Miles eased Sawyer closer, close enough their lips touched in the slightest, most teasing possible way. Somehow, through talent and practice most likely, Miles kept the distance between them as he walked Sawyer back toward the bed. Their stares remained locked as he sat Sawyer down on the edge and wedged himself between Sawyer's parted legs.

"I don't want to have sex," Sawyer whispered, even as he leaned up, reaching with desperation for another taste of Miles's mouth.

"Who said anything about sex?"

Before Sawyer could say a word, Miles pressed his mouth to Sawyer's again and used his body to push Sawyer back on the bed.

The tugging in his groin made Sawyer wish he hadn't said anything about not wanting sex. As it now stood, sex sounded like a phenomenal idea. Sex sounded like the best idea ever. He moaned as he hooked his legs around Miles's thighs and held tight, insisting Miles not stop until Sawyer was fully satisfied.

The kiss broke, and Miles brushed his thumb over Sawyer's lips. "Stay tonight, and I swear I'll hold you and nothing else. You can trust me."

Don't trust him. Think about what Elijah did to you.

"Okay" is what Sawyer finally found himself saying, though his mind warred with his mouth and the notion of being alone in a bed with Miles Eisenberg.

IT TOOK a hell of a lot of restraint for Miles to behave himself, but he'd sworn to Sawyer he would, and if nothing else, Miles was a man of his word. Well, at least he tried to be. He pulled the mussed covers back, then reached around Sawyer's body and situated the pillows.

"We can sleep in the same bed tonight," Miles said one more time for good measure, "or you can go back to your own room. I'd like for you to stay, though, and I hope my sleeping in my underwear doesn't bother you."

"It doesn't."

"Good."

Miles knelt and removed each of Sawyer's shoes, then set them beside the nightstand. Next he stood and relieved Sawyer of his shirt.

"This doesn't bother you, does it?" Miles asked.

"Not at all."

"I don't want to assume."

He looked down at Sawyer's jeans as he hooked his thumbs over the stretchy waistband of his sweatpants. Miles pulled them down slowly, exposing tight briefs and a proud bulge. His underwear wasn't exactly tented, but his cock wasn't exactly ignoring the beautiful man on his bed either. A silent mantra reminded him to keep his libido in check because Sawyer clearly wasn't ready to become "the guy I fucked the other night." Honestly, Miles wasn't sure he wanted to dismiss Sawyer as such either.

Sawyer stood up and proceeded to unbutton his jeans. The sprinkling of dark hair dipping down across his navel caused Miles to purr. He could see himself running his tongue along that happy, fuzzy little trail right before he dropped his mouth down the length of Sawyer's cock.

So much for keeping his own business in check.

He locked his hand over his groin, hopefully hiding his hard-on from Sawyer while keeping his dick in check. The real problem came when Sawyer stood chest to chest with him, and their groins met in a kiss. If there hadn't been two layers of fabric between them, Miles would've bent Sawyer over the bed and gone at it despite what he'd promised.

"Lie down for me," he whispered, voice sounding more pleading more than he liked.

Sawyer did what he asked, and Miles climbed into the bed behind him.

Wrapping both arms around Sawyer, Miles settled in for the night, hoping that having a man in his embrace would bring the sweet dreams Miles so desperately needed. He buried his head in the curve of Sawyer's neck, breathing in the spicy, musky scent of a man he could almost see having a future with. He pressed small kisses along Sawyer's collarbone and when he reached the man's ear, he said a soft, "Sweet dreams to you, Sawyer Taylor."

"Sweet dreams, Miles."

CHAPTER SIXTEEN

TUESDAY MORNING, Miles woke up more refreshed and renewed than he had in a very long time. It felt good to have someone sleep next to him, in his arms, against his chest. The last time he'd slept that way had been six months ago with Gavin in the exact same room. Only difference being Gavin and Miles had passed out in the stupor of postcoital bliss, whereas Sawyer had simply given Miles the comfort to sleep like a baby.

Miles awoke first. Though he didn't want to leave Sawyer lying alone in the bed, he had to. He had to get a shower and get his shit together so he could get to the set before people started showing up. If Miles wasn't there to lead, there was no telling what kind of trouble they would find themselves in. Sometimes the adults in his life could be worse than the child.

He eased out of the bed, careful not to make any sudden movements, careful not to jostle the mattress. Sawyer whimpered and shifted but didn't open his eyes. Soft snores followed and brought a smile to Miles's face. Before his urges had a chance to convince him to climb right back in the bed with that gorgeous man, Miles escaped into the bathroom.

He stripped away his underwear while cool water exploded from the showerhead. Old pipes meant it took a few minutes for the heat to come up. Miles didn't mind. He used those minutes brushing his teeth and checking his face for any of those minute imperfections people noticed and the camera's eye always found. When steam finally rose from behind the curtain, he knew his shower was ready.

The hot water poured down over his body, relaxing his muscles and cleansing his skin. He thought about Sawyer and how adorable the country boy had looked all curled around the pillow and twisted in the sheets. While Sawyer wasn't movie-star gorgeous—like Gavin or the other Hollywood types that always seemed to flock to Miles when they wanted something—Sawyer had a simple beauty about him, unblemished by the coldness of the world, unscathed by numerous heartbreaking encounters. He had an innocence Miles envied.

Foamy shampoo rolled down Miles's face and back, and he'd just begun to wash it away when the shower curtain crinkled behind him. The metal hooks holding it in place scraped along the curtain rod. Miles quickly scrubbed the soap from his face, just in time to catch a completely naked Sawyer climbing into the shower behind him. No way could he deny his libido now, and from the looks of it, Sawyer had every desire to quench his carnal fires too.

"What are you—"

Sawyer pressed two fingers against his lips, abruptly silencing him. He reached down with his other hand and palmed Miles's cock. Miles gasped. He hadn't realized how soft Sawyer's hand was until he felt it riding over his most sensitive flesh. His eyes rolled back. He flattened his hand to the tiled wall to help hold the weight of his body. He didn't know how much longer his quivering legs would do the job.

"Oh, God," he rasped. "What are you…?"

"I'm returnin' the favor," Sawyer said, voice lilting wickedly.

Sawyer tightened his fist and Miles gripped the wall harder. He wouldn't have believed he was getting a hand job from Sawyer Taylor had he not opened his eyes and seen Sawyer standing beneath the spray with one hand around his shaft. Part of him still wondered if this was a dream, if he'd find himself lying awake in his bed and fully erect.

"Holy shit." He whimpered. "Don't stop. Please, don't stop."

The jerking and squeezing became harder and faster. Pressure pushed up from Miles's sac and into his shaft, thundering through his length like a runaway freight train until it exploded from the head of his cock, taking the last breath of air Miles had with it. His head hung. He panted hard and fast, lungs begging for every single shallow breath it could get. He felt his heart thumping wildly from his temples to his thighs. And the best thing he could do for himself was sink into Sawyer's chest.

"Why?" he whispered in a breathy, ragged rush.

"I told you why. I wanted to return the favor. Only seemed fair."

"Fair." Miles snorted. "I guess I can buy that."

"It's honest."

"I'm sure."

Miles lifted the light blue bar of soap in his hand and, without asking, ran it down Sawyer's chest. He moved slowly, tracing every single muscle, tracing the dark patch of hair running over his navel, and down farther to the dark hairs surrounding the base of one gorgeous cock. His mouth watered for a taste of it, to feel the veiny ripples rubbing along his tongue. The thought made his sac tug. He knew if he didn't push away the idea of kneeling in front of Sawyer and swallowing him whole, he'd be rock hard again and wanting a hell of a lot more than a hand job.

"We should get going," he said. Tension filled his voice. "If we want coffee and breakfast before leaving for the day, we need to get dressed and get our asses down there."

"I didn't bring any clothes with me."

"Finish showering. I'll get dressed and go to your room. Anything in particular you want to wear?"

"I have jeans and more jeans, and T-shirts. That's what I brought to work in."

"Right. Jeans and T-shirt." Miles stole a quick taste of Sawyer's lips. "I'll be right back."

"I'll be right here. Well, in your room here." Red crept into Sawyer's cheeks.

Miles had the urge to stay and kiss the red away.

Before he let his body talk him into calling off filming today, he escaped from the shower and Sawyer's incredible body and his delicious lips and his magnetic doe eyes. He dried off as best as he could and threw on some clothes. Then he grabbed Sawyer's room key and laptop, and headed down the hall.

Inside, he found Sawyer's suitcase set up on the stand, with the top unzipped but not open. Carefully, he set the laptop aside so he could fish out something for Sawyer to wear without creating a situation for disaster with the computer.

But disaster didn't come from dropping one of Sawyer's precious possessions and helplessly watching it shatter. No, far from it. Disaster, or rather the kind of ache Miles could've gone without, came when he lifted the lid of Sawyer's suitcase and found a black and white picture of two men pinned to the inside of it. One of those men was Sawyer. The other Miles had seen in the magazines, in the pictures Sawyer had taken. Elijah. After the lunch date yesterday, Miles could put a face to the name.

The two men sat close together, shoulder to shoulder, looking lovingly into each other's eyes. From across their bodies, they held hands. Their locked fingers rested on Sawyer's knee. They appeared to be in love, young and in love, and so lost in each other no one could come between them. If the way Elijah looked at Sawyer in this picture was an act, then Elijah deserved an Oscar, because right now, Miles actually believed in true love.

He stumbled back and sat down in the chair. The picture remained in view to drive home the truth that what Miles was doing with Sawyer was so very, very wrong. He couldn't ever imagine looking at another man the way Sawyer and Elijah had looked at each other. The course of his life didn't lead to great romances and happily ever afters. He'd never once felt something so strong for anyone but Anne, and now Zoe. His heart had an occupant, and he could say with an honest amount of certainty, there wasn't room for anyone else. The fewer people who had claim there, the less likely he was to ever feel the hurt of losing someone he loved again. Sawyer deserved a man who could look him in the eye and tell him without words just how much he was loved, adored, and revered.

Swallowing the painful lump in his throat, Miles stood and went back to the suitcase. He tried not looking at the photo as he dug around, but he couldn't help himself. It drew him in and begged him to witness something he'd denied himself over and over again. When he finally had an outfit in his arms, he quickly closed the lid and sucked in a breath of relief. The photo was gone now, and Miles's heart and head were back on course.

Until he returned to his room and found Sawyer utterly naked, one leg hiked up on the edge of the bed. His cock hung loose and long between his thighs. He lay back with his elbows supporting the weight of his torso. Miles's sac tugged again. In that pose, Sawyer was hot, porno hot, and he had a wickedness in his smirk.

"I brought your clothes," Miles said raggedly. Lust was completely undoing what little resolve he had. Keeping his eyes averted, Miles set the folded clothes on the table. "When you're dressed, meet me downstairs for coffee. Please."

"Sure." Sawyer sat up. The salacious expression immediately drained from his face. Now he looked like the innocent boy he'd seen in that picture with Elijah.

Miles felt like a cad.

He finally closed the distance between them, swept one hand around the nape of Sawyer's neck, and guided him in for another kiss. This time, it was much less chaste than the one he'd stolen in the shower. It wasn't much more than a press of lips and a close of the eyes, but somehow, held so much more passion than Miles had expected. He felt so much more than he wanted to, and the longer he held Sawyer to that kiss, the harder it was for him to let go.

His voice was much huskier than it should've been when he said, "I'll see you downstairs."

CHAPTER SEVENTEEN

SAWYER DIDN'T know how that man did it, but Miles somehow made his heart rush wildly and beat slower all the same. Every touch, no matter how innocent or how heated, seemed to take his breath away, and those kisses…. God help him, every kiss touched Sawyer's soul. Every moment spent with Miles was like walking through a dream—a dream Sawyer didn't want to wake up from yet.

Even in the euphoria of having spent a night in Miles's bed and shared a shower, however, Sawyer knew better than to let himself keep falling the way he had been. His relationship with Elijah had begun the same way. One look. One kiss. One touch. He'd fallen head over heels for the first guy who'd paid him any attention. Eight years later, he had an empty house and a broken heart to show for it. And here he was, letting history repeat itself.

It wasn't entirely his fault, though. Miles was incredible and charismatic. He said all the right things and romanced his way right into Sawyer's life. He was the kind of guy Sawyer had once dreamed about meeting, the kind who could bring everyone in the room to their knees, the kind who demanded respect but didn't have to ask for it, the kind no one could avoid feeling something for. Miles had all those qualities, and he knew it. And holy shit, if that wasn't the hottest thing ever.

Wearing a grin as big as the moon, Sawyer practically danced his way downstairs to join Miles and hopefully Martin in the kitchen for breakfast and coffee. The blondes and Penelope, and even Sawyer's cute little assistant, were most likely still in bed. No one in their right mind would've been as bright-eyed and bushy-tailed as Miles and Sawyer so early by choice.

When he reached the pocket doors leading into the kitchen, all conversation stopped and Martin gave him a cat-that-ate-the-canary grin. Miles looked over his shoulder, and with his foot, eased the chair beside him out from under the table. Sawyer took the offered seat, but couldn't help feeling everyone in the room had their eyes on him.

Conversation continued while Miles ate his fruit and sipped his coffee. Sawyer inhaled the scrambled eggs and bacon and biscuits, chasing the food back with copious amounts of piping hot java.

Together they headed out to the waiting sedan and took turns settling into the backseat. Miles ordered the driver to leave for the set right away, saying he needed to start the day's business before everyone else arrived. Maybe that was truly the case. However, when he reached down between them and took Sawyer's hand, Sawyer got the idea the urgency had more to do with being alone together than it did any sort of "business" Miles wanted to tend to.

"Is this okay?" Miles asked. His fingers tightened enough to let Sawyer know what the question referred to.

"Fine by me. You okay with it?"

"I am."

Thank God.

When they arrived at the set, Sawyer didn't expect Miles to jump right into director mode. He wasn't sure what he expected. Maybe a little light kissing and petting. But definitely not the abrupt game face Miles put on as soon as they crossed the threshold. He learned something very important about Miles then. The man had unwavering focus when it came to his career, and no amount of lustful distraction would interfere. Sawyer sincerely respected that fact.

The week continued on in much the same way it'd begun. They didn't spend every night in the same bed, though. By Thursday, both men were so buried in work, neither had time for making out until they fell asleep and then waking up to hard-ons and shared showers. They did, however, manage to meet every morning at the breakfast table and leave at the same time. They shared a brief conversation and a meaningful kiss before parting ways.

Friday afternoon came and Sawyer was more than ready to spend an evening relaxing and sight-seeing. Anything to take his mind off work for a little while. Anything to take his mind off Miles for a little while. He longed to be in Miles's arms for another night, to sleep with the warmth against his back and the soft noises in his ear, to wake up to a beautiful smile and have his entire day brightened before he even climbed out of bed.

"Cut!" Miles called out.

The sudden sound of his voice jerked Sawyer right out of his fantasies. Good thing too. The otherwise not-so-significant bulge in his groin was quickly trying to tent his tight jeans, making for a *very* uncomfortable situation. His method of ducking for cover was bending down for the camera bag he swore he'd left behind him after lunch. It was gone now.

"Tabby!" he growled.

His mousy little assistant came running. "Yes, sir?" she squeaked.

"Where's my camera bag?"

"Oh, I put it away in the cabinets next to stage two. I…. I'm sorry. I'll not do that again."

"No." Sawyer held up one hand. Tabby immediately clamped her mouth shut. "Just… don't move it in the future, 'kay?"

"Yes, sir."

Groaning under his breath, Sawyer turned on his heel and quietly stepped along the back wall of the building, out of the way of the cinematographers and grips and actors and crewmembers Sawyer hadn't yet learned the purpose of. They were all scurrying to the tables full of food. He'd arrived at the cabinets with moderate ease when he heard someone behind him ask, "What are you doing?"

OH, WHAT a devious thing to do to the unsuspecting, calling out to them with a voice of pure authority while they had their backs turned. Miles could almost feel the devil horns poking up from his meticulous coiffure. But when Sawyer nearly dropped his camera, his pride and joy, all the humor drained from the situation.

"Oh God," Miles said as he bolted forward out of reflex. Luckily for them both, a strap kept the instrument of Sawyer's art from hitting the floor. "I'm so sorry."

"S'okay. That's what they make the strap for."

"I'm sorry. I can't believe…. Sawyer, I'm so sorry."

"Miles—" Sawyer gripped Miles's shoulders. "It's okay. The camera's fine. I'm fine. Everything's okay. Calm down."

Exhaling hard, Miles slumped, back curving, shoulders rounding. The light fluttering in his chest slowly faded away. The knot in his stomach loosened.

"Have dinner with me tonight," Miles said once everything calmed down, and he was certain Sawyer and the camera were in good shape. "We can go someplace quiet. Someplace nice and elegant."

"It don't have to be nice. I kinda liked the little diner you took me to Monday."

"I did too, but let me take you somewhere nicer. Please."

When Sawyer didn't immediately answer, Miles thought he'd crossed the line again and ruined whatever momentum they'd gained in the last week. He had to know that what happened Monday night, then again Tuesday morning, had happened because Sawyer wanted it to, because Sawyer felt something for him. If Sawyer said no, Miles wouldn't push anymore. He'd know the photographer wasn't interested in anything more than a professional relationship with a side of fringe benefits, and Miles swore to himself, if that was the case, he'd leave Sawyer alone and stick to making movies.

Oh, but the longer Sawyer held out on him, the more Miles wanted to get down on his knees and beg for a chance to prove his romantic side to Sawyer. That alone was so uncharacteristic of Miles, he'd begun to believe he'd lost his damn mind.

"Dinner sounds good," Sawyer said, "but—"

"But?" Miles frowned.

"If I go with you, you have to let me take some pictures of you in the garden afterward."

"Take as many as you like. I'll spend the entire night being your willing subject."

DINNER WAS great, better than great, actually. Miles had picked the perfect spot—for a man like Sawyer, anyway. The place was fairly elegant, white cloth draped over the tables, candlelight, and a list of wines Sawyer couldn't pronounce. The steak Sawyer ordered had been divine, and by the time the "date" ended, Sawyer's gut hurt from eating so much and his cheeks hurt from smiling and laughing so much. But he welcomed the change with open arms. It felt good not to be all Debbie Downer, to actually laugh at jokes and enjoy conversation again. It felt good to hold someone's hand and know they would be leaving together, possibly spending the entire night together. In the same bed. In each other's arms. By the time they got back, the sun had completely set and the sky was the blackest black, save for the soft glow of the moon.

Moonlight hung over the inn's garden, drenching it in golden light. The reds and oranges and pinks in the flowers truly popped. Miles's white shirt stood out in the darkness, illuminating his face in an almost angelic way. He was beautiful, more handsome than any man Sawyer had ever seen, especially when he smiled.

"So I promised you pictures," Miles said, reaching for Sawyer's hand. He gave it a little tug, jump-starting Sawyer's feet and forcing him to move forward. "But I want a kiss first."

"I can certainly oblige, Mr. Eisenberg."

Their lips met in the middle. Their bodies eased closer. And as always, sparks burst to life the moment their mouths touched. At least, for Sawyer they did. He wasn't sure what Miles experienced when they kissed. Truth: part of him hoped Miles felt the same, part of him feared Miles felt the same. Falling in love the first time hadn't ended well. The second time around would probably be so much worse. Sawyer couldn't even entertain that idea right now. But he intended to enjoy the companionship as much as he could while he could get it.

The sudden warmth of Miles's hands slipping under Sawyer's shirt and caressing along his back elicited a moan that began as a subtle hum in his throat and ended with a vibration of his lips. He felt Miles's mouth stretch and curl, as if he were smiling rather than kissing Sawyer.

"Do you always moan when men kiss you?" Miles asked as their lips parted.

"Considerin' you're the second man I've ever kissed…."

"Right." Miles's cheeks flushed. "Sorry. I keep forgetting."

Sawyer shrugged. "It's okay. Really. I like to think I'm the kind of guy who would rather save my affection for the right person, rather than havin' a bunch of meanin'less hookups."

"That's admirable, you know?"

Miles leaned against a rock quarter-wall that encircled a round garden of palm trees and exotic plants Sawyer couldn't name and had never seen before. Crossing his legs, ankle to ankle, Miles gripped the edge of the wall and watched with a slightly tilted head as Sawyer dug his camera out of its bag.

One hand on the lens barrel, Sawyer positioned the camera with his eye at the viewfinder and knelt to angle the camera up at Miles. "So tell me about Miles Eisenberg," he said, which resulted in a soft chuckle and the beautiful, dimpled smile Sawyer had become so enamored with of late. He snapped a succession of pictures.

"I think you know as much about him as I do," Miles said. "He can be a complicated sort of man."

"What makes him complicated?" Sawyer asked, moving to his right, still taking picture after picture. "What's the key to Miles Eisenberg's heart?"

Miles's expression darkened, or maybe it turned more serious. He pursed his lips and lowered his gaze, dark lashes beating on his olive cheeks. It was a breathtaking sight, and one Sawyer couldn't resist capturing.

"Be honest," Miles eventually said.

Sawyer raised his head and lowered his camera. "Excuse me?"

"You asked me what the key to my heart was."

"Yeah."

"Be honest." Miles pushed up from the stone wall and paced toward Sawyer, moving oh so slowly, so deliberately. He kept his stare laser focused on Sawyer, leaving Sawyer frozen and barely able to swallow, thanks to the knot in his throat. He reached for Sawyer's free hand, laced their fingers together, and leaned in close. He whispered, "Be real with me. Be honest. Give me a reason to never want to be without you."

Without giving Sawyer time to utter a single sound, Miles locked mouths with him, tongue thrusting deeply into Sawyer's mouth. It was the kind of kiss that stole all movement and function, the kind that made eyelids flutter closed and hearts beat harder and faster. It was the kind of kiss that lingered in daydreams and night dreams and consumed every thought in between.

Sawyer slipped one arm around Miles's waist, hand splayed over the most perfect ass his palm had ever had the pleasure of feeling. And without causing too much commotion, he lifted the camera at his side and snapped off a picture to commemorate the moment.

CHAPTER EIGHTEEN

DISTRACTION CAME in the form of memories of a romantic dinner and a night spent in the garden. It had ended weirdly, though. Sawyer wasn't exactly sure where he stood with Miles Eisenberg—employee or possible lover. For real. Miles had planted one hell of a knee-knocking kiss on him, then as soon as they'd come up for air, Miles had turned cold again. He'd said, "Have a good night" two seconds before disappearing into the house, leaving Sawyer with a whole bunch of "What the hell just happened?"

That ending to their bizarre romance had stayed with Sawyer all night, into the morning and through the remainder of the weekend. It kept him from focusing, kept his mind wandering, which left little room for actually doing the job Miles had hired him to do. And to make matters worse, what Sawyer did see of Miles in the days after—which wasn't much—equated to nothing special in the grand scheme of things. Miles did his job. Sawyer took pictures. They both kept their distance for the first four days of the week, even if Sawyer needed to know what the hell was going on.

The guy with the clapperboard jumped in front of the shot, violently throwing Sawyer out of his daydreams. Sawyer snapped off a quick picture. In the background, the actors were poised, ready to start the scene. The beautiful young ingénue sat at a table in a staged diner, waiting to meet a lover who would end up betraying her and breaking her heart. The man playing the lover stood outside the fabricated scene, waiting for his cue.

Clap. The sound startled Sawyer. As many times as he'd heard it, he still hadn't gotten used to that ear-piercing, silence-stealing sound. Every new scene came with it, and every new scene pushed his heart a little harder.

People started to move in and out of the scene, and Miles sat up in his chair, elbows pressed to the wooden arms, hands locked together like a vise. His hazel eyes darted around the stage as if he were taking stock of every single minute detail. His raw intensity made him ten times more attractive than he had been before. If *that* was even possible.

Sawyer raised his camera again and double-checked that the flash was off and the electronic shutter enabled to dampen the noise when he took the next shot, making sure nothing he did would interrupt the scene. He gripped the long barrel of his lens and aimed it at Miles.

Each picture he took of the director had a beauty of its own, from the intensity in his eyes to the hard set of his jaw to the way he held his shoulders rigid as he watched the magic of fiction unfold. Clearly, Miles took pride in the art he made, and that alone was something to be respected, revered and, dare he say it, adored.

God, yes. In some small way, Sawyer adored Miles Eisenberg. He adored Miles for the story he'd shared about his daughter, the pride in his eyes when he'd spoken of her, and the joy his work brought him. Sawyer even adored the way Miles guarded himself, because it mirrored the way Sawyer felt too. Bottom line, Sawyer adored everything about his boss, and maybe even longed to find out what else there was about him to fall in love with.

"Cut!" Miles called out.

Sawyer nearly jumped right out of his shoes. He'd been so lost in admiration he'd forgotten where he was and what was happening around him.

"I think we can call it a night, guys," Miles added shortly after, checking his watch.

He shot a grin over his shoulder, aiming it right at Sawyer. The slight curl of those kissable lips caught Sawyer's breath. He thought about the way Miles had kissed him. Each time so unrestrained and demanding, passionate and heated, like he'd poured every bit of himself into the kiss. Elijah had never kissed him like that. Never. Nothing Elijah had ever done turned him on like Miles did, especially not so many hours after the fact.

Sawyer cleared his throat, shifting uncomfortably as he leaned down to pack away his camera, part of him hoping once the set cleared, Miles would roughly demand more kisses. He would be happy with the sweeter ones too. It didn't matter as long as Miles's lips found his.

"No, go ahead," he heard Miles say to Penelope, who'd asked him if he wanted the car held. "I have some things to finish up. I'll call the car when I'm ready."

"What about you, Camera Boy?" Penelope asked.

Sawyer stood, turned, and opened his mouth, but Miles immediately cut him off. "No, he has to stay a bit too. We have to send the first batch of pictures to the studio."

"Right," she said with a pursed-lip smirk, almost like she suspected Miles of being a liar. "Well, see you tomorrow." She spun on her designer heels and marched her skinny ass out of the building. Sawyer was happy to see her go, happy to hear the doors slam behind her. The sound meant they were finally alone.

Sawyer knelt on the floor, fighting with his gear bag, or rather, acting like he couldn't get his camera safely tucked away. It gave him a reason not to engage in conversation or look Miles in the eye. He couldn't right now, not while imagining their lips crushing together again. Not with the threat of a major hard-on pushing against his jeans.

"We're alone," Miles eventually said, voice velvety smooth.

"What does that mean?" Sawyer whispered, half hoping he'd spoken so softly Miles didn't hear him.

"I don't know what it means. I...." Miles hesitated. The silence pulled Sawyer to his feet. He faced his employer, keeping his expression as neutral as he could. Miles took exactly one step. "I want... to talk to you. I've missed you. I had so much fun with you—"

"You're the one who said good night and never came back," Sawyer bit out before he had enough sense to tamp down on his attitude. "I mean, you must've been busy."

"Not too busy."

"We both had things to do."

"Maybe." Miles shrugged. "But we could've worked together, side by side."

As the conversation continued, Miles had been inching his way closer. When he'd said the words "side by side," he was close enough for Sawyer to feel the heat brush along his cheek as he spoke, and Sawyer could smell the mint on his breath and the cologne on his collar. The closeness made Sawyer even more aware of the stirring below.

"I took some beautiful pictures of you," he said after clearing his throat. His face felt damn warm. "You're an amazin' subject."

"There's an office setup in the corner." Miles thumbed toward the back of the warehouse. "There's a couch and a table. We could look at them on the studio's laptop."

Right when Sawyer thought that next step would lead to another kiss, or another touch, Miles brushed by him. Their arms barely connected, and Sawyer swore he felt a prickle of energy. Sure, it might've been his imagination, but he wouldn't deny feeling something, whether it had been excitement being alone with Miles or disappointment in not being kissed. Sawyer gathered his bag and followed Miles.

A little metal room with windows on two walls and a windowed door filled the back corner of the warehouse. Each window had a set of blinds, pulled to different levels. Sawyer spotted the "couch" Miles had spoken of. It was really nothing more than a loveseat with a short table in front of it. An old white Mac had been left on the table.

Miles opened the door and waited for Sawyer to step inside.

The lights were dim enough to create a semiromantic ambience, yet bright enough for Sawyer to see where he was going. He sat down on the couch, pulled out his camera much quicker than he'd tucked it away. A black cable followed. Sawyer ran it from the camera to the laptop while Miles settled beside him.

It took a few minutes for the computer to come to life. Sawyer caught his gaze wandering toward Miles's slightly spread legs and the way the lose fabric of his slacks hung at his crotch in all the right places. It didn't leave a whole lot to the imagination, but Sawyer's imagination wasn't as well endowed as his companion appeared to be. He bit the edge of his lip to remind himself they were here in an official business capacity, that gratification of the naughty kind probably wasn't going to be part of the agenda.

White light from the computer screen pulled him away from his fantasies and back to business. Sawyer clicked around, but he didn't have a clue what the hell he was doing. He'd never touched a Mac in his life.

Miles chuckled. "Let me help you."

It took Miles all of two seconds to access the camera and pull up all the pictures Sawyer had taken since he'd arrived in San Francisco.

"I can't believe you rode the BART." Miles wrinkled his nose at the first image.

Sawyer was too nervous to speak. The next picture to come up was a photo of the homophobe, Wes, watching with what looked a hell of a lot like admiration. Wasn't possible. Wes didn't like Sawyer's kind and had made the fact very clear.

"Who's that?" Miles asked. His tone resembled that of a jealous lover's.

"A guy who ended up being a complete dick. Keep goin'."

"These really are beautiful pic—"

The next photo stopped Miles midsentence. These were the photos Sawyer had been nervous about Miles seeing. One black and white of Miles standing at the edge of the set filled the screen, the tip of his thumb between his teeth, watching the actors with unwavering attention. The muscles in his forearm were tight and defined. His thin white shirt caressed his pecs and, from the side, showed off one hardened nipple. Stage lights accentuated the stubble on his face. His profile was utter perfection.

"That's one of the best pictures of me I've ever seen," Miles said in an airy voice.

"Keep goin'. They get better."

"How is that possible?"

"I told you, you're a beautiful subject."

A gentle hand splayed across the small of Sawyer's back, fingers spread and brushing with feather-soft kindness. Sawyer became very aware of how close they sat and how intimate it felt. He laid his hand over Miles's thigh. He couldn't help himself. He needed the touch as much as Miles apparently did.

The last photo filled the screen, and Miles spent a few minutes staring, as if he were committing every curve and highlight to memory. A few minutes later, Miles closed the laptop. It sucked a lot of light out of the room, but Sawyer didn't mind. He preferred the soft ambience over the harsh white.

Miles turned toward him, but kept his hand on Sawyer's back. Sawyer kept his hand on Miles's thigh in turn. "Do you really see me like that?" Miles asked. "I'm *that* beautiful to you?"

"The camera don't lie, Miles. You *are* that beautiful."

"I want to kiss you again," Miles whispered.

"I've been waitin' for a kiss all damn day."

Chapter Nineteen

Cupping Sawyer's cheek, Miles took slow care in lifting his chin. He brushed his thumb over Sawyer's stubbly, warm skin. This wasn't the setup for a rough and dirty kiss, but rather a heartfelt, romantic display of the kindness and beauty Sawyer captured in his pictures.

Miles leaned his head down and their mouths connected, caressed. For a moment, he didn't move, didn't spread his lips and let his tongue take over. For a moment, he simply savored the taste of lips he'd been craving for four agonizing days.

Soft moans encouraged Miles to go further, to allow more and claim more. He loosened his jaw, parting his lips. His body lost all rigidity. Miles melted into the kiss and gave himself over to the warmth and fullness he felt when he had Sawyer close by.

Of their own volition, his arms wrapped around Sawyer. He held that wonderful man against him, guiding Sawyer backward with body and mouth until Sawyer lay on the couch with Miles's weight pressed against him. They were going too far again, and again, Miles didn't want to let it end.

He pressed his tongue through the barrier of lips and slipped it deep into Sawyer's mouth. The taste he'd been craving exploded onto his tongue. Without thought, Miles ground himself against Sawyer, feeling distinctly that they were both thoroughly turned on by what was happening. Thank God they still had their clothes on, Miles thought. While sex with Sawyer sounded like a phenomenal idea right now, what would become of them afterward? Did Miles really want to be the second man Sawyer had ever had sex with, knowing in three months they would part ways?

No. He didn't. Any other man might not have mattered, but this was Sawyer—kind, innocent, compassionate, talented Sawyer. And that'd been the reason for the cooling-down period after their date. Not because Miles had been too busy. Not because Sawyer had been too busy. But because Miles's desire was going to get the best of him if he didn't put a lock on it, which was impossible to do in Sawyer's presence.

Ruefully, Miles broke the kiss and lifted enough to slide behind Sawyer and lie down on the couch to spoon against him. He kept the kid in his arms, holding on tight because it felt wrong to give him any less. Miles closed his eyes, mind and heart at war with each other over the decision each had made.

"Why did you stop?" Sawyer asked. His voice was hoarse, barely a whisper, even in the quiet of the dimly lit office. It echoed off the metal walls and reverberated those four disappointed words for Miles to hear over and over again.

"Do you want the truth?"

"Please."

Even though Miles had made the offer, yet again, to be honest… *yet again*, he didn't think he could be. Being honest meant he would have to admit to himself he cared about Sawyer a lot, more than he should have.

Cared? Wait. Is that the right word?

"Because," Miles finally said, "you're a nice guy, Sawyer. You deserve to have a nice guy make love to you. I'm not that guy."

"I'm not lookin' for love, Miles. I had love… eight years of it. Love burned me."

Miles's eyes shifted, searching Sawyer's face for God only knew what. Maybe a sign that indicated in no uncertain terms Sawyer would be okay with a quick, meaningless fuck.

But would Miles be okay with it?

"How about we order Chinese takeout and watch old movies?"

An answer didn't immediately follow, and he wondered if Sawyer had even heard him, or if the disappointment in the photographer's voice had been more real than Miles had first imagined. "Say something," he wanted to beg. "Tell me I'm making the right choice here."

"That's fine, I s'pose," Sawyer finally said. He shifted slightly, like he'd been clinging to the idea of storming away from Miles. He relaxed, obviously settling into the decision he'd made. Miles couldn't have been more relieved.

"Search Netflix," Miles said as he reached across Sawyer to pull a web browser up on the computer. "I'll call in some food. Anything you don't like?"

"Nah. I'll pretty much eat whatever."

"Good." Miles pressed a kiss to Sawyer's shoulder.

The Chinese restaurant around the corner had cemented its place on speed dial years ago, during the first all-nighter Miles had pulled in this particular location. It'd gotten so bad they even had his order memorized, which was great considering it spared him wasted minutes repeating his order into the phone. "Yeah, this is Miles Eisenberg. I need my regular, but make it enough for two."

"Oh, two." The woman sounded surprised. "Very good. Very good."

Very good indeed.

He hung up the phone and laid it on the table next to the laptop, then settled back into his spot so he could spoon against Sawyer again. A movie was already running, waiting for Miles to pay it some attention. The only attention Miles intended to pay right now was to Sawyer. He wrapped one arm over the photographer's waist and leaned his head against Sawyer's shoulder blade.

"Please tell me if I'm crowding you," Miles whispered.

"No, this is perfectly fine."

No, not quite. Perfectly fine would've been completely naked and making very passionate love to Sawyer, then holding him and painting his flesh with kisses after they finished. Perfectly fine would've been giving in to every single wanton desire Miles had with no remorse when it ended.

"I want to touch you," Miles said, lifting his head and seeking out the slender column of Sawyer's neck with his lips.

"You *are* touchin' me." From the sound of Sawyer's husky, lust-filled voice, he wanted the intimacy as badly as Miles did. Oh, but the photographer had so much more control than he had.

Miles eased his hand down to the button of Sawyer's snug denims. He sprang the button free with ease, then moved on to open the zipper. Sawyer undulated against him as if eager to feel the heat of Miles's palm caressing his shaft again.

This is such a mistake. "This time, I don't want to stop."

"Then don't," Sawyer said. His words were a dare, challenging Miles to give in and take what he wanted. If Miles caved to his desires, he knew he'd live to regret it. Whether from hurting Sawyer or falling for Sawyer, Miles knew he wouldn't walk away from this night unscathed, and neither would Sawyer.

He wrapped his hand around Sawyer's thickening shaft and slowly started to stroke. Each and every moan from Sawyer's lips turned Miles on, made him want to bury his cock deep inside Sawyer's body and not leave until neither of them could move. He'd never wanted something so badly, not even with the myriad men he'd been with in his time. Those whores had nothing on Sawyer. They didn't hold a candle to the man in his arms.

Face buried between Sawyer's shoulder blades, Miles added more pressure to his grip, greater tenacity to his strokes. Sawyer's moans grew louder as he pumped against Miles's hand.

"Come for me," Miles said, voice soft and low but commanding.

One hard jerk, and Sawyer growled out a stream of prayers and curses. Wet heat coated Miles's palm. A satisfied grin tugged the edge of his lips. Admittedly, he loved the music a man's body made when he got off—the grunting, the groaning, the singing of Miles's praises. That carnal song normally signaled the end of a tryst and served as the starting gun firing to signal the next race, but this time, Miles didn't want to go.

Holding his soiled hand out so he didn't accidentally stain the couch or their clothes, Miles leaned up close enough to find Sawyer's lips. Miles kissed him, giving Sawyer a brief taste of the heat and passion he so desperately wanted to share, but then he broke away to say, "Let me clean up. Dinner will be here soon."

Nothing more than a mumbled noise came from Sawyer. His eyes were hooded and his lips curled. Euphoria left behind in the wake of an orgasm, and Sawyer wore it wonderfully. If they'd been in Miles's bed, would he have gotten up right after jerking Sawyer off? Or would he have stayed and moved on to something to sate his body's salacious cravings?

As he made his way to the bathroom outside the office, the pressure in his groin grew stronger, hardening his cock. His body knew the routine, knew it was his turn to seek satisfaction. But that instinctual desire would have to remain unfulfilled because nothing in his conscious mind wanted to do anything harmful to Sawyer, and fucking that man right now would put a crack in both their fragile psyches.

Down, boy. I'll take care of you later.

This dance was ridiculous. Why couldn't he just make himself fuck the camera boy and get on with his life?

You care. Caring makes Sawyer different.

"I know, stop reminding me," he muttered to himself.

In the cramped bathroom, he washed his hands and face. Somehow, he'd managed to talk his erection down, and none too soon. The chiming of the bell meant someone—most likely a delivery boy—waited outside the warehouse with the dinner he'd called in.

He'd almost made it to the door when he heard the photographer's footfalls behind him. They marched in unison. The bell rang again. "I can get this," Miles told Sawyer. "Go relax."

"No, I'll help. It's okay."

Of course, Sawyer wanted to help bring dinner in rather than lying about waiting for Miles to take care of him. The latter would've made him exactly like all the other men, and Sawyer was way too decent to let someone else tend to him.

Shooting a pleased smile in Sawyer's direction, Miles reached for the door. When he turned back, the most unwanted surprise greeted him with arms full of brown paper bags, surrounded in the scent of General Tso's chicken. The sight stole Miles's breath away and tightened every single muscle in his body.

"Gavin...."

CHAPTER TWENTY

SAWYER'S GAZE shifted back and forth, back and forth, between the man who'd had a hand on his cock less than five minutes ago and the man who would be spoiling the evening Miles and Sawyer were supposed to be enjoying.

And who was this guy anyway?

Where had he come from?

God, he was *really* hot. He had the California sun-kissed tan people would kill for but rarely achieved, breath-stealing blue eyes, and bright blond hair. The messy look worked for him too. Judging from his broad chest and thick arms, he probably never left the gym. He was certainly the kind of man someone as beautiful and successful as Miles could easily get if he wanted.

Did Miles want?

Sawyer stood back and watched the silent showdown happening between them, praying this man wasn't a former lover, even though Sawyer sort of knew better. He also knew he couldn't compete.

"Why do you have our food?" Miles finally asked, reaching for the brown bags in Gavin's arms. "And why the hell are you here?"

Those huge, baby blue eyes swung to Sawyer, glaring at him like he didn't have a place in this conversation. He didn't. Not one part of him wanted to hear anything said between Miles and someone who had apparently had stock in Miles's bed long before Sawyer came around.

"I'll take the food," Sawyer muttered, reaching for bags. It was an excuse to dismiss himself before things got any more uncomfortable. He made an abrupt about-face and fled from the scene as quickly as he could without running.

Jealousy wormed its way up through his gut and kicked him right in his sternum, which didn't make much sense considering he had no right to be jealous over anything Miles did, now or before they'd met. They weren't together, weren't committed, and from the looks of it, never would be. Miles probably wasn't the settling-down type anyway. And what did Sawyer want with a relationship? Nothing. Absolutely nothing. His last and first relationship had nearly destroyed him.

Stop lying to yourself. You're a sucker for love.

Sighing, he set the bags on the coffee table, then sat his behind on the couch, but he didn't settle back and relax while he waited for Miles to return. He couldn't. Every instinct inside him demanded he go out there and tell Gavin to hit the road. Miles belonged to him now.

No, Miles didn't belong to him. Miles was his employer, nothing more. Whatever was going on between them walked a tightrope, and this Gavin guy could very well be the man who pushed Sawyer's heart to its death... again.

He stood and eased over to the slightly open office door. Eavesdropping had always been considered a sin in his momma's house. He couldn't help himself now any more than he could when he was a child. He needed to know what the hell was going on and where he stood in the grand scheme of things. He needed to know this Gavin person wasn't there to push Sawyer aside and that Miles wouldn't discard him.

"You have no business being here," Sawyer heard Miles say.

"I owe you an apology. And you deserved to have it delivered in person."

"So you flew across the United States to say you were sorry?"

Oh, that couldn't be Miles's happy voice.

"Yeah... well, I mean.... I was in San Francisco—"

"I see."

Silence fell over the warehouse. Sawyer let out a single ragged breath. It quivered with the inevitability of heartbreak, though why Miles got to him so, Sawyer didn't quite understand. Maybe being utterly destroyed by the man he'd loved had turned him into a big softy and all that business he touted about not falling in love ever again was a lie. What made matters worse was the tone of Miles and Gavin's conversation. Though their words might've been harsh, they held so much passion—the kind of passion that came from having feelings for someone. Good, bad, or ugly, clearly Miles felt something for that wretched intruder.

"So, who is that?" Gavin asked, breaking the silence.

"*That* is none of your business."

"A new boy toy?"

"What part of 'none of your business' aren't you understanding?"

"C'mon, Miles, we both know you don't get close to people. We're toys for you to throw away once we've worn out our usefulness. I get that about you." Gavin's words sounded more like a purr now. "Don't you want someone who understands how you are and doesn't mind? That boy with his big doe eyes will only end up falling in love with you. He won't understand when you don't call him back or acknowledge him in public. He won't understand you not wanting to spend holidays with him and the family. White picket fences and two-point-five kids with you aren't in his future. You don't want that and neither do I. So why are you wasting your time?"

Those words plowed right through Sawyer. He knew he shouldn't have cared the way he did, but he couldn't help it. Miles had depths he didn't readily share. His inner life was colors and fractals, composed of images that made him a work of art to be revered. He wasn't one dimensional. But apparently, the whole show had been a façade for... for what? To make Sawyer fall for him? Why would Miles want that, especially if what Gavin was saying was true? And why couldn't they move their argument somewhere else so Sawyer could leave?

Sawyer quickly busied himself packing away his camera and the attached cable, just to give himself something to do so he wouldn't feel the urge to eavesdrop. It didn't work. He still wanted to listen in on the conversation, and at the same time, didn't. He told himself Miles Eisenberg was a stranger, that he didn't matter and didn't have the power to break Sawyer's heart, but Sawyer's heart had been a fragile muscle already, thanks to Elijah's running a hot, vicious spear right through the center of it.

Stop being so pathetic.

A distant door slammed, and Sawyer immediately tensed. He took the deepest breath he could manage, bowed his chest, and prepared for the worst. He shook like a leaf, waiting for Miles to come back with some sorrowful, pasted-on fake smile. At least Sawyer had his things packed up already, and he could quickly bolt if he needed to.

A second door slammed, and it took everything he had in him to keep his composure.

"What are you doing?" Miles asked.

"I'm just... I'm...." Sawyer refused to face him. "I think I should head back to the hotel."

"Why?"

Sawyer didn't answer.

Miles grabbed his wrist. "Why, Sawyer?"

"Because, I...." Sawyer swallowed hard as he met Miles's intense stare. "I don't wanna be some boy toy, puppy dog, and I don't wanna fall in love."

Once the words gained momentum, Sawyer regretted even thinking them. He wished he hadn't said that last part. He wished he'd simply told Miles he needed to go.

Miles moved his hand down Sawyer's wrist until their fingers met, and instinct nearly made Sawyer jerk away. He realized he was dealing with Miles the same way he'd dealt with Elijah at the end—badly.

"I wish you hadn't heard that," Miles said.

"Why? So I wouldn't know the truth?"

"Is that what you believe?"

Sawyer didn't answer the question.

Miles released his hand. "If you believe what Gavin said, I won't stop you, and I won't try to change your mind."

"I can't do this." Sawyer hoisted his bag onto his shoulder. "It's too soon," he said, more to himself than Miles. "I'm here to do a job, not fall for some guy I don't know."

"You're falling for me?" Miles said as if he couldn't believe his ears.

"I have to go."

Before Miles had a chance to talk Sawyer out of leaving, Sawyer rushed the door and stormed down the hallway. He had his fingers locked on the handle of the last door keeping him from his freedom and out of Miles's grasp when he heard Miles say, "If you ever stop running from me, I might turn out to be the best you ever had and the last you'll ever want."

Sawyer stopped with his hand clenched firmly on the doorknob. One little twist would liberate him. One little twist would prove he was stronger than his heart wanted him to be. All he had to do was walk through that door and not look back.

"I guess we'll never know," he said before taking that last step and walking out on Miles Eisenberg.

Outside, the air was especially cold and sent a chill rocketing straight through his body. He started walking in a direction he hoped would lead him to a taxi. Streetlamps hung over the road, dotting its edge with tight circles of copper-colored light. He stepped to the end of the parking lot, and was just about to make an exit through the gate when Miles called his name. He stopped, and this time he turned around. He found Miles jogging toward him.

Miles galloped to a stop, just barely out of arm's reach. He said, "If you want to go, then leave because you don't want to know me and don't want to find out where this could go. Don't leave because some piece of shit painted a picture of me that reminds you of some asshole who hurt you. Leave because you have no interest in getting to know the real me. Leave because I don't make you feel good. Leave because you hate my guts."

In the coppery light overhead, Sawyer would've sworn he saw the rims of Miles's eyes turning red. He would've sworn he saw the beginnings of tears.

"I don't hate your guts," Sawyer softly admitted. "I *do* want to get to know you."

"Then don't leave."

"I have to, Miles." Sawyer cupped Miles's cheek, just like Miles had done to him earlier. He brushed his thumb back and forth, then leaned in to steal a chaste kiss. "I have to go for my own sake. I'm not in a good place to deal with this right now. I just… I need a little time and a little space. It's not you. It's me."

Jesus, had he really just said that? Those same exact words had been used on him four months ago, when Elijah had broken up with him. Back then, he hadn't believed them to be true, but now….

"Can we please just take things slow and see where we end up?" Sawyer asked.

Lowering his gaze, Miles licked his lips and said, "I'll do whatever you need me to do." His voice wavered, on the verge of shattering, Sawyer suspected.

Sawyer pulled him into a hug and whispered, "Thank you."

Chapter Twenty-One

MILES REFUSED to go back inside until Sawyer caught a cab. In fact, Miles even paid the fare. He wasn't going to let Sawyer wander around in this part of San Francisco alone. Not that it was dangerous, but it wasn't exactly safe either, not for someone who so obviously wasn't from around here. After the taillights disappeared beyond the gate, Miles headed in for the night and locked the doors up tight behind him. He had no plan to return to Martin's quaint little B&B. If he did go back, he knew he would end up at Sawyer's door, begging to be let in and thus ignoring the photographer's request for time and space. No, he couldn't do that. He needed to respect Sawyer's wishes and just stay the hell away for a few days.

He returned to the office, where the Chinese food they'd ordered grew colder by the minute and a light-hearted, romantic comedy waited on the screen. With Sawyer gone, Miles was no longer in the mood to watch a tale of blossoming love, or crack open fortune cookies after chowing down on fried rice. He wanted to lie down on the couch and count sheep until those fuzzy white furballs turned into a faded memory. But when he laid his head on the pillow, he could smell Sawyer's cologne. It made not having Sawyer there with him so much worse.

"Fuck you, Gavin," he muttered to no one. He could've killed Gavin for that. What the hell was the purpose of him coming here in the first place? Wait. Miles knew the answer to that. Gavin wanted to get laid. Or maybe his Virginia gig fell through. Who knew? It didn't really matter what had happened. Gavin had burned this bridge. Hell, he'd strapped C4 to it and blown it the hell up. No words, no good deeds, and no kindness on Gavin's part would repair that bridge, especially if he'd ruined things for Miles with Sawyer.

Miles curled into his Sawyer-scented pillow, hugging it tightly and watching images flicker on the TV screen. He wanted so badly to call Sawyer and beg him to come back to the set, or hell, even offer to go back to the inn if Sawyer promised to spend the night in his bed, but it was too late for that right now. Best thing he could do for himself was find something to pass the time until his eyelids gave up the fight and his mind settled on a siesta.

Watching a movie didn't help. Reading didn't help. Taking a long hot shower in the back bathroom didn't help. He needed to be in a bed… with Sawyer.

His phone vibrated on the coffee table, and Miles debated not checking it. Obsessive need made him give in and reach for it, but he didn't recognize the number.

Martin gave me your cell#. Hope that's okay. Made it safe. Goodnight.

Dearest God in heaven, it was Sawyer, and Miles couldn't have been happier, even if he knew a text wouldn't lead to titillating conversations nor promises to work things out.

Glad you're safe. Miss you already.

Too bad there wasn't an Unsend button. As far as truths went, that was probably the most honest Miles had been with anyone in a long, long while.

No response came after that, leaving Miles with a whole new brand of regret and unease. He cradled his cell phone to his chest as he trailed off into a land where people were perfect and things happened the way they were supposed to—and dreams really did come true.

Emotional exhaustion afforded him a full night's sleep. The need to keep as busy as possible blasted him through an entire weekend. He'd gone back to the inn long enough to grab a change of clothes and get a long, hot soak in a tub rather than a short, cool shower in a cramped cube.

Miles had promised to do his best to give Sawyer the space he'd asked for, and hanging around the inn wasn't a good way to uphold his promise. Uncomfortable meetings could've been explained away as accidental, but an explanation wouldn't roll back time and make their paths not cross. No, staying away seemed to be a much better idea.

When he woke up Monday morning on the lumpy sofa in the studio's office, he felt like half a man and a ball of knotted muscle but ready to face whatever the day threw his way. Coffee infused his bloodstream and gave him a heaping dose of perky. When the cast and crew arrived, he couldn't have been more eager to work, but….

"Where's Sawyer?" Miles frowned.

One of the blondes said, "He wasn't at breakfast."

"He never misses breakfast," the second added.

That couldn't be good. Miles tried hard not to frown, tried to reel in his disappointment before the cast and crew got wind that Miles Eisenberg had a weakness.

"Then I guess we won't have any photography today," Miles said, lifting his chin to save his dignity despite being discouraged by not seeing the one person he'd looked forward to seeing the most.

The day dragged on, but eventually, everyone left and went back to the lives they had outside the studio. They'd worked much later tonight than they had last week. Working kept Miles occupied and his mind off things that would probably never happen. He had nowhere else he wanted or needed to be.

Instead of cozying up in bed with a like-minded creative type who had an eye for all things beautiful, Miles spent his evening reviewing what'd been filmed over the last week, scarfing down leftover Chinese and trying to keep his mind off Sawyer. So far, the movie seemed to be coming along nicely. Save for a few bad shots, nothing needed a retake. That alone should've put him in a good mood, but it didn't. He sat on the couch, massaging circles at his temples, wishing he had two Aleve and a fifth of high-dollar Scotch.

Tuesday turned out to be an exact duplicate of the day before, like someone had shot the scene twice and relabeled it to move history forward. Again, Sawyer didn't come in to work. Again, no one had seen him at breakfast. Miles toyed with the idea of calling the studio for a little managerial intervention, but he didn't do it. Such a move wouldn't help his case and would probably end up putting more space between them.

With a sigh, he sat back on the couch in the office he'd been living out of and held his phone in his hands. He debated sending a text, just to make sure Sawyer was okay, but he didn't. He thought about calling Martin to see if everything was okay, and he couldn't bring himself to do that either. No, he knew a way to better spend his time, and frankly, no one on earth could lift his spirits at a time like this than his little girl.

The phone rang and rang, and for a moment he considered hanging up, thinking maybe his sister had taken her out somewhere, or maybe they were in bed already. After all, it was a school night. One more ring, and he swore he would hang up. The very last ring, she answered with a squealing, chipper, "Daddy!"

Every ounce of Miles's being warmed. He'd neglected her for too many days, and for what? To chase a man who didn't seem to want him.

This reminded him why he'd made Zoe the center of his world, why he didn't get involved in relationships.

"Hey, princess," he said. The smile on his face filled his voice with the kind of happiness only she gave him. "I've missed you."

"I miss you too, Daddy. I want to come see you."

"Two weeks. I promise. Plus, Daddy wants to do something special for your birthday."

Her excited squeal, though eardrum piercing, was the cutest thing he'd heard in a long, long time. He lived for that sound, loved it almost as much as he loved her little giggles.

"Are you having fun with Aunt Karen?"

"Yes, sir."

"Are you behaving?"

"Yes, sir."

"Well, tell me what you've been doing."

"She let Gigi stay the night and we made cupcakes and watched movies, then she took us to school the next day...." His daughter could talk ninety miles an hour, and for the most part, he caught everything she said. Surely, there were details he missed, but that wasn't important. Just hearing her voice made everything better, like a magical elixir for an ailing man. His heart felt rejuvenated. Men weren't important anymore. They never could and never would make him feel as loved and adored as his little girl did.

"Aunt Karen says I need to go to bed," Zoe said. "I love you, Daddy."

"I love you too, princess."

Indiscernible noise came from the other end of the phone. It sounded like Zoe had tossed the device and it had bounced across a few hard surfaces before landing in Karen's lap. "Hello?" his sister said, clearly still fumbling the contraption up to her ear. "Hello? Miles?"

"I'm here, Karen."

"Hey, big brother. How're you? It's been a while."

"I've been dealing with... well, shit. Frankly."

"Sounds fun. Trouble in paradise?"

"That's one way to put it." Miles scrubbed his hand down his face. "What if I told you I met someone special, a man whom I respect and admire?"

"I would say...." She paused, either seriously considering it or goading him on. "Good for you. It's time for you to find love."

"Who said anything about love?"

"Miles, sweetheart, if you didn't feel something intense, you wouldn't be talking to me about it. You never... *ever*... talk about relationships with me. You've never mentioned even liking anyone. I thought you were going to turn out to be asexual or something."

"Please." Miles rolled his eyes. "I love sex with other people too much."

"I'll admit, I didn't know if it would be a man or a woman who finally stole your heart."

"A little girl stole my heart seven years ago. No one else will ever have it."

"That's silly, Miles."

He *almost* took offense at that. It wasn't her place to tell him where his heart belonged, or if Zoe needed to share it with someone else. It wasn't her place to tell him his decisions were wrong. He might've told her so if one very kind, very talented and compassionate man didn't already have one foot in the door.

"Miles?"

"Yeah?"

"Is he *that* special?"

Miles didn't have to think about it. His gut knew the answer before his brain could make it a thought, and "yes" was the right answer, without question.

"Do yourself a favor, big brother. Give it a chance. You might be pleasantly surprised."

"Karen, I want to. I really do, but what about Zoe? I don't want her to get attached to someone who isn't in it for the long haul. I mean, she's already lost a mother."

"So, feel the situation out. You have three months in San Francisco. Get to know the guy and see how things work out before introducing him to Zoe. Just because you're dating doesn't mean he has to meet her too. Not at first, anyway."

"You're right."

"Of course I am."

"I should go."

"Hey, Miles."

"Yeah?"

"I love you, and I know you'll make the right decision. You always do when it comes to Zoe."

Those tears that had been randomly brewing in his eyes since Sawyer had left him finally broke free. The sum of his life, everything he'd worked for and everything he tried to be, came down to what his sister said to him.

"I love you too," he said with a sniffle, hating the idea she might've heard him crying. "I'll talk to you soon."

Immediately, he hung up the phone and shoved it deep in his pocket. Everything inside him told him to drop the bullshit, give in to what he felt and go after Sawyer. Part of him actually *did* want to ride in on a white horse and sweep Sawyer off his feet. The chickenshit part of him wanted to hide in his little metal office, make his movie, and go back home where things were simple and secure, and the only two people in his life who mattered loved him unconditionally. Unfortunately, it wasn't that easy. There seemed to be a third person who mattered now.

CHAPTER TWENTY-TWO

FRIDAY MARKED one week since the big blowup, a whole entire seven days Sawyer had spent in the solitude of his room. Mostly, he'd stayed curled around a pillow, staring at a light blue wall while praying he could rewind time. He would go back to the first time he'd talked to Elijah about marriage. The conversation had gone something like, "We don't need marriage to be in love." Then, maybe things would've worked out between them, and he wouldn't have found himself available and eager to fall in love with the first man who came knocking. He wouldn't have been in Miles's path and wouldn't have set himself up to be hurt again.

Because he hadn't left his room, and only left his bed to shower, Martin insisted on taking care of him. Every morning, the kind old gentleman brought up coffee and breakfast. Then he sat and chatted with Sawyer for a few minutes before carrying on with his duties. The only time Sawyer smiled anymore was in Martin's company.

"Are you ready to talk about this?" Martin waved his hand over Sawyer's fetal form.

"I think it's time for me to go home," Sawyer finally said. "I think I overstayed my welcome here."

"For what reason?" Martin wore the most incredulous expression. It closely resembled pure shock.

No one knew about the time spent with Miles. Both men had done a fine job keeping their secrets. It just seemed better that way. If they didn't tell anyone what they'd been up to, they wouldn't have to explain when things didn't work out, because inevitably, things never worked out.

"I think, I.... I just need to go home, Martin."

"What did he do to you?"

"Excuse me?"

"Miles, what did he do to you?"

Maybe we didn't hide it as well as I thought.

Sawyer had never considered himself to be transparent, not enough that someone on the outside of his little bubble would know. But good old Martin had pegged that nail dead in the center of its head.

Sawyer raked his fingers through his messy hair.

"What do you expect from him?" Martin asked.

"Exactly what he gave me."

"And that is…?"

"Space." A sigh pushed through Sawyer's pursed lips. "I told him I needed time and space, and he gave it to me. Now, I wish I hadn't. I miss him so damn much. Everything was just… it was movin' too fast. Then Gavin showed up."

With a snort, Martin rolled his eyes. "Gavin is a whore. Miles doesn't respect him. Miles doesn't even like him."

"What?" Sawyer frowned. "What do you mean? How do you know?"

Inhaling deeply, Martin reached over and gathered Sawyer's hand into his. "I was angry with Miles when he came back to my inn. He and Gavin singlehandedly destroyed the room Miles is staying in. I don't know, nor do I want to know, what happened. One minute it sounded like they were fighting, the next it sounded like they were screwing. In Miles's defense, he left a hefty sum of money to cover the damages, but my son had to help me do all the work." Martin shook his head, giving Sawyer's hand another squeeze. "He's a very different man around you. He has a light to him I haven't seen in some time. Sawyer, if there's something real between you two, explore it. Give it a chance. He's rough around the edges, sure, but who isn't? I'd hate for either of you to end up like I did."

"How's that, Martin?"

"Old and lonely."

With that, Martin stood. The conversation ended, and it had served its purpose. Sawyer had a lot to think about, a lot to consider where the director and his heart were concerned. Martin reached for the doorknob, and when the door opened, Sawyer heard a choir of angels singing. Not literally of course, but his imagination tended to run a little wild these days.

Miles stood there, looking wrecked and somehow devastatingly handsome all the same. Thick, dark bags surrounded his gorgeous hazel eyes. Deep brown stubble littered his face. Had he showered or slept since Sawyer left? It didn't look like it.

"Take care of him," Martin whispered before leaving the men alone.

At first, neither spoke. They took equal steps and met in the center of the room. Their eyes locked, and Sawyer's breath hitched. When the time came for him to either say something or look idiotic, they both pounced, spewing a nonsensical jumble of words. A shared laugh followed.

"Go ahead," Sawyer said.

"I wanted to give you what you asked for. I wanted to give you space, but I…."

"I've had enough space, if it's any consolation." Sawyer swallowed. "I think I'm just too damn afraid of bein' dumped again to put myself out there. Elijah, he…." His words trailed off as he lowered his gaze.

"I want to tell you I'll never do what Elijah did," Miles said, "but I can't make that promise. I can only promise to be honest with you."

"That's all I ever expected of him."

"My little girl is the most important person in the world."

"As she should be."

Miles didn't ask for a kiss. He didn't ask if he could hold Sawyer in his arms, he went for it, grabbing Sawyer and pulling him tight against him, crushing their mouths together as if Miles were a starving man and Sawyer his only sustenance. And when he held Sawyer, he held him like he never planned to let go. Somehow, that made everything so much better, made the words Miles fed him into something real and tangible.

The kiss deepened. Sawyer drank from Miles's mouth, taking all he could and sparing no amount of intensity or passion when Miles reciprocated. With one hand splayed over Sawyer's lower back. Miles knotted his fingers in Sawyer's shirt and started slowly lifting it. Cool air brushed along Sawyer's spine, causing a shiver to ripple through him.

"You okay?" Miles asked, breaking the kiss long before Sawyer wanted him too.

"I'm better than okay."

"I'm not presuming too much, am I?"

Sawyer frowned.

"By kissing you. I want you, have wanted you since that first kiss. But you have to want me too. Do you?"

"God, yes."

Miles laughed softly. "I like your enthusiasm."

With both hands on Sawyer's hips, Miles walked him back to the bed. He sat Sawyer down, then knelt in front of him. "I'm sorry," Miles said as he delicately lifted one of Sawyer's legs. Sawyer opened his mouth to speak, but Miles stopped him. "Let me do this, please. I've apologized to two people in my life—my sister and my daughter. So let me do this, and please don't take this as idle words I say to just anyone."

Sawyer nodded.

Miles lifted a slipper away and set it aside, then turned to the other leg and repeated the process.

"I'm sorry I didn't talk to my sister about you when I first met you. If I had, I could've spared us a lot of turmoil, and we could've been weeks into building a relationship, rather than repairing what's already been damaged." Miles rose to his feet. He pressed his hand to Sawyer's sternum in such a way the web of his thumb and forefinger framed the hollow of Sawyer's throat, and he gently pushed, guiding Sawyer to lie down on the bed. He reached for Sawyer's pants, slowly untying the drawstring.

"I'm sorry Gavin didn't know not to come around. I'm sorry he ruined what could've been a wonderful night between us, and I would love the chance to make it up to you." He slid the pants down Sawyer's legs, then piled them atop the slippers he'd set to the side. Sawyer lay naked and waiting, hard as a rock and ready to finally take that next step with a man he'd spent two weeks trying to get close to.

Miles pressed a kiss to a spot of skin just above Sawyer's navel. "I want to do something I've never done before."

"What's that?"

"Make love."

CHAPTER TWENTY-THREE

"YOU NEVER made love to anyone before?" Sawyer asked. Surprise filled his big brown eyes, not doubt-filled surprise, the generic sort of surprise that came with learning the unexpected.

"I came close once," Miles said, guiding Sawyer onto his stomach. He eased down, pressing part of his body against Sawyer's backside, and slid two fingers between Sawyer's cheeks as he kissed along Sawyer's shoulder blade. "The night I conceived Zoe."

Sawyer looked over his shoulder with an arched brow. "You made *love* to a *woman*?"

"Yeah, as close as I could come to making love while being mildly intoxicated. I loved her with my whole heart. She was my best friend. She wanted a kid but didn't have anyone special in her life. I told her I had sperm to spare. We got drunk and did the deed.... But I did love her." He pressed the tips of his fingers against Sawyer's hole. "Now, lie down so I can please you."

Miles didn't do tender passion. He did heated trysts. He had never before taken the time to work his lovers' bodies. The sex was always hot and rough and greedy, with nothing sensual after. Yet he was considered one of Hollywood's hottest, a star among stars thanks only to his sexual prowess and the chatty bitches he liked to fuck. This would be a lesson for him, a new adventure in sexual gratification. Thank God he'd chosen to share the experience with Sawyer, a man who'd appreciate it and hold it dear, maybe even remember this night long into old age.

Trailing kisses over Sawyer's back, Miles pushed one finger into Sawyer's hole. The muscle gripped tightly, pulling his finger deeper inside. Then Sawyer exhaled and relaxed.

"Do you have lube or condoms in this room?" Miles asked.

"No, I.... I didn't come to California expectin' to get laid."

"You really are innocent, aren't you?"

He didn't need an answer. What Miles had said had been more of a revelation than a question. He eased off the bed, then carefully removed his finger. Sawyer whimpered in protest. It was the cutest sound Miles had ever heard from a lover.

He positioned himself between Sawyer's legs and splayed his fingers over his lover's rounded cheeks. With his thumbs, he spread those gloriously firm mounds to expose Sawyer's tight, puckered hole. Miles lowered his head, lips meeting skin before his tongue darted out of his mouth. He licked once, twice, letting the taste settle on his tongue. Though it had been done to him a thousand times, he'd never rimmed anyone before, never had any inclination to taste another man's derriere. He wanted to taste Sawyer's, though. He wanted to devour that man, kiss and lick every inch of his body. He wanted to memorize it, so later, when he lay in his own bed and the mood struck, he could fist his cock and think about the way it felt to be inside Sawyer, connected to Sawyer in the most visceral, most physical possible way.

Moans filled the air. Sawyer arched in retreat as if he couldn't take the amount of sensual pleasure Miles was giving him. Then he thrust his ass against Miles's mouth. Tongue lapping hard and fast, Miles reached between Sawyer's legs and palmed his cock. It thickened in his hand, strong and firm, rigid and ready. Sawyer's balls were already tight; he would come soon if Miles kept up what he was doing.

The rhythm of his licking matched the rhythm of his stroking. The sounds of their carnal dance made the sweetest music. Sawyer's body tensed. His cock grew thicker. Miles gripped harder and pumped faster. A low growl rumbled up Sawyer's throat just before wet heat filled Miles's hand.

"That's it," he whispered. He kissed the top of Sawyer's ass, right on the curve where his back met those beautiful cheeks. He kissed the center of Sawyer's spine as he dipped two slick fingers in his lover's hole. "I want to be inside you right now."

"So why aren't you?" Sawyer asked.

"I don't bareback."

"I'm clean." Sawyer looked over his shoulder, eyes hooded, bottom lip swollen like he'd been sucking on it the entire time. "I've only been with one guy… ever."

"I'm clean too, but…."

Rules are rules, Miles. Don't break them because you're in the heat of the moment.

"Do you trust me?" Sawyer asked.

What was there not to trust? Miles had never met a man so pure, so real, and so truthful in all his life. "Yeah, I think I do."

"Then make love to me, Miles."

How could he say no to that?

He couldn't.

Tomorrow, he would freak about having unprotected sex. In a few days or weeks, he would go get tested, then again in six months, like any responsible, sexually active man. But tonight, tonight was about pleasing Sawyer, about giving into whims and desires and consummating a relationship mapped out in the stars.

Slowly, slowly, he pumped two fingers in and out, eyes closed as he listened to every beautiful sound Sawyer made. Miles could dive in right now. He was hard enough, ready enough, turned on enough, but Sawyer's body wouldn't handle his girth. He was too tight, too tense. Nervous?

"You okay?" Miles asked.

"I always topped Elijah," Sawyer said matter-of-factly.

A giant O contorted Miles's mouth, but he didn't say a word, didn't dare ruin the moment. That blast of news explained why Sawyer's hole felt so very virginal.

One more problem: Miles never, ever bottomed.

"Why didn't you say something?" Miles asked, easing the thrust of his fingers. He moved them with a more delicate rhythm now, stretching gently.

"Because I didn't care who topped. I just.... I wanted to be with you."

Miles's breath hitched on an inhale. Those whispered words hit him like a ton of bricks. That decision couldn't have been an easy one for Sawyer to make. God knew, Miles couldn't have made it. If it came down to what cock was going where, Miles's hole would've been off-fucking-limits, but Sawyer didn't mind sacrificing his virginity to be with Miles. That was huge.

Oh dear God, I think I'm falling.

"You're sure you're okay with this?" Miles asked, closing his fingers for the last time before removing them.

"I wouldn't be here if I wasn't."

Swallowing hard, he tucked one arm under Sawyer's chest and wrapped his free hand around the base of his cock. Sawyer's ready hole glistened with the spend from the hand job Miles had given him. The mood had been set and the players were in the game; all Miles had to do was seal the deal.

He looked down at his bare shaft, then up to Sawyer's pucker. Miles wanted to bareback just once, just to experience the feeling of hot tight flesh around hot hard flesh. The thought of it jerked his rigid cock. Barebacking was dangerous, and maybe that was part of the thrill. Who knew? Right now, he had the best possible partner for such an experiment, and if he didn't go for it, he might never have a chance like this again.

Holding tight, he angled his hips and pressed the blunt tip of his shaft to Sawyer's hole. "Don't clench," he softly coached. They all clenched the first time they felt a dick near their delicate holes. If they hadn't been around the block a few times, the surprise made the body react. He waited for Sawyer to exhale, for the softening of tense shoulders and the roll of tight muscles in the back. Then he eased his shaft in, inch by thick inch, until he was buried to the hilt and the sprinkling of dark, coarse hairs kissed the rounded surface of Sawyer's beautiful ass.

Miles didn't move. He stayed buried, nice and snug, reveling in the unabated connection of two male bodies, relishing the heat hugging his cock. He tightened his arm around Sawyer. His throat tightened around the breath he needed to take. Closing his eyes once again, he pressed a single kiss at the nape of Sawyer's neck. Sawyer had just given Miles a gift no other man had been trusted enough to give him.

CHAPTER TWENTY-FOUR

THE PRESSURE was odd, but not uncomfortable. Sawyer liked the way Miles didn't go right into pounding his virginal ass into oblivion. He liked that Miles considered the fact Sawyer had never done this before, but it was the caressing and kissing that really made the moment feel like something special, like love instead of meaningless sex.

He reached under his chest and ran his arm alongside Miles's, and when their hands met, he curled their fingers together to let Miles know that everything happening to him right now—the physical and the emotional—was okay. Even better than okay.

Each move Miles made was slow and deliberate, gentle and savoring. He pulled back until it felt like he was going to stop. Sawyer opened his mouth to beg Miles to keep going, but before he made a sound, Miles slid back in to the hilt, and Sawyer's words turned to moans. Each roll of Miles's hips made his cock pump in and out, in and out. Then he shifted his angle, and his shaft rolled right over Sawyer's sweet spot. It sent a welcome pressure pushing up from Sawyer's sac and into the base of his erection. In and out, Miles brushed that spot again.

"Oh God, I'm about to…."

Sawyer couldn't finish the sentence. The pressure pounded down the length of his shaft and exploded from the head, leaving a wet puddle beneath him. He heard a low growl at the nape of his neck. Miles thrust hard and deep, then the pressure pushing against Sawyer's hole vanished and warmth trickled over his ass, joining the pool of bliss he'd left on the sheets. He felt the weight of Miles's body on his back. Miles tightened his arm. A hot breath gusted over Sawyer's shoulder, followed by another kiss.

Movement wasn't an option at the moment, even with the sheets threatening to paste themselves to Sawyer's body. Hell, he could barely breathe. Coherent thought didn't seem to be happening either. Miles had singlehandedly managed to turn him to mush.

"I think that was the most incredible sex I've ever had," Miles rasped.

"I think I never want to move."

They both laughed.

Before Sawyer could grasp what was happening, the world around him began to turn. Where he'd once looked down at the bed, he now stared up at the ceiling. Miles's glistening, smiling face came into view. Cooling moisture no longer pooled against Sawyer's skin. Miles had rolled them away from the mess, but more importantly, Miles had rolled Sawyer into a cuddle—another new experience for Sawyer. Elijah had never cared about lying in bed together after sex. Maybe he had at first. Sawyer couldn't remember. Their firsts had happened close to a decade ago, and nothing Elijah did struck Sawyer as sacred or special. That could've been because they were so young back then, or it could've been the fact Elijah wasn't Sawyer's be-all and end-all. The fact became clearer and clearer with every minute spent in Miles's arms.

"I like this," Miles whispered against Sawyer's temple.

Frowning in confusion, Sawyer raised his gaze to meet Miles's. "Like what?"

"Making love. Cuddling after."

"You do?" Sawyer could feel the crooked grin contorting his lips.

"I do."

Their lips met again, one kiss in a long line of many kisses Sawyer hoped they would share over the next few weeks.

AND IT was. Nights were no longer spent in cold, separate beds. They were spent in the warm arms of a sated lover. If they left the studio to return to the inn, they would have dinner together, then go back to Sawyer's room because his hadn't been spoiled with the memory of myriad old lovers—Miles's words, not his. If they stayed at the studio, they slept on the couch, Sawyer curled on top of Miles's chest, ear pressed to his heart. Those weeks together passed quickly, the two of them utterly inseparable, even though they both did their level best to keep up appearances and remain professional.

Sawyer stole frequent glances at Miles and caught Miles returning them. He often found himself daydreaming about spending more time with Miles. He imagined Miles on the beach back home in Biloxi—toned, muscled body drinking up the sun. The sprinkling of dark hairs running along Miles's chest, down to his navel and circling around both nipples, danced in the cool Gulf Coast breeze. Sawyer would bury his bare toes in warm sand as he captured Miles's beauty on the digital equivalent of film. Many hours. Many pictures. Always Miles and Sawyer. Always together. That was the life Sawyer now dreamed of. That was how he wanted things to be.

"It's been pretty amazing," he told Lucy during the first phone call they'd had in weeks. He'd been so absorbed in San Francisco life, in making movies and making love with Miles, he'd forgotten to call home. Lucy made sure he'd never forget to check in again.

"So you no longer hate it there?" she teased. "Wow, your tune changed fast."

"With good reason, I promise."

"Who is he?"

"You know who...."

"The director?" She sounded surprised for someone who'd gotten it right after the first try. "You worked things out with the director."

"You could say that."

"Details. Sheesh."

With a chuckle, he proceeded to tell her all about the whirlwind romance, about the ups and downs and how everything finally seemed to level out. He told her how Miles made him happier than Elijah had, how he hadn't known what falling for someone really felt like.

"Whoa...," she said. "You're in love with him?"

Sawyer thought about it for a moment, weighed everything he felt and how Miles had swept him off his feet. He thought about all the things he'd felt the first time they'd made love and how Miles seemed to cherish every single moment they spent together. The answer clearly was "Yes, I think... I think I fell in love with him."

"And this is the first time you've admitted it, huh?"

"Yeah." Sawyer laughed again. "Yeah, it is."

"Well, I'm glad I could inspire your acceptance of your feelings. Now, are you gonna tell him?"

"I think I should."

"Me too, babe. Me too."

"I have to go, Lucy. I'll call you later."

"You'd better. I wanna know what happened."

Looking over his shoulder, Sawyer slipped his phone back in his pocket and watched his lover deal with the business of making movies. Miles's broad shoulders squared. He appeared to be going over the script with two of the actresses. This particular scene hadn't been going well, and tensions were quickly mounting. Over lunch, when Miles had vented and aired his frustrations with the scene, Sawyer had told him no one could fake true love. If the actors behind the characters didn't at least like each other, they'd never convince the audience they were in love. The fact remained proven hours and hours later. Actually, the more the days dragged on, the more the fact became apparent. Each hour made Miles's temper burn hotter.

Miles shook his head and closed the script. The expressions on the actors' tired faces screamed of frustration. The mood looked dire, and Sawyer wondered if now was a good time to tell Miles about the revelation he'd had on the phone with Lucy.

Yes, now was a great time. His feelings were so intense right now, if he didn't tell Miles, he might just explode, and Miles needed a pickup. He needed something to brighten his day.

"Just go home, everyone. We'll start bright and early in the morning."

A chorus of grumbles sang out through the room. Grumbles, because nobody wanted to work on Saturday, but Hollywood slept for no one, and the movie had been slowly falling behind schedule. But even with all the stress, Miles had been incredible to be around. So incredible, it almost felt like a fantasy.

"I want to take my clothes off," Miles whispered to him. He stood but a few inches away from Sawyer. "And I want you to rub every single aching muscle in my body. Please tell me you'll do that for me."

Of course Sawyer would massage him. Massage was a form of foreplay most nights.

From over Sawyer's shoulder, Miles watched as the last person left. That also had become part of the normal routine. When the door finally closed and the last body was gone, Miles pulled him close and wrapped him in a hug. He first kissed Sawyer's forehead, then the tip of his nose, then stole a chaste kiss from Sawyer's eager lips. The tenderness could've melted Sawyer right there.

"I love you," he blurted, then waited with bated breath while Miles processed those three dangerous words.

CHAPTER TWENTY-FIVE

THOSE THREE words lingered in the air, begging for attention. Miles didn't want to say them just because Sawyer had. Doing so would've made them so much less important. But he didn't know if he could say it and mean it. Had they gotten to that point already? Was it love Miles felt every time he looked Sawyer in the eye or kissed his lips? Did love happen this quickly in real life, or were those feelings reserved for fairy tales and romantic comedies?

The need to hold on to Sawyer with everything he had hit Miles hard, like being dropped to his knees by the weight of a million bricks. He tightened both arms and splayed both hands—one at the Sawyer's nape, one at the small of Sawyer's back. He pressed his face to the curve of Sawyer's neck and inhaled deeply. Cardamom and musk, and everything that distinctly smelled like Sawyer, whisked through his nostrils and down into his lungs. For whatever silly reason, the idea of letting go terrified Miles.

"What's wrong?" Sawyer asked, voice quiet and careful.

"Wrong?" Miles raised his head, grinning from ear to ear. "Nothing is wrong, Sawyer. Everything is absolutely right."

"Did I mess up by tellin' you I love you?"

"No." He raised his hands and cradled Sawyer's face, keeping their stares locked. "No, you didn't mess up. I'm surprised, I'll admit. I didn't think anyone other than my daughter and my sister would ever say those words to me."

"But the feelin's aren't reciprocated…," Sawyer ventured, dropping his head.

"I never said that." Miles lifted Sawyer's face so their gazes met again. The hopeful desperation in Sawyer's eyes tugged at his heart strings the way only Zoe had been able to in the past. If that wasn't a sign of love…. "The feelings are there, I promise. I could say the words to you right now and mean every syllable, but there's one thing, one very important thing keeping me from professing those feelings to you."

"What?"

"Zoe. My daughter." Miles stroked his thumb back and forth over Sawyer's cheek. "I'm very protective of her. I don't want her meeting someone, liking them, then losing them. I don't want her to know that kind of heartbreak. Do you understand?"

"I think so...."

"What I'm saying is, I need to know this is going to last and it's serious before I introduce you to her. Her happiness is the most important thing in the world to me. When I know all those pieces are going to come together, then I'll tell you with utmost honesty how I feel about you, and I'll spend hours and days and years showing you. But I have to know this is going to work first."

"I get that. I really do. I spent eight years thinkin' I'd found my forever. If I'd had a child and Elijah left us and broke my child's heart like he did mine, I woulda killed him." Sawyer's eyes shifted about. "Not literally, of course."

"Of course." Miles grinned again.

"But you know what I mean."

"I do."

"So.... I'm okay with waitin' to hear you say I love you. I would rather you mean it. I just.... I *do* love you. Even if things don't work out after we're done with the movie, I love you for what you've shown me, and I love you for freein' me from Elijah's misery."

Miles gathered Sawyer's hands in his and brought his knuckles to his lips. He kissed softly, letting his lips linger over the hard ridge of bone. Miles did love Sawyer, truly loved him. In all honesty, he wanted Zoe and Karen to love him too, and if he'd been a praying man, he might have asked God to make it all come to fruition for the both of them.

"How about we get some food, and we'll give each other massages? We can spend the night in bed, rubbing each other and watching movies until we're forced to get up and come back to this place."

"Sounds amazin'."

Chapter Twenty-Six

ANOTHER WEEK passed with a lot of the same day-to-day. The hours grew longer and more focus was put on the movie. Sawyer had an amazing collection of pictures to turn over to the studio, even had a few epic black and whites of Miles for his private collection. He would cherish every single one of them, maybe even more than he cherished the pictures of Elijah.

Miles had locked himself in the office to discuss things with someone from the studio. Actors and actresses scurried by, getting ready for the weekend. Sawyer knelt on the floor to tuck away his camera. The sounds remained the same as they had been since they'd started filming. Not even the startling snap of the clapboard surprised him anymore.

"Daddy!" a tiny voice screamed from the direction of the double doors. A petite little girl dragged a woman by her hand. Sawyer didn't have to hear any names to know those two belonged to Miles. They both had the same crystal-like hazel eyes. Even the smiles looked exactly alike. But the petite princess had the most precious caramel ringlets framing her heart-shaped face. She was more beautiful than Miles had described.

"Daddy!"

"He's in his office." Sawyer righted himself. The little girl stared at him with curiosity. "I'm sure he'll be done soon."

"Say thank you," the woman said.

"Thank you," the little girl parroted.

Sawyer offered a hand to the woman. "You must be Miles's sister. You look just like him."

"I like to think I'm much prettier." She winked, and when she smiled, she could have lit up the room, just like Miles. She took Sawyer's hand and gave it a shake. "I'm Karen, and you're…?"

"I'm Sawyer Taylor."

"Oh, the photographer."

The photographer? Was that all Miles had said about him? Had he not told his sister about the man he'd been dating? Oh God, was he even out to her?

"Yeah, the photographer," Sawyer said, immediately pulling back his hand. He shoved it in his front pocket, for what reason, he didn't know. Maybe to hide his fidgeting.

"I like pictures," Zoe said. "Will you take a picture of me? I can be a movie star."

He let out a high-pitched, nervous laugh. Truthfully, she was adorable enough to be on the silver screen. Certainly cute enough to be in pictures.

Karen arched her brow and nodded toward the kid. Sawyer got the distinct feeling if Miss Zoe asked for something, she got it without question. He couldn't imagine a childhood like that. His parents hadn't spoiled him. Being the only child meant double the chores. It also meant, when it came time to help with their business, he'd had no choice.

"So…. You gonna take a picture, or what?" she asked.

"Well, I s'pose I should," he said.

The smile that stretched across her face and filled her big hazel eyes would've crumbled his willpower had he not said yes already. That child would be a heartbreaker in a few years. Damn, Miles was going to have his hands full.

He knelt and dug out his camera again. When he straightened, she was already posing like a little pro. Another soft laugh escaped him.

"Tomorrow," she said, "I'll be seven years old." She put both hands on her hips and posed with a wink. Sawyer snapped a picture. "I'm here to celebrate it with my daddy." After the flash went off, she gave him the Macaulay Culkin in *Home Alone* pose all the cute Hollywood kids seemed to be trying to pull off now. She wore it better than most. "He lets me visit the set and meet the actors and actresses." She spun around and grinned over her shoulder, holding the smile as she spoke. "My daddy is the most awesomest like ever!"

"Yeah," Sawyer said reminiscently, thinking over everything that made Miles the awesomest… like ever. "He really is."

He took a few more shots in quick succession, and then she stopped midspin and her smile changed dramatically. It became more real and less fabricated for the camera's eye. Her cheeks turned rosy red. Her eyes widened.

"Daddy!" she squealed, running past Sawyer in a dash. She ran right into her father's arms, and he scooped her up in a hurry.

"Princess," he said, before planting a kiss on his child's cheek.

He carried her back to where Karen and Sawyer stood. However, instead of kissing Sawyer's cheek, or even smiling in passing, Miles all but glared as he walked by. It was one of those *we'll talk later* looks that usually meant the receiver of said look was in some sort of trouble. Sawyer and Lucy had often found themselves on the receiving end of a look like that when they were kids. Mostly after they'd done something they shouldn't have.

What the hell had Sawyer done to get in trouble with Miles, though?

"Daddy needs to take care of something," he said as he set her back on her feet beside his sister. He looked up at Karen. "Take her outside for a minute. The car is on the way. I'll be out shortly."

Without question, Karen took Zoe by the hand. Zoe didn't argue when they headed toward the doors. Miles waited until they were gone before turning to Sawyer.

The silence in the room doubled, heavy with a tension Sawyer didn't understand. There was no gentle explanation that Miles had to go and Sawyer couldn't come. Sawyer would've understood. Miles had rules when it came to his daughter, and there was absolutely nothing wrong with that. But Miles didn't say anything of the sort. He looked at Sawyer and said, "What the hell were you doing?"

"Excuse me?"

"With Zoe. What were you doing?"

Sawyer's brow furrowed and his lips wrinkled. Just what the hell was Miles accusing him of? "She wanted her picture taken...."

"I'm not ready for you to meet her, Sawyer. It's too soon."

"But, I—"

"You can't just push your way into my life."

"I didn't—"

"When... *if* I want you to know my child, I'll let you. Don't think you can just insert yourself in my family. You can't."

"I...." Sawyer didn't know what to say. Not that Miles gave him a chance to say anything. By the time his head stopped reeling and his stomach stopped turning, the loud crash of a metal door against its jamb was all that was left of Miles. Had Sawyer not been in shock, he might've broken down in tears.

What the hell just happened here?

He set his camera on top of his bag and put it aside without bothering to tuck it in, and then he half stumbled, half walked back to the office. Absently, he sank down on the couch and stared at a windowed wall and discolored blinds. The last time he'd felt this lost, Elijah had just left him.

"WHAT WAS that about?" Karen asked when Miles climbed into the backseat with her. Zoe sat, posture perfect, in the front seat, checking out all the buttons and dials.

Miles spoke low so only Karen could hear him. "It's not time for him to meet Zoe."

"What does that mean?"

The car jerked from side to side as it lurched forward and pulled out of the battered parking lot. Over the purr of the engine and the noise from the tires, as long as he kept his voice low, Zoe wouldn't hear him.

"I wanted him to meet her eventually, but not yet, not right now."

"You *wanted* him to…."

"Yeah."

Brother and sister stared at each other. A mix of confusion and understanding passed between them. They understood what a big deal it was for someone to meet Zoe. Miles had been careful about that since she was born. Obviously, Karen didn't understand why Miles wouldn't make Sawyer the exception to the rule.

"He loves me," Miles said, answering the question that had to be running through her mind right now.

Karen didn't humor him with a response. Her silence meant she saw right through Miles using that truth as an excuse to overreact the way he had.

"Okay, and…?" she said, crossing her arms.

Miles's throat tightened.

"Say it," Karen said. "Say what you really mean."

"Okay, I love him too," Miles blurted. "Are you happy?"

Victory filled his sister's expression, filled her eyes with the joyful twinkle she would get when they were kids. It was a smirk that wasn't exactly spiteful or mean, just triumphant and pleased, a testament to her truly competitive nature.

"I *am* happy, but…. Miles, why did you get mad at him?"

"Because I told him I would let him meet Zoe when I was ready, not a moment before."

"Sweetie." She turned toward him, one hand on his leg. "I mentioned he was a photographer, and Zoe wanted her picture taken. He had his camera put away and didn't seem to want to do it. I powerfully suggested with these evil peepers"—she pointed at her eyes—"that he give the kid what she wanted. I thought he was just a member of the crew. Why didn't you tell me about him?"

"I did," Miles insisted.

"No. No. No." Karen waved her finger in his face. "You said you met someone you were really into. You didn't say anything about it being the photographer you were all crazy about. How was I supposed to know? You didn't tell me!"

"I haven't told anyone about him, Karen."

"I'm not just anyone, Miles Gregory Eisenberg. We're family. We don't keep secrets from each other. Now you're mad at him for no good reason."

Their parents had never scolded Miles quite like Karen did. She had a way about her, didn't even have to raise her voice. It raised hairs and twisted spines, and blessed if she didn't know how good she was at verbal lashings. He deserved to be scolded like a spoiled brat, though, he supposed.

"I wasn't trying to fall in love," he said, voice lowering as he turned his head toward the window. He could barely see the warehouse's fence now. "The man walked into my life, smiled, and stole my heart. I never thought anything like that would ever happen to me."

"Why, Miles? You have so much love to give, so much heart. Why did you plan on living alone for the rest of your life?"

"Because I never wanted anyone to come between me and Zoe."

"Oh, sweetie." The hand she had on his leg moved up to cup his cheek. She lifted enough to kiss his forehead. "Nothing in the world is ever going to come between you and Zoe. You're her hero and she's… she saved your life, Miles. No one will ever take that away, and you would've loved to see how good that man was with her."

"What if he leaves us?"

"There's always a chance of that happening, Miles. But you have to accept the risk and hope for the best, have a little faith in the heart. Have a little faith in him."

He leaned over and laid his head on her shoulder, then let out a sharp sigh. Everything his sister had said was absolutely true… in a mushy, romantic sort of way, but that was her way. What he lacked in a love life, she made up for in her fairy tales. This time, she was right. In his heart, he knew Sawyer belonged with him, with them. In his heart, he knew Zoe would love Sawyer as much as he did.

Now, he just needed to make things right again.

CHAPTER TWENTY-SEVEN

"ZOE, I need you to sit back here and be very, very quiet, okay?" Miles tousled his daughter's caramel curls. She scrunched her nose at him, carefully rearranging her hair. She sat up straight in his official director's chair, looking much like a miniature, cuter version of Miles. Karen stood behind her.

"Yes, Daddy."

He kissed her forehead, then turned his gaze up to his sister. She looked back with concern. He hadn't slept at all last night. The rings under his eyes were thicker and darker this morning, telling the world he was a lovesick fool who couldn't seem to sleep unless he had Sawyer curled up beside him, lightly snoring in his ear. Somehow, he needed to make things right with Sawyer, but most importantly, he needed to be honest and tell Sawyer he loved him.

"Is the photographer coming back?" Zoe asked as if she'd been reading her father's mind. "I want my picture taken again."

Karen smirked, a silent "I told you so."

"He should be," Miles finally said.

A second and third director's chairs were pulled up by a stagehand and set on either side of Zoe. Miles's sister took the left. He took the right, closer to the action so he didn't have to yell over his daughter's head. He kept one eye on the goings on in front of him, but the other kept straying toward the door, watching and praying for Sawyer to step through it.

Through an entire Saturday morning of filming, Miles kept looking for Sawyer, but his lover never made an appearance. Miles—the boss— tried to make himself get mad about the fact his employee hadn't made it to work, but Miles—the lover—was too heartbroken and too afraid he'd lost Sawyer for good to be upset about his absence. He was so preoccupied he barely paid any attention to what was going on around him. If anyone missed a cue, if the cameras or lighting weren't right, he wouldn't have caught it. That pretty much made anything they attempted to do today a waste of everyone's time.

He checked the clock on his phone. It was nearing lunchtime already, so since his heart wasn't in it, and he had a little girl to celebrate a birthday with, he yelled over the bullhorn, "Let's call it a day."

Everyone cheered.

His sister eyed him hard, quietly letting him know he'd better use the time off wisely, find the photographer, and fix his mistake.

"Give me a minute," he said, sliding out of the chair.

As he ducked into his private office, he fished out his phone and pulled up Sawyer's number. His feet kept busy, making small circles on the floor as each ring sounded, then faded into empty silence. Each unanswered ring killed a little more of his hope. Each unanswered ring made him feel like a bigger ass.

When the voice mail finally picked up, all the warmth and hope and happiness were gone, utterly obliterated. His voice sounded solemn and devastated. "Sawyer, I'm sorry. I overreacted. Please call me. I need to hear from you. I need to talk to you. Please. Please, call me back."

PEOPLE RUSHED by, hurrying to get to one place or another, just like they always seemed to do in San Francisco—a far cry from the lazy days spent strolling the beaches back home. Home. That's exactly where Sawyer needed to be, and if all went well, he'd be on a plane heading back there first thing in the morning.

"Mr. Rockwell's office, may I help you?" a perky voice on the other end of the line asked. The sound knotted Sawyer's gut.

"This is Sawyer Taylor. I need to either speak with Mr. Rockwell or his assistant."

"Mr. Taylor, it's Saturday. Mr. Rockwell doesn't work on Saturday."

"This can't wait."

"Very well. Please hold."

Sighing, he reached for the cup of coffee cooling in front of him. Distorted elevator music blared from the phone. He'd rather have listened to staticky silence and the sound of trollies going by than that garbled noise.

The longer the minutes dragged on, and the more incessant the noise in his ear became, the closer Sawyer came to giving up on his quest to be free of San Francisco, Miles, and everything that had caused him any sort of heartache. He thought about packing up and taking Lucy to some place like New York City, where there was mountain-sized architecture and every possible walk of life to capture on film, where he could be like Miles and Elijah, free to do whomever he wanted to.

That's not really what you want, silly boy.

No, it wasn't, but he knew his fragile heart couldn't take any more caring only to be discarded like yesterday's news.

"I'm sorry, Mr. Taylor." The woman had come back. Her voice gave him a start. "I can't reach Mr. Rockwell or his assistant. Would you like me to leave him a message?"

"No." *You can't tell someone you quit over voice mail.* "No, I'll call back Monday."

"Thank you for calling. Have a great day," she said, as if it was part of a script and she had to say it regardless of how gloomy the caller's mood might be.

Elbows on the table, he scrubbed both hands over his face. Actually, the move covered the tears welling in his eyes so some curious onlooker wouldn't see him turning into a misty-eyed baby, brooding over a love he'd never really had. He should've known when Miles gave him that speech about Zoe and love that things would never work out between them. Miles made excuses just like Elijah did. Men like those two turned men like him frigid, turned lovers into whores, and here Sawyer was, ready to move off and take the plunge.

His phone vibrated, skittering across the metal table. The screen said he had one missed call and one voice mail. He chose not to acknowledge it. If the call had come from Rockwell's office, he needed more time to think things through before abruptly resigning from his position on the movie set. If it was anyone else, they could wait until he had a clearer head and could rationally talk things through.

"HE DIDN'T answer," Miles said to his sister. "Obviously, he's avoiding me. I can't apologize to him if he's avoiding me."

"Calm down." She laid both hands on his shoulders and met his worried stare head on. "He works for the studio, right? You're bound to see him soon."

"Yeah," Miles muttered.

"Okay, then. Stop worrying. Let's take Zoe out for her birthday, take her shopping and have some fun with her before we have to head back home."

Miles nodded. His sister was right yet again. The affairs of his heart could wait one more day. Nothing in the world was more important than treating his little princess to one of the best days of her life.

He bent down and scooped her into his arms. The toile ruffles of her pink dress tickled his skin when he hugged her tight. Someone had placed a sparkling silver tiara atop her head. It even looked like the makeup artist worked a little Hollywood magic on her while Daddy had been busy with work.

"And what would my little princess like to do for her birthday?"

Zoe pursed her tiny pink lips and tapped her forefinger over her mouth, tilting her head to the side in consideration. The child had done almost everything there was to do in San Francisco, some of which she might've been too young to remember.

"We could go to the zoo," he suggested. "See the Komodo dragon?"

"Ew." She wrinkled her button nose. "I'm soooo too old for the zoo."

Karen and Miles laughed.

"Shopping at Union Square?"

Her face lit up like the sky on the Fourth of July. Proof positive his little girl was quickly becoming a little woman. Before he knew it, she'd be asking for the keys to the car, credit cards, and permission to go on her first date.

Dear God, save me now.

They wrangled a driver and limo from the studio instead of the sedan Miles often traveled in, then piled into the back for an afternoon out on the town. Zoe blustered with excitement, mouth moving ninety miles an hour, and she wasn't losing steam. Even with all her cheerful carrying on and the absolutely contagious joy she exuded, Miles's mind kept wandering back to man he loved, the man he stood a good chance of losing.

ONCE HIS cup of coffee became too cold to enjoy and the baguette he'd been picking at lost its appeal, Sawyer pitched them both in a trashcan and started for the Mission station to catch a BART train back to his side of town. He might've called for a car if he hadn't needed the downtime away from the insanity of being anywhere near anything relating to Miles Eisenberg.

He leaned against the cool concrete wall, waiting, waiting, waiting. It seemed as though the pastime he kept returning to these days was waiting—waiting for Miles to say I love you, waiting to meet Zoe, waiting for an apology, waiting to grow a set of balls and tell Miles where to go and how to get there. Waiting to feel his final heartbreak.

A crumpled piece of paper tumbled down the tracks. Immediately, Sawyer reached for his camera and realized he didn't have it with him. That alone summed up nicely how his mind hadn't been with him for a while. He couldn't remember the last time he'd had his hands on it or where it was, couldn't remember if he'd tucked it away in its special bag or left it lying about like unwanted junk. That wouldn't do. He needed to know his camera was safe and sound, especially if his heart didn't have a chance of being safe from anything.

Chapter Twenty-Eight

ANOTHER WEEKEND passed without Sawyer leaving his room any more than necessary. Sawyer stared at the empty, open suitcase at the end of his bed. He debated whether he should fill it with his clothes and go back to Mississippi, where he belonged, or man up and face everything that had happened between him and Miles. Confront Miles for overreacting. Force Miles to once and for all accept the way he truly felt and let those feelings be known.

Sawyer knew better, though. Even as he sat on the bed, sad and lonely, he knew he couldn't force anyone into anything. He'd spent the better part of his adult life as a speed bump in his lover's fast track to... whatever the hell Elijah had been looking for. He might've slowed Elijah down, but he'd never once made Elijah stop and own up to anything. And he damn sure wasn't going to be able to make Miles own up to anything. Those were the facts. He just had to face them.

A soft knock on the door pulled his attention away from the fork in the road of his future. He couldn't tell by the sound who might be on the other side and sort of wished for a visitor ID feature, like the caller ID on his phone. It seemed rude to ask who was there and not let them in.

"Comin'." He resigned himself to facing whoever wanted to steal him away from his ruminations. Barefooted, he padded across the room, opened the door, met his visitor face-to-face, and froze. Even his breath stilled before he had a chance to exhale it.

"I'm sorry," Miles said.

Sawyer hadn't even opened his mouth.

"I seem to be saying that to you a lot." Miles stepped into the room. "But I mean it when I say it."

"'Sorry' isn't workin' for me no more."

"Understandable."

Miles looked away first. Maybe he'd been unable to bear the weight of Sawyer's disappointed glare. Maybe this whole situation hurt Miles as bad as it did Sawyer. Who knew?

He was about to ask if there was anything else when a wide-eyed Miles Eisenberg brushed by him and all but stumbled farther into the bedroom. "Are you leaving?" he asked, voice nearly breathless with a mix of sorrow and surprise. He stared at the empty suitcase on the edge of Sawyer's bed.

Sawyer joined him, staring too. In a fragile voice, he said, "I don't know. I'm not sure what I'm doin' anymore or where I'm goin'. I just…."

"It's because of me, isn't it?"

"Partly. Then again, it's partly me too, Miles."

Miles turned his head enough so Sawyer could see the reddening rims of his eyes and the flush of his cheeks. The slight curl of Miles's delicious lips turned southward. "I understand," he said. Sawyer detected a hint of a tremble. It sounded like Miles was doing everything in his power not to fall apart. "Can I convince you not to go?"

Convincing Sawyer not to leave would've been an easy feat. All Miles really had to do was say the words. Three little words that true believers didn't sling around simply to get what they wanted. Three little words that had the power to heal all wounds and erase all scars. Three little words to fix Sawyer's broken heart. Miles only had to say them once and truly mean them. The suitcase on the edge of the bed would be put back in the closet, and he'd give this thing they were doing another honest try.

Please, just say it….

A hand wrapped around his, fingers gripping tight as if Miles needed to hold onto something to keep himself anchored. Miles's palm felt as warm as it ever had. His touch was a healthy mixture of strong and kind. As sad as it sounded, Sawyer would've been happy spending an entire lifetime holding that hand, whether Miles loved him or not.

"It's time for you to meet Zoe," Miles said. He turned to face Sawyer completely, then reached for his other hand. "I'm still afraid she'll love you and you'll leave us, but I…." Miles exhaled, then swallowed so hard Sawyer could see his throat ripple. "I know I have to have faith in you. I have to have faith that if this is meant to be, it will be."

"What changed your mind?"

"Honestly?"

Sawyer nodded.

"I couldn't even enjoy spending the day with my daughter because you weren't with us. I was so miserable. My sister saw it and she read me the riot act. She made me realize my heart needs to be happy too. Sawyer, you make my heart happy."

"I do?"

"Yeah, and... well, I want you to be a part of my life and my family."

"You do?"

"I do."

That warm, fuzzy, tingling sensation Sawyer had felt when Miles first kissed him came back in a rush and spread through his body. Miles released his hands and pulled him into the tightest hug. No kissing and no groping followed. It was a warm, genuine, meaningful embrace between two men. The embrace spoke of deep and genuine caring, the kind no amount of time or space could ever erase. Even if the declaration of love couldn't be reciprocated right now, the feelings were there, and that's what mattered, despite Sawyer wishing Miles would say those three words to him.

"I want you to come back to Malibu with me when we're done here, at least for a few weeks, just because.... Well, I know I won't be ready for you to go home after this is over."

He felt Miles relax, felt the warmth of breath brush along his neck and the weight of a head on his shoulder. Fingers splayed over his back, Miles obviously wasn't going to let go of him, and Sawyer didn't mind it for a second. He loved being held like this. He loved being in love.

He wrapped both arms around Miles's waist and held on with the same tenacity. Their bodies felt so perfect together. Sawyer closed his eyes and laid his head on Miles's shoulder, content with standing there, hugging, for as long as Miles needed.

Then Miles whispered, "I love you."

The world finally felt right again, as though they hadn't had the first fight, as if they'd laid eyes on each other all those weeks ago and it had been love at first sight. Their worlds collided and birthed something beautiful, something magical, and something holy in Sawyer's eyes.

"I love you too," he said, tightening his hold.

CHAPTER TWENTY-NINE

"I DID it," Miles whispered. He had his cell phone pressed to his ear with one hand and held a flame to the wick of a tall, white taper with the other. "I told him I love him."

"Aww," Karen cooed. Miles could almost picture that wistful, happy expression she often got after reading a romance novel or watching those silly romantic comedies she loved so much. He called it her lovesick puppy face, a face she *never* used in regard to him and his love life. "I'm so glad you finally said it. How did he react? What did he say?"

"He told me he loves me too, but I already knew that."

"Right, so what are you doing now?"

"He's taking a shower. I told him we would go out to an expensive dinner somewhere on the wharf, but I sort of lied."

"Lied?"

"Yeah. Martin and Pearl are making a gourmet, four-course meal for us. I'm setting the table with linens and candlelight. When I told Martin I wanted to romance Sawyer, he volunteered to do anything he could to help. So… he's getting the garden ready for—" The sound of the doorknob jiggling silenced Miles momentarily. "I think that's him. I gotta go. I'll call you later," he whispered.

Quickly, he pitched the phone onto the chaise longue in the corner of his room. The door opened and dim light from the hallway spilled inside, but rather than his handsome suitor, a friendly, portly gentleman with salt-and-pepper hair backed in, tugging a rolling cart into the room with him. "A hand here?"

"Sorry, Martin. Sorry."

"It's okay, Miles."

Miles held the door, and when Martin cleared the opening, he closed it up tight.

"It warms my heart to see you finally opening up to that boy," Martin said with a smile as he shifted the first course onto the table. "I grew so very tired of seeing you with all those men, my friend. I knew none of them would ever please you."

"Oh?" Miles stopped setting the folded linens on the table and arched a brow at Martin. "And just how did you know that?"

"Because they didn't demand your respect. They didn't appeal to the artist in you. They didn't intrigue. You're not a man easily satisfied, Miles Eisenberg. You knew they were fleeting flings, and you fancied them about as much as you fancy a vintage sauvignon."

Martin knew his favorite wine. Impressive. And speaking of which, Martin pulled an uncorked bottle from Napa Valley from the bottom of the cart. Nothing in the world could've made this plan come together better. It was the most romantic, loving gesture he'd ever made for another human being.

"Martin?" The older gentleman raised his head. "Thank you for doing all this for me. I couldn't have pulled it off alone."

"I know. And you're welcome. Now—" Martin paused to settle the last dish on the table. "—make us proud, Miles."

"Oh, I plan to."

One last smile, and Martin vacated the room, leaving Miles standing there in his black Armani dress suit and tie. His hands shook and his palms sweated. The last time he'd been this nervous had been the first time he'd sat in the director's chair. His first shouted command to his crew had come out sounding more like a winded squeak. That first day on the set as a full-fledged movie director had marked a new course in Miles's life, and he hoped this day did the same.

A soft tapping at the bedroom door stole Miles's breath. This was the moment he'd been waiting for, preparing for. "Come in," he said, fighting the urge to run his fingers through his immaculately styled hair. Everything had to be perfect and in its place, even his hair. Anything less simply wouldn't do.

Haloed in golden light from the hallway, Sawyer appeared in the opened door. His handsomeness had reached a whole new level of devastating. His cheeks were rosy from the shower he'd taken. The suit he'd chosen hugged the important parts, giving him a long, lean contour and making his shoulders appear much broader than his hips. Beneath the black suit, his shirt was a beautiful shade of cobalt blue, and a black tie finished him off. He smiled, and it made his big brown eyes twinkle with the kind of happiness Miles planned on spending a lifetime giving him.

"Wow," Sawyer breathed, "you look… this looks…."

"You like it?" Miles started toward him, grabbing the single red rose he'd left on the edge of the table, the single rose being the universal symbol for love.

Sawyer met him halfway. "I love it. You didn't have to go through all this trouble, though."

"Yes, I did. I needed to show you I was willing… *am* willing… to go through all the trouble in the world to make you happy, Sawyer." Miles took his hands. "And I don't mean tonight. I mean every single night for as long as you'll have me."

Sawyer searched his face but didn't say anything. For a moment, Miles thought maybe he'd said the wrong thing. If he had, he didn't know what to say or do to backpedal out of the mess he might've created.

"Why me?" Sawyer finally asked. There was no sense of doom or melodrama in the two words or the sound of his voice, simply casual curiosity.

The answer was quite easy, actually. Miles didn't even have to put any real thought into it. "Because you're the first man who made me want better. You're the first one I've had a desire to put up on a pedestal and the first one I've wanted to shower with love. You're the first one who has ever appealed to every fiber of my being and…." Miles lowered his head. "And you're the first one Anne would've been proud of."

His voice choked on the last few words. A burning knot had developed in the back of Miles's throat. The burn trickled up to his eyes. This wasn't supposed to be a sad occasion. He'd meant to sweep Sawyer off his feet, but instead Miles found himself on the edge of breaking down.

"Are *you* proud of me?" Sawyer said.

"Yeah." Miles raised his head and met Sawyer's gaze despite the threat of tears beating against the backs of his eyes. "Zoe is the only other person who's made me this proud."

"I'm proud of you too, Miles. Sincerely."

"OH MY God, I'm so stuffed." Sawyer tossed the linen from his lap onto the table. He had every desire to unbutton his slacks and let his bloated belly hang out, but how unattractive would that be? *Yuck.*

"Did you enjoy it?" The same misery painted creases in Miles's handsome face. From the jerking of his shoulders, it looked like he was having a hard time breathing too.

The dinner could've ended at the second course, and Sawyer would've been okay. It had started with some sort of bread and oil dip Sawyer had never heard of before. The second course was a generous portion of Caesar salad. Baked salmon and sautéed green beans followed. The bow on top of that delicious gift was a tiramisu and warm beverage combination that left a hint of flavor on Sawyer's mouth. Every time he licked his lips, he experienced it all over again. Now, he couldn't make himself move. He silently prayed sex wouldn't be the second dessert.

"I have another surprise for you," Miles said.

Shit.

"Yeah?" There was more than a hint of caution in Sawyer's voice.

"Yeah. If you want, though, you can change into something more comfortable first."

"What kind of 'comfortable' do I need for this?"

With a wicked grin, Miles popped up from the table and faded into a darkened corner of the room. It was hard to see what he was up to with only a few candles to light the space. Curiosity *really* took hold of him then.

Only a minute or two passed before Miles reappeared. In each hand he held a black gift bag tied closed with a satiny red bow. "When I took Zoe shopping, I picked something up for each of us," Miles said. His gaze slowly, hungrily wound down the length of Sawyer's body, then back up to meet Sawyer's curious stare. "I could picture you in them when I picked them out.

"Them?"

Miles passed over one of the bags.

Sawyer fingered one tip of the red ribbon. Inside was a bunch of black fabric. A hint of gold shimmered in the folds; it was the candlelight reflecting on black silk. When he pulled the fabric from the bag, it unfolded into drawstring sleep pants. Another piece of not-so-shiny black fabric was beneath it.

"That's a tank top to go with the pants," Miles said. "It's not the sexiest thing in the world, but I bought it with this night in mind."

"So… you knew I'd say yes before you even apologized to me?"

"No, I…. I did a lot of hoping and praying."

"Looks like it paid off."

"Yeah." An adorable, crooked grin kicked up one edge of Miles's lips. It took a lot restraint for Sawyer not to lean in and press their mouths together. "Do you want me to strip you, or do you want to change yourself?"

"If you strip me—" Sawyer stepped closer. "—we won't be leavin' this room anytime soon. So if you have something planned…."

"Good point. Go change."

Sawyer had started toward the bathroom when a hand on his upper arm stopped him. "I love you," Miles said, before stealing a kiss.

Their lips touched, warm and moist and sensual. Mouths opened and closed, caressing with gentle passion. The sweetness of the tiramisu and the drink served with it colored the kiss. Nothing in the world had ever been so heavenly, not even Elijah's most perfect kisses, for those had been empty of the love he now felt.

The kiss broke, and Sawyer couldn't stop the grin spreading across his face. His eyelids lowered of their own volition, and if he hadn't known better, he'd say he was well on his way to swooning. "I love you too," he said, before disappearing into the bathroom with the gift Miles had given him.

CHAPTER THIRTY

THE SILK felt amazing on Sawyer's thighs, soft and almost billowing along his legs. The tank top hugged his torso, spreading tight across his pecs. Admittedly, in the bathroom mirror beneath three bright lights, he looked handsome. He could see why Miles would've picked out this combination, but why for a night like this? Why go from dress suits and gourmet dinners to silk pajamas?

He returned to the bedroom and found Miles wearing exactly the same thing. A thick, white, fuzzy blanket was cradled in his arms. Seeing him made Sawyer's heart soar. He'd fallen so hard and so fast despite being afraid so afraid of love.

"I knew these clothes would look great on you," Miles said, holding out his hand.

Sawyer took it, lacing their fingers together. "You look pretty amazin' yourself, lover."

"Are you ready for the next part?"

"I s'pose I am."

"You suppose?" Miles arched a brow.

"Okay. Okay. The anticipation is drivin' me insane."

"Then follow me."

Hand in hand, they walked out of Miles's bedroom, along the hall, and down the stairs. The place felt like a ghost town tonight, and Sawyer wondered if Miles had pulled strings to get everyone to vacate for their special night together. Surely, Miles didn't have *that* kind of clout... did he?

Miles led him through the foyer and down a hall Sawyer hadn't previously traveled. It took them through a dimly lit wing of the old house. The wide hall separated two rooms, both with pocket doors spread wide open. On the right was a living room he'd never seen anyone use, with antique furniture and glass hurricane lamps. A huge painting of a garden hung over the fireplace. The room on the left looked equally unused and equally antique—an office, maybe.

At the end of the hall, a set of french doors greeted them. Tiny flames flickered in their panes. The doors opened as Sawyer and Miles approached, like magic, though Sawyer assumed people stood on either side, waiting for the couple to appear. The doors opened onto a dark garden. The flames belonged to torches that lined a rose-petal-covered walkway.

"Miles…," Sawyer whispered, in absolute awe of everything Miles had done to make the evening romantic.

"Shhh… Enjoy it, okay? Don't think about it. Just enjoy it."

The path disappeared behind the towering trees. They continued to follow it through the gardens, away from the house and what felt far away from civilization. It seemed like paradise on common soil, like a romance novel nestled in reality.

"Stop for one second," Miles softly requested.

They did and Sawyer turned toward him.

"Tell me you're going to stay with me. Please."

"That's the plan," Sawyer said. Miles's fingers tightened around his.

"This is silly." Miles laughed, averting his gaze. "I actually looked at rings while we were out shopping. I've never looked at rings before, Sawyer." Miles raised his stare again. "I thought about what it would be like to go ring shopping for you, what it would be like to slip one of those bands on your finger. Everything inside me warmed, Sawyer. I swear to God, it did."

"So, what'd you do?"

When Miles swallowed, his throat rippled. Sawyer saw it as clear as day in the low, golden glow of the torches' flames. "I bought two things from the jewelry store that day. I bought a watch, and I bought a set of matching bands."

"Bands?" Sawyer's throat tightened.

"Yeah." Miles licked his lips. "I debated hanging onto them and waiting until we were years into a relationship, but that didn't feel right to me. I guess what I'm trying to say right now is I want to be committed to you and only you, and if everything goes the way I think it will, I want to make the commitment official. I want us to be a family."

"And what about Zoe? What if she don't like me?"

"She'll love you. I know she will. You're impossible not to love."

As if he were being pulled by some mystical force, Sawyer stepped up to Miles and their lips met again. The blanket in Miles's arms kept them from getting too close to each other, and Sawyer silently cursed it for getting in his way.

"Are you ready to keep going?" Miles whispered against Sawyer's lips.

"Do I have to stop kissin' you?"

"Only long enough to walk a few more feet."

Sawyer had to stop himself from whining in protest.

A slight part in the foliage revealed more golden light, more flames. Miles pulled back the vines, creating a sort of doorway within the mass of greenery and flowers.

Inside, the path opened to a tight clearing where a round bed hung from a wooden canopy. Pillows were piled at one end. In the center, set up on a silver server tray, was a bottle of Miles's favorite wine—a flavor Sawyer had come to love—and two wine glasses. A white screen hung from a stand in front of the opening. More torches lined the clearing. More rose petals made a beautiful, red floor.

"If you'd chosen tonight to propose, I wouldn't have been able to turn you down," Sawyer said, voice airy and as dreamy as the scene laid out around them.

"I plan to do even more when that day comes."

"I don't know how you could possibly outdo this."

"Oh, I have my ways." Miles lifted the bottle and glasses from the bed. "Sit," he said, and Sawyer did without question. Miles handed him the two glasses, then uncorked the bottle and filled them both halfway. "The second part of your surprise—" Miles set the bottle down on a tiny stand right beside the bed. "—is a sneak preview of what we've been working on. Postproduction isn't done, but they sent me what they've put together so far. I didn't want to watch it without you. And just so you know, I normally do this alone in my office."

"But you're sharin' it with me now?"

"Yeah, I am."

Miles aimed a tiny, silver remote at the laptop beside the bed. A colorful ray of light shone from a device fastened beneath the canopy. The man must've gone through a lot of trouble to do all this. For the briefest of moments, Sawyer wondered if Martin had helped Miles put it all together. For some reason, it was important to Sawyer that Martin approved of this union, maybe because Martin knew Miles so much better than Sawyer did. If he disapproved, there had to be good reason for it.

"The studio sends me a rough cut halfway through filming. That way, if there's something horribly off and I need to fix it, I can without wasting too much time," Miles said, settling onto the bed. He held out an arm, and with his other hand, patted the spot beside him. "Come here. You're too far away."

With a smile and a flutter of his heart, Sawyer slid back on the bed and settled in next to his lover. He curled against Miles's chest, one ear over his heart. Each beat sounded like a soft thud, each breath a gentle whisper. There wasn't a time in Sawyer's life he could remember being so relaxed or feeling so loved. Then two arms wrapped around him and held on tight.

CHAPTER THIRTY-ONE

THE SCREEN died down to black after about forty minutes of video. So far, there wasn't anything Miles had seen that made him want to reshoot any scenes. If time permitted, he might consider tackling the first bedroom scene again, but other than that, everything looked great. Then again, he might've been going easy on himself because of the euphoric feeling of having Sawyer nestled against him.

"You awake?" he whispered.

"Yeah." Sawyer cleared his throat and lifted his head. "Is that all we get?"

"Unfortunately. The rest of it either hasn't been shot or hasn't been composed yet." Miles leaned his head down and brushed his lips over Sawyer's temple. "What did you think?"

"Mmm…. I think it'll be a very good movie."

"Yeah?"

"But."

"But?" Miles frowned.

"But I'd rather be watchin' you make love to me than some man and woman I don't know makin' love to each other."

Well, wasn't that the best kind of "but" Miles could've asked for?

A slow grin spread his lips as he rolled out from under Sawyer's body. The thick white blanket still covered them both, and the warmth they made together defeated the cool of a crisp Bay City evening. Miles positioned himself between Sawyer's legs—groin against groin, stomach against stomach—and pressed a kiss to Sawyer's exposed shoulder. He slowly painted kisses across his lover's collarbone and over the hollow of Sawyer's throat, then up the side of his neck to his jaw, finally stopping at a delicious set of lips.

Miles rolled his hips, pressing against Sawyer. They were both semisoft but growing harder the deeper their kiss became.

The love they made beneath the stars, with the flickering of torches surrounding them, was as magical as it was romantic—a fact that remained true no matter how many times they came together throughout the night. And they didn't stop at one orgasm. One orgasm wasn't enough to sate the hunger Miles had for Sawyer. A lifetime of orgasms wouldn't be enough. He'd known the first time they had sex his body would always crave this man. No one else had ever had that effect on him.

Utterly naked, glistening with sweat, Miles collapsed on Sawyer's chest soon after the fourth—or maybe fifth—time he'd come over the course of many hours. His lungs burned when he tried to breathe. His heartbeat pounded with alarming speed against his eardrums. Maybe if he just lay there, his body would even out.

With the tips of his fingers, Sawyer brushed wet curls of hair away from Miles's face. His touch was so gentle, so kind. "I love you so much," Sawyer said. He was still winded, voice hoarse from all the screaming and praying and moaning.

"I love you too," Miles said. It seemed like every time he said the words, they fell from his lips so much easier than they had the time before.

The only sound between them now was the intense, raspy breaths. Miles enjoyed the sound, enjoyed the feeling of being so emotionally connected even after the physical connection dissolved. Anne had given him that feeling at one time. While he wasn't really attracted to women, Anne had been different. Now, Sawyer took her place. He gave Miles something Miles had sworn he would never find with another person. He'd thought Anne would be the very last, that his heart had grown cold to everyone outside his tight circle, that he'd never find his one true love. As sure as he lay there with Sawyer beneath him, any doubts he'd had about loving again were gone. Not even a ghost of those doubts remained. He hoped he'd given Sawyer the same peace of mind.

They fell asleep like that, with Miles lying on Sawyer's chest, listening to the sound of his lover's beating heart. It wasn't until he felt the warmth of the sun raining droplets of light on his face that he bothered to peel open his eyes.

"You're awake," a velvety voice said from beside him.

Ribbons of sunlight kept him from making out a face, but he knew by the feel of muscle and the musky scent that Sawyer lay next to him. By the smoothness of the voice, he knew Sawyer had been awake for a while.

"You didn't have to wait for me to get up," Miles said. His voice contrasted Sawyer's to an extreme degree.

"No, I wanted to. I like havin' you curled up with me like this. Wanted to enjoy it for a spell."

"Did I talk in my sleep again?"

"Just a little." Sawyer grinned. "Nothing intelligible. It was cute, though."

If Miles were a man capable of blushing, he might've done it then.

His stomach gave a grumble, begging for a little sustenance not in the form of his lover's body. No, this hunger could only be sated with coffee and something breakfasty and warm, like Pearl's buttermilk biscuits and the fresh preserves they often bought at the farmer's market. But Miles wasn't ready to climb out of bed, and certainly wasn't ready to leave that comfortably firm chest. It was Sunday, anyway; why rush to get dressed?

"I wonder if I can convince Martin to serve us breakfast in bed," Miles said.

"After last night, I think he deserves a break, don't you?"

"I suppose," Miles sighed. "But God help me, I don't want to get up."

"Me neither."

Talking gave way to more cuddling. Any thought of moving ended right there. Miles couldn't remember a time he'd been so content to lie around, and not because some random act of sex had taken everything out of him. This time, he was well rested, and his body had all normal function, but he simply didn't want to move. He had paradise surrounding him and paradise in his arms. Who in their right mind would want to abandon something so perfect?

"May I come in?" Martin asked from outside the wall of trees, flowers, shrubs, and vines.

Miles raised his head, but only enough to make sure their naked bodies were completely covered with the blanket they'd slept wrapped in last night.

"Yeah, come in," Miles said.

An arm tightened around him, fingers resting on his hip.

The scent of coffee filled the cool, morning air first, followed by something that smelled a lot like pancakes and hot maple syrup. The scent of maple was unmistakable, and it roused a hard rumble in the pit of Miles's stomach. Sawyer laughed softly.

"What are you laughing at, mister?" Miles turned his head, brow teasingly arching at his lover. "Your stomach's complaining too, you know." He playfully poked Sawyer in the gut.

Martin set the tray of food on the small table by the bed, then turned to leave the garden paradise his family had created over the years, only to stop and look both men over. His expression was approving. He said, "You both had a good evening, I assume."

"I did," Sawyer said.

"Best night ever," Miles added.

"Good," Martin said. "I love to see good things happen to good people. Now, please enjoy your breakfast, and don't worry about cleaning up. It will be taken care of for you."

"Thanks, Martin."

"Thank you, Martin."

Chapter Thirty-Two

Filming ended a few short weeks later. The final "Cut!" sent a painful ripple down Sawyer's spine. Three months hadn't been long enough. He'd gotten too used to sleeping in Miles's bed, lying in those strong arms, having Miles rest his head on Sawyer's chest. Sure, Sawyer had agreed to go to Malibu and spend some time with Miles and Zoe, but like all good things, eventually Malibu would come to an end too.

The bittersweet clicking of studio lights coming up in the background drove home the reality this dream was coming to an end. Sawyer managed to snap off one final memorable photo of the cast and crew clapping and raising their arms in celebration. This didn't feel like a time for celebration to Sawyer. It felt much more appropriate to mourn, for this signaled the loss of the most perfect, most passionate three months of his life.

He packed his camera away on the edge of the set for the last time, knowing Malibu would come next, but then what? What if Sawyer arrived at Miles's home and the people in Miles's life didn't warm up to him and accept him like Miles had? Would that bring a one-way ticket back to Biloxi for him? What if they did? Would he still go home alone eventually? Would they make promises to visit each other when they found time? Or would those rings Miles mentioned that night in the garden become a reality? Could they possibly find a happily ever after in each other?

"Hey," a soft voice said above him.

Sawyer still knelt on the floor, cradling his camera against his chest. The bag lay open. A single, soggy tear dripped from Sawyer's eye. He hadn't even realized he was crying. That tear hadn't come with the tightening of his throat or the burning of his eyes. It had given no warning but simply dripped from his chin all tragic and embarrassing. Before standing, he quickly wiped it away, but doubted the moist tracks on his cheeks disappeared.

A hand gripped his shoulder, the strength willing Sawyer to his feet. He stood, turned, and met Miles face-to-face, but couldn't make himself speak.

"Why are you crying?" Miles asked, brushing his thumb over Sawyer's cheek. Such a gentle touch. It felt so good, Sawyer nestled his face against Miles's palm.

"I'm not cryin'." Sawyer sniffled. "I got something in my eye."

Miles laughed and pulled Sawyer into his arms. Sawyer almost broke down completely. Tears like Niagara Falls. Thank God, he had a little more control than that.

"You're still coming to Malibu, right?" Miles asked.

"Of course." Sawyer raised his head. "You still want me there, right?"

"There's no place I'd rather you be, Sawyer Taylor."

Those were the most refreshing words Sawyer had heard all day. They compelled him to lay his head on Miles's shoulder and snuggle in tight. Thank God most of the cast and crew had already vacated the premises, off to post-filming parties Sawyer didn't care to go to. Right now, he wanted the comfort of his lover's arms, and nothing else would do.

"What if we get to Malibu," he spoke softly, "and the dream ends? What if we get there and things fall apart? What if Zoe don't like me?"

"Zoe's going to love you, babe." Miles's lips brushed over Sawyer's cheek when he spoke. "Karen's going to love you. They're going to love you as much as I do. How could they not?"

"Simple. Not everyone finds me as dashin' as you do."

Laughing, Miles hugged him tighter. The silent *please don't let go* didn't remain unheard, or maybe they were so connected and tuned in to each other, Sawyer didn't have to say anything. He took comfort in that, comfort in the way Miles knew how to treat him and knew what he wanted.

"Finish packing," Miles said. "We need to get back to the inn so we can get ready for tonight."

"Tonight?" Sawyer frowned.

"The party. There's always a party."

"And we *have* to go?"

"It's tradition, Sawyer." Miles brushed his hand up and down the center of Sawyer's back. His beautiful "I can conquer the world" smile stretched across those kissable lips. Sawyer would've willingly handed Miles his soul if he asked for it. "We don't have to go, but I would love to have you on my arm. I would love to stop hiding our relationship from everyone."

A sense of pride overcame Sawyer. Someone wanting to show him off was another first for him. Elijah had never wanted to hold hands in public, never invited him anywhere they would have to hide for mixed company. The gay bars were okay. They'd make out on the dance floor there. Anywhere else, Elijah barely looked at him.

He was quickly becoming more and more aware of how little Elijah had cared.

"You can borrow something of mine if you don't have anything to wear," Miles said.

"I have something. I….I guess I just wanted another night alone with ya."

"Sawyer, this isn't the end of us. I swear."

"I know." Sawyer swallowed, only pulling away from Miles to reach for the strap of his camera bag. He settled it onto his shoulder and pasted on the most fake, most agreeable smile he could pull off. "I keep tellin' myself nothin's gonna change, that you're my true forever, but…."

"But you're afraid I'm going to do what Elijah did."

"I guess."

"I don't know him, and I can't say he didn't love you, but I can tell you that I want to be settled down. I want to settle down with *you*."

No words could've expanded on what Miles said. They were few and perfect and everything Sawyer needed to hear.

He leaned in and kissed Miles's cheek. "I'll go to your party."

"Perfect. Meet me in the foyer at eight."

"I'll be there."

"YOU LOOK fine," Martin said to Miles, who was stealing yet another look in the floor-length mirror hanging to the right of the foyer table. Miles worried the crimson-colored button-down he'd chosen washed him out. He worried the open collar made him look like he belonged in porn, not at an A-list party. He worried Sawyer wouldn't approve.

"It's our last night in San Francisco. I want it to be perfect." He ran his hands down over the shirt, silently debating tucking it into the Armani dress slacks hanging loosely from his waist. "Does my hair look okay? Do I smell okay?"

"Jesus, stop being a diva. You're fine."

A step at the top of the staircase creaked. Martin gasped and Miles swung around. Taking the steps one at a time, slower than Miles could stand, was a devilishly handsome Sawyer dressed in designer jeans and a sage-colored button-down shirt. A pair of leather Prada boots finished him off. It looked like Mr. Taylor had been taking advantage of couture while in San Francisco. The first time Miles had laid eyes on the photographer, he'd been wearing a nondescript T-shirt and faded denims. Now.... "Stunning," Miles rasped.

"Do I look okay?"

"Right off the cover of *GQ*."

"I wanted you to be proud to have me on your arm."

"Baby—" Miles reached for Sawyer's hand. As soon as Sawyer moved, a blast of his cologne nailed Miles hard. The scent made his mouth water. He could've easily said screw the party and taken Sawyer right back up those stairs. "The clothes don't matter. The look doesn't matter. I'm proud of you."

"Yeah?"

"Yeah." Miles grinned wickedly. "I'll be fighting men off you with a stick."

"There's only one man I want," Sawyer said, bringing their locked fingers up to his lips.

"He wants you just as badly, I promise."

Chapter Thirty-Three

INSTEAD OF the sedan, Miles thought it would be a great close to Sawyer's California excursion to take a limo, complete with iced champagne and a dozen red roses in the back. He couldn't remember ever feeling so compelled to romance someone, and not for fear of losing that someone, but simply because he wanted to. Sawyer brought out the hopeless romantic in him, made him want to be one of the good guys, not some random lay forgotten once the euphoria of orgasmic bliss wore off. Miles wanted to be a keeper.

He held Sawyer's hand and walked his lover over the threshold and onto the porch. "Wait a moment," Martin called to them. "Wait. There's something I must do."

They stopped on the edge of the wooden porch. Moonlight hung in the distance, breaking through thin patches of treetop canopies. The air was brisk, wind bustling enough to make it cool outside, cool enough their thin dress shirts didn't warm either of them.

"Would you like a jacket?" Miles asked.

"No, I'm fine. This is nice."

Before Miles managed another word, Martin reappeared with a much less impressive version of the camera Sawyer toted around all the time. "I need a picture of you two." The older man held up his camera and aimed in their direction, waving his hand to signal them into position.

"This isn't our prom, Martin," Miles said.

"I'm aware, but there isn't a picture of you two together." Martin arched his brow, shooting an accusing stare over the top of his camera "Not a clean one that I know of anyway."

Both men laughed. "Let him take the picture," Sawyer said. "It'd be nice to have one. Not of us kissing." The last was said under his breath.

Miles threaded one arm around Sawyer's waist and tucked his lover tight against his side. The flash went off. Then another and another. Every flash of light made him tighten his hold on Sawyer. By the time it was done, Miles was clinging and fighting to breathe steadily.

"Can we go now?" he asked in a low, uneven voice.

"Have fun," Martin said with a grin before ducking back into the house.

The chauffeur held the door open, and Miles let Sawyer climb inside first. It was the gentlemanly thing to do, even if Miles hated missing the look of surprise when Sawyer found the roses and champagne. When Miles joined him, the wide eyes and huge smile were still there, and the sight of Sawyer's pleasant shock made everything in him warm at once.

"You didn't have to go through the trouble," Sawyer said, leaning down to sniff one of the blossoming buds.

"But I wanted to."

They sipped champagne all the way to the party. The driver—as instructed—took the most scenic possible route, allowing them time to enjoy each other's company, allowing them time for toasts. When they finally arrived, Sawyer was all cheeky grins and sparkling eyes. Miles was relaxed and ready to face the cameras.

In all his years of being in the public eye, Miles had never had a man at his side. Pictures like that never surfaced because he took precautions. He didn't hold anyone's hand in public, wasn't seen leaving hotels with anyone, didn't vacation with anyone, and most of all, Miles never let anyone take a picture of him with anyone other than his daughter and his sister at his side. To say the decision to be out and proud with Sawyer was a big one put the situation in very casual terms. No, the decision had been huge: easy, but monumental nonetheless. And there was no better man for the job than Sawyer Taylor.

"Wait," he called to the driver. "Don't open the door yet."

"Yes, Mr. Eisenberg."

Sighing, Miles dragged both hands down his face. Even through the dark tinted windows of the limo, he could see all the flash photography and hear the yelling voices. Actors and actresses were making their way up the red carpet to the nightclub that normally hosted their end-of-filming parties.

"You okay?" Sawyer asked.

Miles hated the concern in his voice, hated the idea he'd made his lover worry.

"I'm fine. I promise."

Normally, such would be true, but right now, saying he was fine was a terrible lie. Putting his love life on display for the world scared the shit out of him, not for himself, but for the little girl waiting back home.

"We don't have to do this," Sawyer said. "We can go back to the inn, pack our things, and go to Malibu."

"No, I have to make an appearance. Studio figureheads will be here. They expect me to be. I can't leave. I'd never hear the end of it."

After a moment of silence, Sawyer said, "I don't have to go in with you."

The thought of not having Sawyer by his side didn't set well at all with Miles. Funny, he couldn't imagine not having his lover with him when there had been a time in his life he wouldn't have considered doing anything hand-in-hand with anyone he wasn't related to by blood or obligation. Now, he didn't want it any other way.

"No. I want you here. I want the world to know I'm taken. I just...." Miles swallowed. "I need a moment. I really didn't think about how this might impact Zoe. What if the kids start to bully her?"

"Do you honestly believe that'll happen? It's not like y'all live in the South where kids are taught every wakin' day to hate anything that isn't white, Christian, and heterosexual."

"No, but...."

"Miles, you don't have to show me off to the world for me to know how much you love me. Keepin' Zoe safe is much more important. So go to your party. I'll go back to the inn and get packed, then I'll see you in the mornin'."

"You're sure?"

"I most certainly am."

Leaning over, Miles pulled Sawyer into his arms and held on with everything he had in him. The love he felt for the man in his embrace was consuming, and the last thing he wanted to do right now was let Sawyer leave. A bigger man might've said fuck the haters and naysayers, but the decision he made now didn't just impact him. It impacted an innocent little girl who deserved the best out of life.

"I love you," Sawyer whispered, "and I'll see you in the mornin'."

"I love you too." Miles stole a quick kiss and a lingering stare, etching into his memory the way his lover looked right now, the kindness in his eyes and the sweetness in his voice. He would remember this as the first time Sawyer had selflessly sacrificed something for Zoe's sake. Sawyer had put Miles's little girl above himself, and Miles fell in love all over again.

FROM THE limo's window, Sawyer watched Miles plaster on his most fake smile. People and paparazzi clamored to get closer to the door, but security did a good job keeping them corralled. What did those people hope for? A candid shot to go viral on the Internet and make them a huge name? A big break? A night of passion? A fulfilled fantasy? If only they knew how not-so-easy it was being in love with someone who consumed the spotlight, how many sacrifices had to be made sometimes.

"Take me back to the inn," Sawyer finally said.

The limo pulled away from the curb as smoothly as it had arrived. Sawyer sat back in the seat—head against the rest, eyes closed. He wanted to be there with Miles, making a stand and showing the world they belonged to each other, that men like Gavin would never come between them. But other things, other people, took precedence over Sawyer's selfish wants. Besides, he knew he didn't have to make a show of things with Miles. Miles wasn't Elijah.

It took all of twenty minutes to get back to the inn. This time, there were no scenic routes, no meandering through the bustling streets of the fair Bay City. A quick interstate ride and he was back at the place he'd been calling home for the last three months. Home and alone.

The chauffeur let him out, and Sawyer did his best not to look disappointed as he trudged up the steps to Martin's beautiful Victorian-era home. All the trying didn't do any good, however. The closer Sawyer got to the front door, the more he wished Miles had returned with him.

"What are you doing back already?" a familiar voice asked from the darkness at the edge of the porch. "And where is Miles?" The wood floor creaked as Martin hurried across to where Sawyer stood. "Is everything okay?" Martin wore the most worried frown. Hard lines dimpled his brow.

"Everything's fine," Sawyer said. "I couldn't do it. He looked so worried about being seen in public with…." He inhaled sharply and the air burned all the way down to his lungs. "I wanted to do the right thing for him and for Zoe."

"Ah…. Zoe." Martin patted his shoulder. "He's always been very careful for her sake. I imagine it pains him not to have you there too."

"Yeah." Sawyer gave him a nostalgic sort of smile, returning to the moment Miles had pulled him into a hug and told Sawyer he loved him… right before getting out of the car to go to his big fancy Hollywood party. *You're a better man than this.* "I told him I'd start packin' up so we can leave first thing in the mornin'."

"How about I make some coffee and warm some muffins?"

"Sounds perfect."

In the dining room, Martin insisted Sawyer have a seat, even though Sawyer asked more than once if there was anything he could do to help. Martin loved playing the role of caretaker, even if getting on in age made it harder for him to do. Upon Martin's insistence, Sawyer took a seat at the table and tried his best to relax.

"Sugar and cream?" Martin called from the kitchen.

"Please."

A few minutes later, the smell of brewing coffee wafted into the room. Martin followed, carrying a plate of blueberry muffins so warm steam rose from their little rounded tops. He set the plate down on the table, then disappeared again. Sawyer hated idly sitting there while the much older gentleman scurried to care for him. Sawyer hadn't been raised that way. The kids took care of the elders, no exceptions.

"Martin, I—"

"Don't you dare move from that spot, young man."

Sawyer pinched his lips shut.

Martin returned with a carafe of coffee and two small white saucers and matching cups. He set everything down on the table and carefully arranged it all before serving one of those delicious-looking muffins to Sawyer.

Despite the pastry smelling so good, Sawyer really had no desire to eat it, but he wouldn't be rude. He peeled back the ruffled, pastel paper and tore away a little piece. It melted as soon as it hit his tongue, but didn't hit the spot. Nothing would hit the spot, not with Miles at that party without him.

"You okay?" Martin asked.

"Yeah." Sawyer nodded.

"You don't look okay."

"I am. I have to be. He gave me the option to go in with him, but I wanted to be the understandin' partner. I wanted to be what Miles needs me to be."

"Sweetie." Martin patted Sawyer on the hand and sat down beside him. "You're exactly what Miles needs. I've never seen him put so much effort into making someone feel special. I've never seen him want to keep a man around."

"He's right, you know."

The new voice in the room spun Sawyer around in his chair. Miles stood in the doorway with a grin on his face and a single rose in his hand. He looked so handsome, like something out of a romantic black-and-white movie.

Sawyer rose to his feet and crossed the room.

"You're back already," Sawyer said, words breathy and whimsical with surprise.

"I couldn't stay. I made an appearance for the executives, said hello to the investors, but I couldn't stay. It didn't feel right staying there without you."

"I'm glad you came back." Sawyer laced their fingers together.

"Me too." Miles kissed Sawyer's cheek, then pulled back with a smile. "Let's go pack. I'm ready to get out of here. I miss Zoe and Karen, and I really want you to see my place."

Chapter Thirty-Four

The early morning sun rained on dew-covered grass. A cool wind pushed through the clearing and rustled Miles's bed-weathered hair and his loose-fitting clothes. He carried the last suitcase down and settled it in the trunk of his little silver sports car. With Sawyer's baggage, the trunk didn't have a whole lot of space left, not that Miles would complain. In fact, he loved having Sawyer's stuff crowding his, even looked forward to more of it.

"I can honestly say I'm not ready for you to leave," Martin said from the doorway.

Miles threw a glance over his shoulder, grinned, then looked back to the car where Sawyer was pacing back and forth at the hood, phone pressed against his ear. It sounded like he was talking to his friend Lucy in Mississippi, explaining to her he wouldn't be home for a while, to take care of his baby, whoever *that* was.

Wanting to give his lover a little space, Miles stepped up on the porch and went right to Martin. "Thank you for everything." Miles pulled his longtime friend into a tight hug. "I mean *everything*."

"You can thank me by taking care of that man."

"Oh, I plan on it."

"Good. He's a keeper. And I think you both deserve to be happy."

"I honestly believe that now." He released Martin. "He makes me feel like I deserve a lot more than meaningless one-night stands. You know what I mean?"

"I certainly do, and you *certainly* are."

"Thank you, Martin."

"I'm ready," Sawyer said, slipping his phone into his pocket and bounding up the porch, taking the steps two at a time. It was his turn to give hugs and say good-byes.

"You two please be careful," Martin said as he released Sawyer.

"We will. I promise," Miles offered.

MILES DECIDED to take the Pacific Coast Highway from just outside of San Francisco all the way down the coast because Sawyer had never seen the Pacific Ocean before. The experience was a hell of a lot different from the white sandy beaches of Mississippi. The ocean was turbulent, with waves soaring high, then cresting against dark sand. They pulled off about four hours in, above an empty, forgotten stretch of beach along the highway.

"Get out and stretch your legs for a bit," Miles said.

"You comin'?"

"Of course I am."

Sweet-scented saltwater air hit Miles as soon as he climbed out of the car. It smelled nothing like the cool smog hovering over San Francisco, and nothing like the bay. No, the Pacific Ocean had its own smell, a scent nothing in the world compared to, at least nothing in Miles's world. Until Sawyer came along.

Sawyer stood on the edge of the pavement, right before the sandy hill rolled down into the beach below. He held his shoulders square and his back properly arched. One hand cupped the long barrel of the lens. The other held the camera to Sawyer's eye.

"I wish I could see the world the way you do," Miles said.

Sawyer turned the camera on him, lowered it long enough to wink, then snapped off a photo. "How's that?" he asked. Miles wished he could see his lover's expression.

"As varied forms of artistic expression. As beauty where other people would find filth. As a collection of poignant views."

"I don't know that I'd call 'em poignant. It's just... pretty."

There was the innocence Miles loved so much. With a grin, he tucked his thumbs in Sawyer's belt loops and tugged him close. The shutter clicked. Sawyer had taken a very close-up photo. It clicked again and again, and every time Miles heard the sound, his smile grew a little wider.

"Sit down on the rock," Sawyer said. He set the camera down, and that's when Miles saw the exuberant twinkle in his eyes. It wasn't like anything Miles had seen from Sawyer before, like this moment on the beach took him back to his happy place, like for the first time since they'd met, Sawyer had let go of whatever held him back and the wall that remained between them was finally gone. Sawyer looked at Miles like a life partner. No... like a husband, not just some lover who would eventually leave him.

Miles sat down and Sawyer unbuttoned Miles's shirt. It fell open, and Sawyer eased the fabric down Miles's arms. Their lips were but inches apart, restrained, so close but so far away, and despite his wanting to, Miles didn't lean up to close the space for a kiss. He simply kept his gaze locked on Sawyer's.

With a grin, Sawyer grabbed his camera and stepped back. He held it up and started taking pictures again. He would kneel, then stand, circle the boulder, then kneel again. It absolutely fascinated Miles to watch him. And Miles imagined spending every single day for the rest of his life watching Sawyer take pictures. He imagined himself doing so happily, longing for the moments they had together, moments when Sawyer was at his most content.

"Marry me," Miles blurted.

EVERYTHING IN the world stopped. The seagulls silenced and the ocean stilled. Sawyer couldn't even hear his own breath or the beating of his heart. He was only aware of its existence by the fluttering in his chest.

"Sawyer?"

Even Miles's low, husky voice didn't snap him out of his shock immediately. Surely he hadn't heard that right. Surely Miles wasn't asking for marriage already. That wasn't the plan.

"Sawyer?"

"Yeah. Sorry, I…." He blinked a few times.

"Did you hear me?"

"Yeah, I…." Sawyer's throat tightened. Why did his voice keep dying on him? Why the hell couldn't he take a deep breath? "I thought we were waitin'."

"Me too, but—" Miles slipped off the boulder and stood nose-to-nose with Sawyer. Again, he was so close Sawyer could feel every breath leaving Miles's slightly parted lips. "You're my future, Sawyer Taylor." He knelt down, pressing the knees of his expensive slacks into the sand, pulling Sawyer's hands into his. "My sister will love you. My daughter will love you. And I…. I can't imagine life without you. Please, say yes."

"Yes," Sawyer said without wasting a single second. He didn't need to think about the answer. The yes was imprinted on his heart, had been for a while now. He'd only needed Miles to ask the question so he could give the answer.

"Yes," he said a second time, voice ragged from the tears clogging his throat. He nodded convulsively as he dropped to his knees and threw both arms around Miles's neck. Sawyer pulled him into the kind of kiss that rocketed people to the moon. Their lips melded and their tongues twisted. The connection created in that moment was built purely on passion, though not sexual at all. Love built their connection. Love made it strong.

He knotted his fingers in Miles's hair. The moan from his lover's mouth was the sweetest sound his ears had ever heard. He dipped his tongue in and out, in and out, lips caressing and dominating, and somewhere, in all that passion, Sawyer realized he'd shed a tear.

One dripped from his chin, then another, and another. Miles cradled his face, thumb brushing over the wetness. The kiss broke and Miles frowned, "Why are you crying?"

"I don't know." Sawyer half laughed, his grin so wide it pushed his cheeks up against his soggy eyes. "Because I'm happy. Because I didn't think I would find love again. Because.... I don't know."

Miles pulled him back into his chest, cradling the back of Sawyer's head so Sawyer could rain his joyous tears into the curve of Miles's neck.

"When we get home," Miles said, "I can pull out the rings I bought or—"

"I want to wait. When it's official, then we'll wear the rings."

"Anything you want, Sawyer Taylor. Anything in the world."

CHAPTER THIRTY-FIVE

THE SUN had already given way to a light blue night when they finally pulled up to Miles's Malibu beach house. His two most favorite women in the whole entire world greeted him in the driveway, smiles wide, arms waving in the air. He couldn't have been happier. He couldn't have felt more loved.

"You ready?" he asked Sawyer, squeezing the hand he'd been holding over the sports car's console since they'd left the beach.

"As ready as I'll ever be."

"Remember what I said? They'll love you."

Miles leaned across the console and gave Sawyer a reassuring kiss before climbing out of the car. When he didn't see Sawyer immediately follow, he stopped at the hood and looked back through the windshield. Poor Sawyer looked petrified. Miles waved his hand to encourage his lover to join him.

He didn't make it up to the path before his little girl plowed into his legs. She hit him with a force that would've knocked a more unsuspecting man on his ass. Not that Miles would ever complain about her enthusiasm. It always made him feel more loved than words ever could. He immediately scooped Zoe into his arms, then turned to find Sawyer joining him.

"Do you remember—"

"The photographer!" she squealed, cutting off her father's question. Apparently, she did remember Sawyer. "He took pictures of me."

"This is Sawyer, sweetheart. He's Daddy's...."

How did Miles explain this? Men never came around and for good reason. He'd never wanted to try to explain to his little girl that Daddy didn't like women *that* way. Now, he didn't have much choice. A stir of panic set in. He opened his mouth and closed it. His arms tightened. His eyes shifted back to Sawyer.

"I'm your daddy's friend," Sawyer said.

Miles exhaled, giving his lover a thankful smile.

"Are you going to stay with us?" she asked.

"For a little while." Sawyer gave a nervous laugh. "I have a home in Mississippi."

"Where's Mississippi?"

"Far away from here."

"How far?"

"Sweetheart," Miles interrupted her interrogation. "Let Daddy and his friend get settled in. Our drive was long, and we're both tired."

"Yes, sir," she said as she climbed down from his hold.

She darted off past Miles's sister and into the house. Her excitement made both men laugh, but when he looked up and saw his sister watching them with curiosity, his laughter died down.

"I should explain this to her," he whispered.

"Is this a bad thing?"

"No. Not at all. I'm sure she wants to know what's going on. That's all."

Sawyer thumbed over his shoulder. "I can wait by the car."

"No. No." Miles locked his hand over Sawyer's. "Come with me."

Lacing their fingers together, Miles guided Sawyer up to the front door of the house he hoped to share with him soon, and hopefully, forever. The idea of going to sleep with Sawyer in his arms and waking up in the same bed, to that beautiful smile and those mesmerizing brown eyes, made Miles feel like he was floating.

His sister stood by the front door, watching each step they took. Her expression was warm, curious, but welcoming, like she hoped for the good news their locked hands alluded to.

"You made it," she said.

"I did. It took a while, but…."

"Pacific Coast Highway?" She let her gaze drift Sawyer's way. "It's incredible, isn't it?"

"Yes, ma'am," he said. His chest deflated a hint, like he'd been saving all his air on the off chance he found himself unable to breathe.

Miles didn't blame him. Karen could certainly be scary when the mood suited.

"You don't have to call me 'ma'am.' I'm younger than Miles. You don't call him sir…." She smirked. "Do you?"

"Karen!" Miles exclaimed after he noted the red creeping into his lover's otherwise peach-colored cheeks. "Behave yourself, for God's sake. You're insane."

"It's part of my charm, big brother."

"Charm. Right."

"So, are you moving in?" she asked Sawyer.

"Karen," Miles responded.

"What? I'm just asking."

"I'm stayin' for a few weeks...." Sawyer said. Miles hoped the fading words were followed by a "maybe longer" that remained unspoken for the sake of avoiding an argument... or Karen's twenty questions.

Miles looked at Sawyer, thumb stroking his forefinger with purpose. It somehow fed a little tenacity, a little strength, and a lot of pride back to him. "We're getting married," he said as he turned back to his sister.

Her mouth gaped and her eyes widened. "Are you serious?"

"Yeah." Miles nodded. "Yeah, very serious."

Her expression didn't change, not even an involuntary muscle twitch. "Can you please say something?"

She blinked a few times. "I can't believe *you're* getting married."

"That's not what I was hoping you would say," he said flatly.

Sawyer appeared to be getting a little more scared as the sibling banter bounced back and forth. Holding Miles's hand didn't seem to matter either. Clearly, what Sawyer needed and wanted was some sign of acceptance from Karen, and no amount of reassurance from Miles would do the trick.

"Karen...."

"I'm happy for you."

Both Miles and Sawyer exhaled, relaxing in unison. Miles didn't even realize he'd been holding his breath.

"Thank you, Karen," Miles said, leaning in for a kiss. He didn't let go of Sawyer's hand.

The kiss on the cheek turned into a hug. "Well, I'm going to let you guys get settled in," she said, then let go and pulled Sawyer in for a warm embrace. "Welcome to the family," she whispered, then gave him a kiss too. "Take care of my big brother."

"I plan on it."

Karen went inside and said her good-byes to Zoe while Miles and Sawyer unpacked the trunk. It didn't take long to get the luggage hauled inside. Miles insisted Sawyer let the maid take care of his suitcases and laundry tomorrow. Sawyer was resistant. It took Miles saying, "Let's do something fun with Zoe instead" to make Sawyer give in.

THE IDEA of spending time with Miles's kid excited and terrified the shit out of Sawyer. If this went badly, his stay in paradise would be short-lived for sure. If it went as well as he prayed, then moving forward and starting their life together shouldn't hit any roadblocks.

Shouldn't.

"What are we going to do?" Sawyer asked. He didn't know what the hell six-year-old girls were into.

"She loves pizza and movie nights. We'll take her shopping or something this weekend, but tonight, we'll just be… a family."

A family. Nothing sounded more wonderful. That's all Sawyer had ever wanted. He'd thought he'd been on his way to having a family of his own with Elijah, but that hadn't worked out. He'd gone as far as to buy a house and fence in the yard, even started stashing money to buy a reliable car a family could travel in. He never thought he'd mature enough to want the stability before Elijah did. He'd thought they were in it together. *Together* didn't really mean anything until he met Miles.

"What does she watch? What does she eat?" Sawyer asked.

"Pizza." Miles laughed. "Preteen comedies these days. Disney is *so* first grade."

"Disney. First grade. Right," Sawyer muttered to himself, taking mental notes.

"Sawyer." Miles gripped his shoulders. The remnants of an amused laugh clung to his smiling lips. He stepped close, close enough Sawyer became hyper aware of the little space between them and the sudden pressure against his crotch. Sawyer bit down on his bottom lip. Miles kissed the pursed skin. "Relax, baby. You don't need to freak out over her. This is going to work out."

"You have to be right, Miles. You have to be. I can't—"

"Shh…." Miles gently pressed one finger over Sawyer's lips. "This is going to be perfect."

Tiny feet pitter-pattered down the hallway. The wood floors amplified the sound. Using his hip, Sawyer urged Miles back far enough to put a comfortable distance between them, comfortable because they wouldn't have to explain any of this to Zoe yet. Right now, he could just be her daddy's friend. That truth would be easier to get used to.

"I found a movie!" she exclaimed, sliding into the kitchen on pink, fuzzy-socked feet.

The cover of the DVD matched the neon pink of her clothes. In fact, the whole case was neon. And Sawyer had to pretend to like it? This was going to be a disaster. He so sucked at lying.

"Help me," she said to Sawyer, grabbing for his hand. "I can't reach the DVD player."

Miles gave him an "I told you so" look. "Go. I'll order the pizza."

"Extra cheese," Zoe said.

"And pepperoni," Sawyer added before being dragged around the corner.

She pulled him all the way into the living room, never once letting her little fingers loosen. She had an adorable determination about her, much like Sawyer had had all his life. He remembered doing the same thing to his mother whenever he'd wanted something. And Zoe had Miles's crystal-like hazel eyes. So there was absolutely no way he could say no to anything she asked for.

"You're gonna sit right there." She pointed to the left end of the couch. "Because Daddy sits at that end and I get the middle." Zoe gave him a huge, toothy grin.

CHAPTER THIRTY-SIX

EMPTY PIZZA boxes lay open on the coffee table. Crumbs and hardened cheese and dried sauce clung to the cardboard. The closing credits of the movie they'd been watching rolled down the television screen. The entire two hours, Zoe lay against Miles's side, and Miles had his arm stretched across the back of the couch, hand at Sawyer's nape.

Soft snores trickled up beside him. He looked down and found Zoe completely crashed, half on his lap, half on Sawyer's. Miles smiled and looked up, ready to say something about how adorable she was when she slept, only to find Sawyer sleeping like a rock at the other end. Sawyer was almost as adorable as Zoe.

This was probably the best homecoming he'd ever had.

As soon as he shifted Zoe into his arms to carry her to her bed, she whimpered and her socked feet dragged across Sawyer's lap. Sawyer's eyes sprang open. He stared straight through Miles as though he had no clue where he was or what had happened.

"You okay?" Miles whispered, careful not to wake his daughter.

Sawyer blinked and responded with a grunt.

"Let me put her to bed. Then you and I can get settled in."

Sawyer responded with a nod.

Miles carried his daughter to her pink bedroom and tucked her into her adult-sized bed. Pink and white tulle cloaked the bed from the canopy above and hung loosely over the tall posts. One day, probably soon, she would tell him only little girls had princess beds and she needed something more grown-up.

He sighed. The time was going by so fast. She was getting so big.

Big enough to understand her daddy having a boyfriend?

Kissing her forehead, he pulled the blanket up to her chin. When he turned around, he found a sleepy-eyed Sawyer watching from the doorway. Miles wasn't used to having someone waiting for his attention like that. He was used to having all the time in the world with Zoe, not having to share with anyone else.

Miles crossed the room. He laid one hand over Sawyer's stomach to ease him back so Miles could close the door before their voices woke his little girl. They stood in the dark hallway without saying a word. Something awkward lingered between them, awkward and uncomfortable. Something Miles didn't care for.

"What's wrong?" he asked.

"Nothing. Everything's great. I just…. I'm excited to be a part of your family, and scared as hell at the same time."

"I know you are."

"I want her to be okay with us. I want to tuck her in bed with you."

"I know."

"Do you think we'll ever get there?"

"Of course," Miles immediately said. Truthfully, he didn't know when or how they would get to that point, but he knew it had to happen, preferably before the wedding plans started. "Let's get to bed. I'm exhausted, and I know you have to be too."

"I am."

The door at the end of the hallway led to Miles's bedroom, a room that had never before been shared with another person. Within inches of the door, he paused. If Zoe woke up in the middle of the night and came looking for him, what would she find? Her daddy cuddled in with another man? How would she take that? Would she hate him?

Miles turned around and said, "Maybe you should sleep in the guest room tonight."

As soon as Miles said that, he wished he hadn't—even before he noticed Sawyer trying to hide his hurt-filled expression.

"I understand," Sawyer said.

"I'm sorry. I just—"

"Don't be. I do understand. I promise." Sawyer stepped back. "Can you show me where it is? Maybe help me get my suitcases in there?"

"Yeah. Sure." Disappointment seeped into Miles's voice, but it wasn't disappointment in Sawyer or the situation, but disappointment in himself. He needed to garner the bravery to tell his little girl she was going to have a second daddy. He needed to be okay with sharing everything in his life with another adult.

He led Sawyer down the hall to a door directly across from Zoe's. Before they stepped inside, he flipped the switch, and the entire room filled with harsh white light. "I'll fix that," Miles mumbled.

Inside, the room was virtually untouched as always. The maid came in once a week to dust and change the linens. She also left a fresh bouquet of flowers in a vase on the dresser. Miles had never understood that. No one used the room, and more frequently than not, they went unappreciated and died before anyone had a chance to enjoy them. Regardless, now he was happy to see them there. The carnations and roses and flowers Miles couldn't identify added a burst of color to the stark white and soft blue palette of the room, a palette only truly enjoyed when the surf could be viewed through the french doors.

He pulled back the heavy curtains to expose thin white sheers. The light from the full moon managed to cut through them. He reached over and turned on the table lamp next to the bed. "You can kill the lights now, if you like."

"You don't have to be so morose," Sawyer said, flipping the switch.

The brightness vanished, leaving behind the softness of the table lamp and the small, yellow circle of moonlight beyond the sheer white curtains. It was utterly romantic and a perfect opportunity for Miles to show his fiancé how much he loved him... had his daughter not been sleeping across the hall.

"Morose, huh?" Miles arched his brow.

"Yeah, morose. I think you're takin' this a lot worse than I am. Believe it or not, I understand not sleepin' in the same bed. Yeah, I'm disappointed, but I understand. If I had a kid, I'd probably handle this the same way."

"You would?"

"I would."

Thank God.

Feeling a little better about the situation, Miles approached Sawyer and pressed a chaste kiss to those beautiful, waiting lips. He tucked his hands into Sawyer's back pockets, fingertips gently massaging the rounded mounds of his perfect ass. He held Sawyer tight against him as the kiss deepened, as their tongues twisted and their lips merged.

A tug in his groin tensed every muscle in Miles's body, and Miles abruptly ripped away from the kiss. He cleared his throat, exhaled raggedly, and said, "Let me get your stuff," before he ended up with a huge problem downstairs.

He headed back to the foyer where he'd left their suitcases for the maid, practicing even breathing with each step. When he reached the luggage, he flattened one hand against the wall and one hand over his crotch, applying enough pressure to relieve the subtle throbbing.

Maybe he hadn't thought this whole plan to live together through. They'd spent every night in the same bed for the last month, probably longer. They'd made love nearly every night since they'd gotten together. Now that the job was over and they had to return to real life, had the dream ended too?

"This was a bad idea?" Sawyer said from somewhere behind him. The lilt in his voice phrased the sentence more like a question than a statement.

Miles wanted so badly to tell Sawyer exactly what he needed to hear. Wanted to say no, it wasn't a bad idea, that everything would be okay and they'd work through this. He wanted to give Sawyer all the reassurance in the world, but he couldn't do it. Even as he stood there, thankful for having Sawyer, he couldn't reassure anyone of anything.

"I don't have to stay," Sawyer said.

"No, I want you to." Miles licked his dry lips, then turned to Sawyer, realizing too late that he still had his hand locked over the bulge between his thighs. He promptly let go and balled his hand at his side. "I want you here. If we're going to be married, I have to face this and talk to my daughter openly and honestly about what's happening."

"It's really too late to talk about anything tonight," Sawyer said as he reached for one of his suitcases. He firmly locked his fingers around the handle and hefted it up from the floor. "Tomorrow maybe we can talk about things and figure this all out."

"Tomorrow. Right." Miles gave a tight nod, grabbing the second suitcase.

He followed Sawyer back to the guest bedroom—the last place Sawyer should be sleeping. Everything inside Miles begged him not to go through with this, to have Sawyer in the bed beside him where he belonged, where he would always belong. The idea of having Sawyer so close and so far away at the same time felt so damn wrong. Miles even considered telling Sawyer to come to the right bed, that they could lock the door and Zoe would never find them, but even that idea felt wrong. He'd never locked Zoe out of his room, never in her young life.

"Tell me good night." Sawyer spoke softly, reaching for Miles's hand.

Their fingers intertwined and Sawyer gave a gentle tug. Miles closed the remaining space between them. He closed his eyes, head slightly lowered. Their lips connected.

Please stay with me tonight.

Miles's mouth lingered, kissing and caressing Sawyer's lips. Their hold on each other didn't break, didn't falter in any way. This was right, being together was right. Zoe knowing about her father, even at such a young age, felt right.

"You're not staying in here," Miles finally said.

Sawyer frowned. "What?"

"In this room, by yourself, without me. It's not right. You're not staying in here."

With a firm hold still on Sawyer's hand, Miles started toward the door, tugging Sawyer along with him. Something that felt a lot like an anchor stopped him dead in his tracks. His head whipped around, and he found Sawyer planted firmly, wearing an awkward smile.

"What are you doing?" Miles asked. "Come to bed with me."

"I'll sleep in here."

"But I don't want you to."

"Miles…." Sawyer inhaled deeply, eyes softening. "You were right to make this decision, okay? We'll explain to Zoe together what's goin' on, and then… then we'll share a bed, and we'll play family, and we'll see how all this works out."

Miles didn't speak. He wasn't sure what to say.

"I love you, Miles." His voice was a whisper, soft and sweet and heartwarming. His words touched Miles's soul. His words made the decision to sleep in separate rooms for tonight feel okay, maybe even bearable.

"I love you with all my heart, Sawyer Taylor."

He begrudgingly released Sawyer's hands. Every step he took away from Sawyer pushed little slivers of pain into Miles's wildly thumping heart. He quickly ducked inside his bedroom, feeling the burn of tears in the back of his eyes, not because he was sad, but because he'd chosen the best man in the world to be his partner… or rather, the best man in the world had chosen to say yes to him.

CHAPTER THIRTY-SEVEN

IT WASN'T bright golden rays of warm sunlight, or the musky, earthy scent of fresh-brewed coffee that woke Sawyer the next morning. None of those things waited to ease him back into the land of the living because Sawyer's eyes had spent the better part of the night wide-awake. After months of sleeping in another person's arms, being without that comforting embrace made getting a solid night of good rest impossible.

He rolled toward the door, curled around his pillow, and listened as the waves crashed into the shoreline. In his bedroom, even through the closed doors and windows, he could hear the seagulls cawing, and it reminded him of home.

As if the universe had sent his thoughts all the way from the coast of California to his home in Biloxi, Mississippi, his cell phone answered by vibrating across the nightstand. It was a text message from Lucy. *Anyone alive in there?*

Instead of sending a cold, impersonal text back, he called her. Part of him needed to hear her voice, to feel close to home again. It wasn't for wanting to be away from Miles, but missing his beautiful small town.

"Oh my God, you're awake!" she squealed instead of saying a simple hello. "What is it, like five in the morning there?"

"Six."

"Why are you awake?"

"Couldn't sleep." Sawyer sat up and settled against a pyramid of fluffy white pillows stacked against the headboard. "We didn't stay in the same room last night."

"Why not?" She sounded disappointed for him.

"We agreed to talk to his daughter before sleepin' in the same bed."

"Okay...."

"It's okay. Really, it is. It's the right thing to do."

"If you say so."

"Lucy...."

Silence filled the airwaves. He could hear her breathing, hear her shuffling around on the bed. It was eight in the morning in Biloxi, way too early for Lucy to be up and at 'em. That woman made a religion out of lying in bed and watching talk shows until lunchtime. He heard Maury in the background: "You're not the father."

Lucy still hadn't spoken, which was weird for her, especially considering they hadn't had a phone call in weeks. They were the kind of friends that didn't normally miss a day.

"You should let me have a kid for you and Miles," she finally said.

"Come again?"

"You heard me."

"Yeah, I…. Why do you wanna have a kid for us?"

"I don't know. I want a kid, but I don't want a kid. Does that make sense?"

"Not really."

"Well…."

The bedsprings squeaked like she'd finally gotten up. Her feet thudded across the hardwood. Lucy wasn't huge, but she wasn't a small woman either. *Comfortably middle*, she called it. Enough to hold on to. Enough curves to make her sexy. She was right. Sawyer had always thought she was incredibly beautiful and would probably make gorgeous babies. Yes, he'd thought about it. Every time she brought it up, he'd thought about it.

"We're not ready for kids, Lucy. He just proposed to me yesterday."

"Wait. What? He proposed? Seriously?"

"Yeah."

She squealed so loudly he had to pull the phone away from his ear to keep from going deaf. The sound made him laugh. He couldn't help it.

"You're comin' here for the weddin', right?" Sawyer asked.

"There?" Lucy paused. He could sense the frown in her silence. "What about the lighthouse? What about the gazebo?"

"Same-sex marriage isn't legal in Mississippi."

"Right."

The sound of little feet, echoed by the footfalls of much larger feet pulled his attention away from the conversation he'd been having with Lucy. Zoe very loudly declared she wanted pancakes with strawberries and a big glass of milk; then she wanted her daddy and his new best friend to go swimming with her.

Daddy's new best friend.

Sawyer blew out a sharp breath. "The family's up. Can I let you go?" he said to Lucy, keeping his voice just above a whisper.

"Think about what I said."

"I will. Love you, Lucy."

"Love you too, Sawyer."

He ended the call and slipped his phone back onto the nightstand. It could stay there for the rest of the day for all he cared. The only business he'd had to deal with was Miles's studio, and that project had wrapped already. Most importantly, he didn't want the phone interfering with family time.

He climbed out of the bed and swiped a shirt from the suitcase he'd left open on the floor after digging out his sleep pants the night before. Then he tugged it down over his head. It wasn't the best look, but decent enough to join Miles and Zoe for breakfast.

In the kitchen, a short, round Latino woman dug through cabinets with a smile on her face. She must've been the maid Miles mentioned the night before. Though, she wasn't wearing one of those little outfits. She had on jeans and a T-shirt and looked like just like everyone else.

"*Princesa* Zoe," she said, accent thicker than any he'd ever heard. "Take your milk to the table and sit down. Your *panqueques* will be ready *en un momento*."

Miles stood at the coffeemaker, pressing buttons and grumbling. He looked like hell, like he hadn't slept much either. Thick, dark bags circled his enchanting hazel eyes. He had the worst bedhead Sawyer had ever seen, as if he had maybe spent all night tossing and turning, just like Sawyer had.

Sawyer decided to stand back and simply observe the way a typical morning in the Eisenberg house got its start. From the looks of it, the maid handled most everything while Zoe and Miles slid into their own routines. Granted, this was a Sunday, and she didn't have school today. Didn't look like they went to church either. Not that Sawyer minded or judged. He'd stopped going to church when he was old enough to decide for himself he didn't want to go.

The coffeemaker beeped and Miles moaned. The maid immediately handed over a mug as if the sound were a softly offered command. When Miles lifted the steamy mug to his lips, all the weariness in his face turned into an easy, happy expression. But it was Zoe who finally noticed him standing there.

"Sawyer!"

A smile stretched across his lips. Her excitement made him feel good.

"Sit with me!" she demanded, pushing out the chair beside her with her foot.

He did as she asked, and as soon as he settled into the chair, Miles came around the table and slid a cup of coffee in front of him. Then Miles took the chair on the other side of his daughter.

Silence, save for the sound of Zoe smacking on pancakes and the maid doing dishes, surrounded them. In fact, the only truly unnerving silence came from the two very uncomfortable men sitting at the table. They exchanged glances, then looked down at Zoe, then back at each other. Should they, or shouldn't they?

"Sweetie," Miles said. "Can I talk to you for a minute?"

Zoe rocked in her chair, happily scooping up maple-covered strawberries. She mumbled something around the fork in her mouth. Miles obviously understood.

"What do you think of Sawyer staying with us?"

Her tiny hazel eyes grew about as big as the saucer beneath the boat of hot syrup on the table. She swallowed her food fast. "Can he?"

"Yeah, he can. In fact, maybe he'll come live with us. What do you think about that?"

"I love it!"

Not only her acceptance, but her excitement warmed his heart. He'd been so afraid she wouldn't want him here. That clearly wasn't the case, and nothing in the world could've been a better sign that they were doing the right thing. Miles stared lovingly at them both. Sawyer gave him a nod, a signal to keep going.

"Zoe, look at me for a second," he said.

Miles shifted his gaze back and forth between the two of them, like he wasn't exactly sure what he would say to her, and he looked to Sawyer for a little help. At that point, Sawyer didn't know what the boundaries were, what would offend and what would be helpful. He wasn't sure what Miles would appreciate and what he might get upset over.

"What if he slept in my bed?" Miles finally asked.

"Like a slumber party?"

"Sure." Miles laughed. "Like a slumber party."

"Can I have a slumber party too?"

By the flushed look on Miles's face, that didn't go the way he'd hoped. He took a huge gulp of coffee, set his mug down, then ran his fingers through his messy hair. His chest rose, then fell. He licked his lips, forced a smile, and asked, "What if he was your daddy too?"

CHAPTER THIRTY-EIGHT

EVERY SECOND that passed without Zoe responding, every second she spent staring at him like she didn't understand the question made Miles a little more uncomfortable. He couldn't even hide it. The fidgeting with his coffee cup, the running of his fingers through his hair, the shifting in his seat: it all gave him away. He knew it did. What really did it for him was how worried she suddenly looked.

"But…." Her bottom lip quivered. "You're still gonna be my daddy, right?"

"Oh God, yes, sweetie." He exhaled so deeply his shoulders rounded.

"Then why do I need another daddy?"

Nothing in his parenting tool kit had prepared him for this conversation. He'd honestly never thought he'd be having *this* conversation. Marriage and family aside from Karen and Zoe had never crossed his mind before. Sawyer made him want it though, made him dream about and aspire to have it.

Not really knowing what else to do, Miles stood and then knelt on the floor between Sawyer's chair and Zoe's. He took one hand from each in his. He kissed the top of Sawyer's hand, then kissed the top of Zoe's.

"Sweetheart," he carefully continued, "Daddy loves Sawyer."

"Like you love me and Aunt Karen?"

"Sort of. He's um—" He smiled up at Sawyer, squeezing his hand tighter. "—special to me."

"Well, Daddy…." She crossed her arms. "If he's special to you, that means he's special to me too, because you're special to me."

Who could argue with that logic?

He released Sawyer's hand only to pull his little girl into a hug. If he didn't bury his face in her soft curls soon, she would catch his eyes watering again. The only time in his life he'd ever shed this many tears in such a short span was when Zoe was born and his best friend in the entire world died.

"Can I hug Sawyer now, Daddy?" she whispered into his ear.

He laughed softly and let her go, but not before sniffling back whatever tears might be lingering in his eyes. "Hug him now. Please." Miles pushed up to his feet and stood out of the way.

The legs of her chair scraped the tile as she slid back from the table. She slipped out of the chair in time for Sawyer to catch her in both arms. Miles watched his little girl hug the man he loved and accept him into the family with open arms. Nothing could've made Miles more proud than what was happening in his kitchen. If he'd believed in God, he might've thanked the big man upstairs.

"Zoe, why don't you go grab your bathing suit so we can hang out on the beach?" he said. It was an excuse to get Sawyer all to himself for a moment.

"Can Gigi come over?" she asked.

"That's fine, honey," Miles said, and when he noticed Sawyer's frown, he explained, "Gigi is her best friend. She lives down the beach. Actually, I think she lives here too. The kid never goes home, I swear."

"Because our house is sooooo awesome!" Zoe said, voice lilting excitedly.

"Child, go. Before I change my mind." Miles pointed in the general direction of her bedroom.

Without another word, Zoe darted out of the room and disappeared down the hallway. The maid had disappeared long before the conversation at the table had begun, leaving Sawyer and Miles alone, now, and essentially out to the only person who really mattered.

"You okay?" he asked.

"I um…." Sawyer's lips tugged at the corners like he wanted to smile, which contradicted the red rims of his eyes. He blew out a breath. Who knew how long he'd been holding onto it. The tears he'd been holding back slipped down his cheeks. "I'm happier than I ever been in my life."

"Is that true?"

"Yeah," Sawyer answered without hesitation. "It is."

"I want to make all your days happy."

"I'm pretty sure you will. I wanna make you and Zoe happy too."

"I know you will."

Before the conversation had a chance to go any further, Zoe's tiny bare feet were slapping against the tile. She had her bathing suit on and a towel over her shoulder, ready to go for a swim, even if her daddies weren't. She put both hands on her hips and glowered at the two of them. No one on earth had a glare quite as intimidating as hers.

"You're not ready," she declared, stomping one little foot on the ground. "I thought we were going swimming."

"We are, honey." Miles nudged Sawyer. "Go before we get into trouble."

They walked down the hall together, but didn't hold hands or anything like that. Any kind of intimacy in front of Zoe would have to wait until things became more comfortable. But before they ducked into their respective rooms, Miles stole a quick, innocent kiss.

Miles changed quickly. He heard the guest bedroom door open and shut and raced to meet his lover in the hallway. He wanted one more kiss, just one, before returning to the kitchen.

"Hi," he said with a grin when his eyes met Sawyer's. His fiancé had on the cutest pair of light blue board shorts that settled right beneath his navel. A loose, white button-down hung open, showing off Sawyer's rippled abs and the sprinkling of dark hair trailing down toward his crotch. The sight was mouth-watering, and the biggest turn-on. Miles had to compose himself before he dared to step foot in front of another human being. "You taking the camera?" He nodded toward the gear bag hanging from Sawyer's shoulder.

"Yeah, I like takin' pictures on the beach. Elijah and I...." Sawyer licked his lips.

"It's okay. You can talk about him."

"I don't wanna. He's not important anymore. I have someone much better, someone who really loves me."

"Someone who will never stop loving you," Miles added. He pushed off from the doorframe and met Sawyer in the middle of the hall. Habit had him reaching for Sawyer's hand. He simply couldn't stop himself. "We should probably get back. Little girls aren't very patient."

Miles gathered the beach towels and blanket from the deck, grabbed the umbrella and sunscreen and portable radio he listened to while watching his daughter play with her best friend. In the past, he'd sat alone and enjoyed her happiness, but now he had someone to be happy with, someone to talk to and laugh with while she played in the sand and ocean with her friends. The thought prompted a grin in Sawyer's direction.

As a family, the three of them walked down to the beach, Zoe giggling and talking ninety miles an hour, constantly looking over her shoulder to make sure they were still following her. Miles and Sawyer didn't hold hands. They appeared to be nothing more than close friends, and that worked for them both… for now.

When they got closer to the shoreline, Miles and Sawyer set up their spot while Zoe jogged across the sand to meet her bestie halfway. The sun had risen high above, but it wasn't scorching hot. Malibu rarely did get unbearably hot.

"I'm cold," Sawyer said, as if he were reading Miles's mind. "The beaches back home are never this cool."

"You'll get used to it. The weather is always great here."

Miles pushed the umbrella's pole deep into the sand and cocked it in such a way its colorful fabric would protect them both from the sun. Each man had fair enough skin that too much direct light would burn them.

"One night," Miles said with a grin as he sat down on the blanket, "while Zoe is at Karen's house, I want us to come down to the beach and make love. Have you ever made love with the ocean crashing behind you and stars twinkling in a pitch black sky?"

"No." Sawyer took the spot beside him, sitting close enough to touch but not be too obvious. "But you make it sound beautiful."

"Oh, it will be, I promise."

EPILOGUE

Twenty-seven months, four days, and three hours later….

"SHE'S HAVING the baby!" Karen yelled through the phone.

At first, Sawyer's brain didn't process. The one word that stuck with him was baby. *She's having the baby.* "Oh, shit! She's havin' the baby!"

The phone slipped from his ear and hit the hardwood with a thud. It probably broke, but he didn't care. Lucy was having the baby… his baby.

Every internal alarm fired at once. The receptors in his brain were going haywire. His feet were ready to get a move on. His heart thumped wildly. And yet, he couldn't take a single step, couldn't move a single muscle.

"Baby, you okay?" Miles asked, waving a hand in front of Sawyer's wide but unseeing eyes.

"She's havin' the baby," he mumbled.

"I know. I heard. Come on, let's get you to the hospital."

"Right." Sawyer still didn't move.

A hand curled around his bicep, squeezing lightly. When they started moving forward, his brain began working and answering thoughts again. *Where's Zoe? She's at Gigi's house. Where's my wallet? It has the doctor's number in it. You need to call him. Where's my phone? On the floor where you dropped it. Wait. No. It's in Miles's hand. Where's Lucy's overnight bag? By the door just like we practiced.*

"You okay? You're as white as a ghost," Miles said.

"I'm f—" Another thought interrupted that one. "The baby is early, Miles. It's not supposed to be here for another six weeks."

"Listen to me." Miles wrapped his hands over Sawyer's shoulders and looked him in the eye. "Babies are born early all the time. That doesn't mean anything is going to go wrong. It just means we get to meet our little bundle of joy sooner rather than later, okay?"

Sawyer nodded slowly.

"Now breathe."

He inhaled deeply, held it, and then exhaled slowly.

"We need to go, and you need to pull it together. You're Lucy's birthing coach, and she needs you right now, okay?"

Sawyer nodded again.

Now that everything important was settled, they headed out to the SUV, acquired after Miles traded in his cute little sports car. Sawyer's cherished, rusty Jeep Wagoneer was parked beside it, dead and needing a new lease on life. Sawyer didn't want to part with it, even after two years' worth of being offered every amazing car under the sun.

A lot had happened in those two years. Miles's family had doubled in size. Well, would double as soon as Lucy gave birth to their son. Lucy had relocated to Malibu and lived with Karen. They had a really odd relationship. It had started as a friendship, and somehow, they'd ended up dating the same guy. Nuclear-type fallout followed, and then they were best friends again. Now, they dated each other and had a steady guy they both saw. It worked for them. They were happy, and Lucy was ecstatic about Sawyer finally giving in to the whole baby thing.

Miles and Sawyer married exactly one year to the day after Miles had proposed on the beach next to the Pacific Coast Highway. They had an intimate beach wedding with twenty or so of their closest friends, complete with paparazzi failing miserably to hide in the bushes while snapping photos of their special moment. Even Tabby, the assistant who'd become the topic of many a joke over the years, and Penelope made it out.

Martin and Pearl and their son had come down from San Francisco and spent the week prior helping Miles and Sawyer prepare. In that week, Miles had learned a little bit about the mystery that was Martin. The kind old gentleman had been head over heels in love once, the same brand of love Sawyer and Miles shared—complete with the desire for a trip to the altar and as many kids as the old Victorian would hold. Pearl, a dear friend to Martin and his beloved Felix, had been happy to give them children, as long as she was allowed to be a part of their lives. But Martin's true love never lived to make the trip. Disease, one Martin wouldn't elaborate on, had claimed his partner's life, and Martin had simply had no desire to replace him. He had a son with Pearl, and that gave him the family he needed and enough love to keep his heart warm. Save for the occasional melancholy, he was happy.

Days later, wedding photos started surfacing in the tabloids. Neither Miles nor Sawyer cared. They were already out to the people who truly mattered and had no plans to keep their nuptials a secret.

Zoe was still as sweet and beautiful as ever. She spent more time with Karen and Lucy now that adolescence was on the horizon. She remained best friends with Gigi, but a third had been added to their circle—an eleven-year-old boy who reminded Sawyer of himself at that age: too cute for words and absolutely aware of the fact. Zoe had a crush on him. He was too young for Gigi—her words, not Zoe's. Miles and Sawyer did their best to keep the fear of God in that boy. If he did anything to their little girl….

"Hey," Miles whispered, "where are you right now?"

Sawyer turned his head, gaze slowly following. "Reminiscin'? I guess." He sighed and rubbed his hand over his sternum. "I'm scared, Miles. What if I'm not a good father?"

"Hello, you're already a great father. Just ask Zoe."

"Yeah, but—" Sawyer turned in his seat so he could face Miles a little better. "—she wasn't an infant when I came into the picture. She was practically grown." Miles laughed. "The point is, Cooper is going to be so… needy and fragile."

"They're not as fragile as you think," Miles said flatly. "Trust. Me."

Sawyer laid his head against the seat, taking in his spouse's expression: the slight curve of Miles's lips, the faint dimples hugging that adorable grin, the hint of wrinkles at the edge of his squinting eyes. This was the man he would grow old with, raise kids with, have a life with. This was the man he'd given his heart to, and Sawyer couldn't have made a better choice. Let Miles tell the story and this romance was all his doing, but Sawyer knew the truth.

"You're staring at me like you're daydreaming again," Miles said.

"Just rememberin' how I landed the hottest man in Hollywood."

"You mean how I convinced a talented young photographer to fall in love with me?"

Sawyer laughed. "Sure, we'll go with that." Another thought made him raise his head. "Hey, does Zoe know her little brother's bein' born?"

"I doubt it. I didn't call her."

"Where's my phone?" Sawyer held out his hand. "I want to tell her."

Miles reached in the center console and pulled back an iPhone. He held the contraption out for Sawyer to take. Of course, number one on his speed dial was the cutest little girl on God's green earth.

In fear of interrupting something important in the world of the preteen mind, he decided to send her a text instead of calling. *I have huge news for you. Call me.* Not two seconds later, his cell phone rang. "Your brother is bein' born," Sawyer casually said in lieu of a hello.

She squealed.

He pulled the phone away from his ear.

Miles laughed.

"Lucy's at the hospital?" Zoe asked.

"Yeah, can you get there? Will Gigi's mom bring you?"

"I think so. Ooohhh… don't let her have Cooper before I get there."

"Sweetie, I don't think I have a say in the matter. Just hurry. Daddy will be there waitin' for you."

"Yes, sir."

The call ended and Sawyer slipped the phone into his pocket. He felt all warm and fuzzy now, warm with the sheer happiness of having his life come together in such a magical way. He couldn't have dreamed better for himself.

The SUV jostled and jerked as Miles wheeled into the maternity ward's driveway. He pulled to a stop in front of the sliding glass door. It took a minute to register with Sawyer where they were and what he needed to do. His brain still hadn't gotten in the game.

"Baby," Miles said, laying a hand over Sawyer's. "We're here. I'm going to park. You get in there and take care of Lucy."

Sawyer nodded as he absently climbed out of the car.

Inside, the waiting room was filled with people anxiously awaiting the arrival of a new family member. Their faces all looked happy, like the joyous occasion had descended upon them at the right time, like it was expected and welcome. Sawyer sympathized. At first, he hadn't known if they were going to be able to get pregnant. It took six months of talking about it, a little over a year of trying and countless doctors' visits, but eventually, Sawyer's little swimmers did their job and here he was—at the hospital, waiting for his son to be born.

"Can I help you?" an older lady asked, jerking him out of his barely tethered hysteria.

"I'm going to be a dad," he mumbled.

"Well, congratulations. When is the little one due?"

"Right now." Sawyer frowned. "She's havin' him right now."

"Oh. Oh!" The second *oh* came with a burst of realization. The old woman took Sawyer by the hand and guided him down the hall to a nurses' station, where Sawyer exchanged Lucy's name for a room number and an escort back since he clearly wasn't capable of doing much of anything on his own.

MILES GRIPPED the wheel of his SUV, staring out over its enormous hood. It wasn't as sexy as the sports car, but life had more purpose these days. Life had taken a dramatic turn. He was about to be a father for the second time. It had been nine short years since he'd been in Sawyer's situation, confused and on the verge of panic, wanting to be the best man he could be for a little girl who had yet to grace the world. He remembered the fear and dread like it was yesterday, and here he was, right back in the same boat. Funny thing about that: he'd loved every second of it. Wouldn't trade it for anything.

He grabbed both cell phones and his wallet, stood, and stared at the interior again. Nothing was left. Nothing forgotten. Then, he locked the family truckster up tight and headed across the parking lot, back to the maternity ward entrance. This time tomorrow, his family of three would be a family of four. Sleepless nights and dirty diapers, empty bottles and endless pampering would be his future for the next few years. There was no other man in the world he could imagine going on this adventure with. No one he wanted to share the laughter and tears with, the first steps and first dates. He couldn't wait for Zoe to meet her little brother. She'd always wanted a sibling, and he'd felt so bad for not giving her one. She was at the perfect age to nurture and care for a baby brother, the perfect age to be a big sister and role model.

"Daddy!" she yelled from across the driveway, arms waving in the air. She took off at a run, charging toward him full speed. When she finally collided with him, she folded her arms around his waist and held onto him with remarkable strength. "I'm going to be a big sister," she exclaimed.

"Yes, you are, princess."

"Congratulations, Mr. Miles," Gigi said, joining in their hug.

"Thank you, Gigi."

The hug broke in time for Miles to catch a glimpse of the new boy from down the beach making his way up the driveway. *That boy* had been following his sweet Zoe around since the first day they'd met, and Miles had an ever-present feeling he was going to have to give the kid a piece of his mind.

"Congratulations, sir." The kid held out his hand for a shake, proper and honorable, especially for an eleven-year-old. As long as he *only* shook hands with that hand, then Miles wouldn't have the drive to wring his little prepubescent neck. Miles may have known at a very young age he had a thing for boys, but he also remembered very clearly what kind of things had gone through his mind at that age.

"Thank you," Miles managed through the gritted teeth of his most fake smile. "Shall we go inside?"

In the waiting room, Karen was pacing back and forth, chewing down her nails. She looked up at the clock, then back down at the floor. Miles could almost imagine a hole worn in the carpet. She looked scared shitless. He certainly sympathized.

"Guys, go sit down over there and entertain yourselves, okay?"

Zoe nodded like a good girl and led her pack over to a set of chairs pulled into a tight circle. Miles watched them for a moment before joining Karen. His arrival apparently startled her because when she raised her head to look at the clock, she gasped. She blinked a few times before having the presence of mind to throw her arms around his neck.

"I'm so glad you're here," she said, squeezing him so tightly he could barely breathe.

"You thought I wouldn't be?"

"Oh, no." She finally let go. "I knew you would be. I'm just happy to see you."

"How long have you been pacing?"

"Since they took her back. Her water broke in the middle of the mall. We were on our way to American Cookies to get some of those chocolate chip minis she likes so much. She knew it was going to be soon, but...."

"Didn't expect that one, huh?"

"No, she didn't. They let me ride in the ambulance because she was freaking out, but they didn't let me go any farther once we got here."

His sister looked utterly terrified, much like she had the day Zoe was born. He remembered being shoved out of the delivery room while they prepared his best friend for surgery. One of the doctors had said she needed a C-section if there was going to be any chance of saving the baby. That had been the last time he'd seen Anne alive. Karen had held his hand through the entire ordeal, had even spent the first few months of Zoe's life by his side because his breakdowns came suddenly and they came with fury.

"Lucy's going to make it," Miles finally said. His voice sounded strained, ragged and on the verge of tears. "Everything's going to be fine this time. It has to be."

It had to be because he knew he wouldn't be able to handle watching Sawyer break down the way he had. Nothing in the world would tear at his heart like seeing Sawyer go through that kind of pain. Well, seeing his sister suffer the loss of someone she loved would definitely do it too.

The real concern right now was for the baby. He wasn't due for another month or so. Miles wasn't sure about the science of babies and how they grew, but felt pretty certain coming into the world a month early probably wasn't the best way to get a jump on life, regardless of what he'd said in his efforts to calm his husband.

"Come on," he said, hoping to take his mind off worries about birthing babies. "Let's sit down before we both wear ourselves out."

Reluctantly, his beloved sister followed him over to the circle of chairs where Zoe and her friends sat, though Miles and Karen didn't interrupt their little party. The children's spirits were certainly higher than the adults', and frankly, both Miles and Karen could've used a little uplifting.

Miles was restless as hell, sitting up in the chair, then leaning back, picking at his nails and running his fingers through his hair. Every little while, he looked up at the clock. It felt like hours when really it had only been a few minutes. His stomach grumbled in protest. It was nearing lunchtime, and he knew Zoe would probably be getting hungry soon too.

"Sweetheart," he said to her. Conversation in their circle immediately ceased. She looked at him and smiled. His heart melted... again. "If you're hungry—"

"I'm not leaving until Sawyer comes back and tells us Cooper is okay."

And again. "Okay, but if you and your friends start getting hungry, you can take my credit card down to the cafeteria to get lunch."

"We're fine, Daddy. Thank you."

Well, that ended a lot quicker than he'd wanted it to. The conversation bought him about two worry-free minutes, if that. He went right back to ringing his hands.

The fourth or maybe fifth time the waiting room doors burst open, Miles almost didn't raise his head. Those doors had been crying wolf for hours now. Something inside him told him he needed to look up, though, that when he raised his head, the greatest gift in the world would be waiting for him. And sure enough, when he looked up, he found the most handsome, glassy-eyed, disheveled, disoriented man standing there grinning from ear to ear.

Without thinking, Miles rose to his feet and quickly crossed the room. He didn't utter the first sound, didn't say a word. All he wanted was to feel Sawyer in his arms again and know that everything had gone okay. He held Sawyer tight. Sawyer sniffled back his tears.

"Where's Cooper?" Miles whispered.

"They have him on oxygen right now. His color's good. He's a little bitty ol' thing, but everything looks okay."

"And Lucy?"

"She's fine. Sleepin' probably." Sawyer let out a soft laugh. "You should've heard all the things she called me. I don't think she's my biggest fan right now."

Miles joined in the laughter, tears streaming down his face. He was just about to turn and tell Karen the good news when her arms encircled them both. They pulled her into their hug. "I love you guys," she said through her tears.

Both men laughed harder.

"Zoe," Miles called over his shoulder. "Let's go see your little brother."

As a family, they headed down the long corridor—Sawyer held Miles's hand, Miles held Zoe's, Zoe held Karen's, Zoe's friends followed close behind—to the grouping of windows where people could visit the newborns. And there in the very center, with a tiny tube in his nose, was baby Cooper Taylor Eisenberg, son of Lucy Cooper and Sawyer and Miles Eisenberg. His face was red and wrinkled, tiny fists in a tight ball, and he was the most perfect little boy Miles had ever laid eyes on, the most perfect son in the world.

"I love you," Miles said to the glass window, knowing good and well Cooper couldn't hear him. That didn't matter. He felt compelled to say it, so he did.

"He loves you too," Sawyer whispered, laying his head on Miles's shoulder.

ALLISON CASSATTA was born and raised in Memphis, Tennessee, where she lives happily with her amazing husband of over a decade. She has written more than twenty books with gay, lesbian, bisexual, and heterosexual pairings. Her passion is the beauty of love and the art of words.

Allison's accolades include 2013 Top Pick of the Year from The Novel Approach, 2013 All Romance Ebooks Bestseller, 2012 Rainbow Book Awards Honorable Mention Winner, 2011 Best-selling Author, and 2011 Best Anthology. She is currently published with Dreamspinner Press, Silver Publishing, Amber Quill Press, and MLR Press.

You can find more of her works by visiting http://www.allisoncassatta.com. You can also connect with her via Twitter at https://twitter.com/allisoncassatta, on Facebook at https://www.facebook.com/allison.cassatta.page, and you can follow her blog at http://allisoncassatta.blogspot.com. She also welcomes any and all e-mails to info@allisoncassatta.com.

http://www.dreamspinnerpress.com